Praise for *The Returnees*:

'[An] evocative tale of identity,
friendship and unexpected love'
Mail on Sunday

'An exciting new voice in
contemporary fiction.'
AnOther magazine

'A brilliant read'
Closer

'An intoxicating tale of love,
identity, and friendship.'
Lunate.co.uk

'Brilliant'
Bella

'The perfect August read.'
Frizzandgo.com

LONDON B
D1149236

About the author

Elizabeth Okoh is a British-Nigerian writer, content creator and photographer. She holds a degree in Psychology and Sociology from the University of Sussex. Her work has been published in various online and print magazines, as well as curated at exhibitions in London and Athens. Her work is inspired by social justice, culture, immigration and living in the diaspora.

THE RETURNEES

ELIZABETH OKOH

HODDER

First published in Great Britain in 2020 by Hodder & Stoughton
An Hachette UK company

This paperback edition published in 2021

I

Copyright © Elizabeth Okoh 2020
The right of Elizabeth Okoh to be identified as the
Author of the Work has been asserted by her in accordance
with the Copyright, Designs and Patents Act 1988.

All rights reserved. No part of this publication may be reproduced, stored in a
retrieval system, or transmitted, in any form or by any means without the prior
written permission of the publisher, nor be otherwise circulated in any form
of binding or cover other than that in which it is published and without
a similar condition being imposed on the subsequent purchaser.

All characters in this publication are fictitious and any resemblance
to real persons, living or dead, is purely coincidental.

A CIP catalogue record for this title is available from the British Library

B format ISBN 9781529380569
eBook ISBN 9781529380552

Typeset in Plantin Light by
Palimpsest Book Production Ltd, Falkirk, Stirlingshire

Printed and bound in Great Britain by Clays Ltd, Elcograf S.p.A.

Hodder & Stoughton policy is to use papers that are natural, renewable
and recyclable products and made from wood grown in sustainable forests.
The logging and manufacturing processes are expected to conform
to the environmental regulations of the country of origin.

Hodder & Stoughton Ltd
Carmelite House
50 Victoria Embankment
London EC4Y 0DZ

www.hodder.co.uk

For every artist who's on the arduous path to making their dreams a reality.

THE NAMING

Present Day

I

Osayuki

The sweet smell of Fairy Dust wafts into my nostrils from where it burns on the marble stool I've placed by my white stone bathtub. The scented candle had been hand delivered only five days before by Cynthia, one of my closest friends, who had picked it up from a boutique shop in Covent Garden on her way from London. That candle shop had been one of my guilty pleasures. Back in the day, I could easily have spent hours in there, watching as the small batches of handmade candles were set into jars and then left to cool at the far end of the shop. When I'd finally leave, I'd be on a sweet-smelling high with a new stock of Fairy Dust and sometimes Wild Berries in my bag; but that was years ago. Now living in a beautiful house in Lagos, tastefully decorated thanks to Pinterest boards and 3 a.m. calls to suppliers in China, I am still the same carefree and adventurous girl, but in a different city – one that, equally, does not sleep.

The bath water is beginning to feel lukewarm, so I pick up my sponge and start scrubbing my neck, then my arms and enlarged breasts, which now hold milk and are a size that I've only come to know over the last couple of months. I do ten reps of the Kegel exercise and massage my thigh, just below my moon tattoo, and then scrub my belly. It is no longer as firm as it once was. Giving birth does that to you. I have expected these changes, but living through them is still a wonder on the days I feel like my old self and can't believe that I am now a mother.

Through the small slit between the bathroom door and its lock, I hear the voices in the other room. Someone has come in and I think I hear Cynthia saying the guests have started to arrive. This information doesn't make me rush; I know Mum will knock on the door when it's time. I lean back again and rest my head on the edge of the bathtub.

Twenty minutes later, I walk out of the bathroom to find that my red-and-silver-coloured aṣọ oke is laid carefully on the bed. I sniggered when Mum told me the market seller had assured her that the woven fabric had been made by the best hand-loomers in Ibadan. 'Ahn ahn . . .' Mama Fola had drawled, neither confirming nor disputing the claim, although her coy smile had attested to the latter.

I get ready in the bedroom that I had prepared for my mum and step-dad, Bob. He is already downstairs with our guests while Mum and some female relatives are helping to prepare me for my baby's naming ceremony. I pick up my iro – a Yoruba word for a large piece of fabric worn as a wrap-around skirt – and look it over. It is beautiful. Mum made a good choice at the market weeks ago when I was still heavily pregnant and unable to leave the house. It is crazy that only eight days ago, my baby boy, Nimi, was still inside me. I didn't expect my last trimester to have been so testing, but now my son is here, I am happy to announce his arrival to the world in the way required by my husband Fola's Yoruba tradition.

I wonder what Fola is doing. I guess that he is most likely ready and waiting for me, but I am in no hurry. We still have to get Nimi dressed. I put on my iro and buba – a blouse – and then sit on the bed while a friend of Mama Fola ties my gele on my head. Mum is dressing Nimi, and when he stirs and begins to cry, I know he needs another feed. We stop the head tying and Nimi is passed over to me. He latches on with toothless gums and I flinch. I am still getting used to being a new mum and it still hurts whenever he clings to my breast. Eight days in and I am still figuring out what being a mother entails. No one told me that it would hurt for this long. But I love my son and would do anything for him. This was once a cliché to me, but now I fully understand it.

An hour later we are all dressed and ready to start the ceremony. Fola joins us outside the room. I pass Nimi to him and we all make our way downstairs to the waiting party. The house, a three-bedroom duplex, is in a coveted area in Victoria Island, only a fifteen-minute drive from my Aunty Rosemary's house. I fell in love with our place the first time we went for a viewing, despite the previous owners' questionable taste in decor. It still pains me to think of all the garish furnishings adorning the interiors of Lagos' most lavish houses. 'Money can never buy class!' said my friend Wendy when I aired my frustration. We signed the papers and put down a deposit for the house a few days later, and thus began my task of making it fit to move into with my new family. I had initially worked with my own ideas and then completed the makeover with an interior designer, and the house that Fola and I would call our first home was ready to be inhabited just in time for our baby's arrival.

Our families quieten down as Fola and I walk into the brightly lit living room, decked with gold accents and large framed illustrations. When we were decorating, I had ordered an oval gold-framed mirror and asked that it be hung on the wall just before the marble staircase. When I instructed that another be put in the living room, Fola had protested. He said we 'weren't vain people'. So instead, we hung pictures of us in our traditional wedding attire and at our reception, both of us smiling like we had won the lottery. Perhaps we had.

Our new chandelier with teardrop diamonds is glittering above our families and guests. Just behind my parents, I can see my friends and my Aunty Rosemary, along with her husband Osi and my cousins. There are some other relatives I don't know too well – I smile at them all as we walk in. Fola's family and friends are there too. We beam with pride and take our seats at the head of the gathering, with our parents on either side of us.

Mama Fola's pastor is already at the front of the room waiting to proceed with the naming ceremony. It is a tradition that has to take place on the eighth day after the birth of the child. On the table next to the pastor are bowls containing substances the Yoruba people believe are essential to a child's start in life – honey, salt, sugar, alligator pepper, palm oil, kola nut, bitter kola and water, all of them a representation of goodwill and prosperity. Fola passes Nimi to the pastor and the ceremony begins. A prayer is said, followed by the recitation of a hymn from an Anglican hymn book.

Nigerians say that when your palms are itchy, money or good fortune is coming your way. But itchy palms have always spelled trouble for me, and I wonder why it has to be at this moment when I am carrying Nimi in my arms that my left palm decides to itch its way to madness. I badly want to scratch the damn thing, but I can't let go of my son, so I try my best to ignore it. I smile as the salt is rubbed on the tip of his tongue and he contorts his face. That there is the beautiful thing I love about the Yoruba culture. But I have also learned that tradition is something that can hold someone captive; that can turn them stone cold to any concept of reasoning and make them refuse to grow or think for themselves. I once heard a lady on a yellow danfo bus swear that culture and religion stunt the growth of Nigerians more than anything else, after a preacher stopped by to deliver a sermon in the fifteen minutes it took for the bus to load full of passengers. 'Na inside this hot sun where person dey find peace, wey him kon dey shout on top of our head? Abeg, make we hear word!' she hissed. I couldn't have agreed more. So when I do fawn at the beauty of culture, I do so with finger-measured adulation.

The Yorubas believe that just as honey is sweet, so will be the life of the child, and just as salt adds flavour to food, so will the child's life be full of substance and happiness. The sugar also represents a sweet life, and just like the plentiful seeds in an alligator pepper, the child's lineage will multiply. Palm oil is to signify a smooth and easy life, while the kola nut is to repel evil. The bitter kola is for a very long life and, finally, water is present so that the child is never thirsty in life and so that no enemy will slow its growth. I taste each and rub them on my poor baby's mouth, this small creature of mine who is still breathing new, unrecognisable air, another life in a terrible yet wondrous world. I hope the world won't be cruel to him.

I have already decided that my Nimi will be a feminist. Fola nodded in agreement, knowing better than to argue with me. I want him to play with dolls just as much as he does with cars. I want him not just to enjoy egusi soup but to know how to cook it too. I want him to know what it is to love a woman whole-heartedly, so that her submission is never a conversation at the dining table. As well as knowing how to repair a car, he'll know how to do his own laundry. By God, he'll learn to do it all, and where I fail, Fola will come to the rescue, teaching him what I cannot. The world desperately needs more feminists and my Nimi is going to be one.

II

Osayuki

I am upstairs in my bedroom taking a much-needed break from the celebration downstairs. I have fed Nimi again and he is peacefully asleep in his grandmother's arms. I can already tell that Mama Fola will spoil him. She had happily taken him from me when I said I was coming up to the room. 'Go and rest a bit my dear,' she had nodded in understanding. The formal part of the ceremony is over and everyone is helping themselves to the food we prepared for the big feast. But before this, the pastor called on both grandparents to hold Nimi, to give him a name and pray for him by declaring great things into his life. Later on, other relatives were also given a chance to give him a name if they wanted to, but they were first required to put money into a bowl. At the end of the ceremony, Nimi came away with five names. But Fola and I know that there are only three that will make it to his birth certificate. The one we have given him – Oluwalonimi, a Yoruba name meaning 'God owns me', due to the circumstances of his conception; Ifẹlẹwa, another Yoruba name meaning 'beautiful love', given by Fola's mother; and Osazẹ, given by my mother, meaning 'chosen by God' in our Edo language. Our little boy will be known to the world as Oluwalonimi Ifẹlẹwa Osazẹ Morgan, beautiful names rooted in love and God's grace.

I take off my heels and relax into the flower-patterned chaise longue adjacent to our king-sized bed. I stretch out my legs and turn on the TV to distract me from the headache I am beginning to feel, thanks to the tightness of the gele on my head. I look for the knots. While I loosen them, I watch the news on the BBC. They're talking about a young man who died a month ago while on a trip to Nigeria. The reporter says that he was a third-generation British-Nigerian man, and had been in his mother-land for over a year before his untimely death. *Not today, oh not today. I can't breathe, I can't breathe.*

I am shocked to the core and, all of a sudden, I feel numb. I stare at the TV in silence, my lips trembling, watching flashing images transition from a solemn crowd in London gathered at a graveside, to a bustling junction in Lagos, overflowing with market sellers. I try to process what I am hearing. I knew that the day would come when I'd have to make a decision. But why today? The day of my baby's naming ceremony. Is it a sign? I realise I am covered in goosebumps and the once humid room now feels cold. I grab my throw and wrap myself in its faux fur. Without warning, tears begin to race down my cheeks.

Moments later, I hear the loud clickety sounds of stilettos on the marble floor outside, coming towards my room, and I grab a pocket tissue and quickly dab my face, making sure I don't ruin the makeup Cynthia had perfectly applied this morning. I fluff my buba, pat down my iro and compose myself. No one must know what is unravelling in my head. The news on the TV continues to recount the events that led to the young man's death by the roadside. I bend over and tie the straps of my heels back up. I look up to find Cynthia leaning against the door frame, staring at me with arms akimbo, accentuating her hourglass figure even further.

'Yuki what are you doing here? Hiding away while the rest of us attend to the guests huh?' she drawls. 'You're lucky today is your day, you know I dislike babysitting adults at parties, especially these aunties we all know are here just for the food! I don't know what it is with Nigerians and party jollof,' she continues, exaggerating the last two words as they roll off her tongue.

She walks over and joins me on the chaise, nudging her big bum against mine, an order to scoot over.

'Don't tell me you're already tired? You've only worn that head tie for like . . . an hour? Come on, give me a break!' she goes on, relaxing into the chair and making herself comfortable.

'So why are you sitting down then?' I smirk.

'Well if you can sit, so can I!' she counters.

She picks up the remote and I attempt to collect it from her, but she is too fast. She sways it out of my reach and turns up the volume. I can tell that she is going to sit for a while.

'Oh God, he looks familiar,' she says.

'Who?' I ask, pretending not to understand.

'Were you not just watching this? He looks familiar, but I don't remember where.'

'I'm sure every good-looking guy looks familiar to you Cynthia. Please, let's join the others downstairs. Who's with Nimi?' I change the subject.

I get up, take the remote out of her grasp and turn off the TV, even though I know that she still won't follow me immediately. With shaky legs, I walk towards the door, glad that my back is now to her, hiding the tremor in my lips and the tears welling up again in my eyes.

I pause. 'Let's go, I don't want people wondering where the mother of the day is,' I say, and walk out.

'Go on, I'm right behind you,' Cynthia says while still seated, one foot now crossed over the other.

I don't bother urging her any further. I need the time it will take to walk from my room to the winding staircase and down into the living room to get myself together and be the proud, smiling mother that I was a few minutes ago. Even though my sanity is beginning to crumble, I have to put on a facade for the rest of the day until the last of the guests are seen out. Like a swan, I have to be regal and glide with charm, even though underneath I am swimming for dear life.

III

Cynthia

Finally alone, I turn the TV back on and take off the corset that is holding my tummy in. It had been amusing to watch Fola's mother try to convince me to eat that mound of pounded yam. She had got quite upset when I had refused to, seeing as it had been dished out with my favourite soup.

I had followed Yuki upstairs, hoping to chat to her about my latest struggles with setting up my beauty academy back in London. The road to being self-employed is definitely not as linear as I had imagined when I first thought of the idea to create a brand to help women build their self-esteem through makeup. Yuki always knows how to put things into perspective, so I had hoped we'd get a chance to chat properly before I returned to England.

'I'll just close my eyes for five minutes,' I think as I stretch my legs on the chaise longue. But just a few seconds later, I am brought out of my dreamland by the news reporter's solemn voice. I sit up and watch with keen eyes. Something is amiss. I'm not sure what it is, but I know exactly who can explain it to me. I head back downstairs.

I've been watching Yuki for an hour now, and something is definitely up. She no longer has that spring in her step or that glow in her eyes. If anything, she looks on the brink of tears. It might not be visible to the undiscerning eye, but I know her well and I know that something is wrong. I look at Fola who is seated beside her, and wonder if he too can tell.

'Of course he can.' I answer the daft question in my head and fan myself with a newspaper as the help runs out to turn on the generator again. For the second time this afternoon, the power has gone out. 'Ah NEPA!' comes the familiar lament. Nigeria's National Electric Power Authority, long ago privatised and given a new name, has been providing such treats for years. But the disappointment is fresh every time, like a mother who suddenly realises that her son is now grown and no longer wants to be kissed in public.

Some hours later, when everyone has eaten their fill, I try to help Yuki cut the cake to serve to the guests, but she shoos me away. This isn't unlike her. If there is one thing that I know about Yuki, it is that she loves to keep herself busy whenever she is stressed or on edge about something. She would rather move around, sing, dance, or do anything other than sit twiddling her fingers, or try to keep still while her body involuntarily fidgets. I look at her closely before I leave to help the other women in the kitchen bring out more drinks. The guests are clearly still enjoying being merry, and the quick wave of her hand gives just enough time to blink back tears. She isn't fooling me.

The day carries on gallantly. Everyone is all smiles, especially the proud parents. That sweet smile of Yuki's easily captures the hearts of most, but I can tell it is sometimes forced. Fola, on the other hand, beams with pride, as any new father would. It is a wonderful ceremony for a wonderful couple.

We eat, dance and share many stories that evening. I have never seen Fola's mother as excited as she is today; she is known for her dramatics, but she has surpassed even herself. And Yuki's family are no different. Her mother, who was up the whole previous night, helping her to tend to Nimi, is still on her feet seeing to everyone's needs. She is clearly a doting mother. Although she was shocked to find out that Yuki was expecting a child after only being away from London for a year, she was still very supportive of her choice and new life. It has been a perfect ceremony, and knowing Yuki, it couldn't have been better executed. However, I can't shake off the feeling of foreboding.

I wait until most of the guests have left, and believe me, it is a long wait. It is no news that Nigerians love to party and at any given opportunity will turn a small ceremony into an all-night event. But thankfully, at about 9 p.m., the guests start to go home, and it is clear that there will be no partying into the wee hours of the morning. Mother and child both need their rest, after all.

After seeing Aunty Rosemary and her family to the door, I cast my bait.

'Yu-ki,' I drawl, as I usually do when I need a favour. I want to make her feel comfortable. 'You must be knackered, let's go upstairs for a bit.'

I can tell by the way she pauses that she would rather busy herself in the kitchen than go upstairs with me. But she must know I'm onto something – she's caught me staring at her several times so far this evening.

'Come on, you've been up since morning. Most of the guests are gone now, let's take a break. Fola can see the rest of them out.'

'Let's take a break, or *you* need a break?' she jokes.

I play along and give a fake laugh, but the walk up the winding stairs to the room is clearly awkward and I don't know what I'm going to say when we get there. I just hope she opens up and tells me what is troubling her. When we get to the landing, I lead the way into the bedroom. As soon as she enters, I close the door – I want to make sure no one will walk in on us. Then, immediately, I pounce.

'What's going on? Come clean!' I demand.

'What do you mean?' she asks shakily.

'I know you well enough to know that something's wrong. What, did you think I wouldn't notice?' I say.

'Cynthia, I'm tired, I thought we were coming up to rest?'

'Now you want to rest? Come on, it's been quite obvious. You've been acting weird since this afternoon. I mean, don't get me wrong, you've been hiding it well, but I know something's up. I'm surprised Fola hasn't said anything to you yet – or has he?' I continue, ignoring her evasion.

'You've started with your exaggerations again. I'm fine, just a bit tired, that's all.' We both know that isn't true.

'If you won't tell me, I'll have to force it out of you one way or the other or should I ask Fola?' I challenge.

'Are you mad? Don't get him involved in this!'

'Oh really? So are you going to tell me what has upset you? Does it have to do with what was on the TV?'

As soon as I mention this, her demeanour changes. Faced with my stern look, she sits down on the bed and breaks into a flood of tears.

'I don't think I should tell you,' she starts. 'You don't need to know . . .'

'Clearly I do, and if you don't tell me, I'll find out one way or another before I leave for London. Osayuki, start talking!' I haven't used her full name in a long while.

Her next few words leave me in shock. With my head spinning, I reach for the bed. I sit next to her, head in hands and mouth ajar as I look on, incredulous. It's an expression every Nigerian knows all too well.

'How did this happen? When?' The questions tumble out of my mouth.

It doesn't make sense. None of it does. From the little that I can recall, she disliked Kian from the start. How has she found herself in this mess? I look at her for answers, and her eyes begin to well up again.

'It happened so fast,' she manages in between sobs.

'I thought you had only been with Fola since you arrived?'

'I know what you must think of me. It only happened during our break!'

'Ahh . . . the break that only lasted for like three weeks?'

'It was a month, but that's beside the point. I thought I was never going to get back with him. He was dead to me, remember what happened?' she says, trying to choke back fresh tears.

'Hold on. You need to start from the beginning. How did it happen? You definitely didn't like Kian at our first encounter,' I reply.

'No, I didn't. But when we bumped into each other again at your leaving party, something was different about him, or maybe

I was mad from the whole Fola situation. I don't even know,' she says, exasperated.

This is the first I have heard of her meeting Kian again. 'Have you kept in contact with him all this time?'

'No, I ignored all his calls and eventually he stopped calling. It was just that one night. And now it's turned into an episode of Jeremy Kyle. Ah!' she sighs.

'So, he's Nimi's father?' I ask, not wanting to believe the words as they stagger out of my mouth.

'No. I mean, I don't know!'

'How can you not know? OK, start from the beginning.'

OVER A YEAR AGO

CHAPTER 1

Osayuki

I was heading back from the toilet when I first saw her. She was a few years younger, perhaps a year or two I guessed. She looked like she belonged somewhere other than sitting at the connecting lounge at Milan airport. Long wavy weave (human hair no doubt), black leather jacket, Chelsea boots and red-stained lips (Ruby Woo most likely) – she fit the description of what I liked to call the classic 'London babe' look. I was getting bored, and with two hours till boarding, I decided to have a wander.

'Is that your real hair?' she asked in awe as I strolled past.

'Yeah.' I grinned, stopped, fiddled with the handle of my cabin luggage, then plopped myself on the opposite chair.

After introducing ourselves, I learned she was in fact four years younger than me, and was also waiting for the connecting flight to Lagos. From the look of things, she wasn't exactly happy to be heading there. She asked what I knew about Nigeria's National Youth Service Corps scheme, commonly known as NYSC – I told her I didn't know much. She disgruntledly revealed she was due to start her service year in the capital, Abuja. I didn't want to pry but I was curious, so asked why she was heading to Lagos instead. I had always valued the sense of openness and shared anxiousness amongst Nigerians at the state of affairs in our home country. Meet a Nigerian anywhere, and you'd soon be bonding over stories about NEPA, fuel scarcity and mad traffic.

The most familiar phrase amongst our generation was '*African parents*'. It usually explained why someone was doing something they'd rather not do, or not doing something they wanted to do. Cynthia, my new friend, revealed that returning to the motherland hadn't been voluntary; she had had no say in the matter.

'African parents,' she said, and rolled her eyes.

I shook my head and mouthed 'Tell me about it.' But we didn't share a similar story. The chain of events that had led me to the airport on that very cold February morning was far from familial. Like her, I *was* being pushed to return to the motherland, but in my case, I was running away from the life I had known in London. It was still a new year of sorts, and a fresh start was needed.

'Ladies, ladies. You buff tings, you going to Lagos yeah?' a voice intruded.

I looked up to see who had brazenly drawn our attention. Six foot two, toned, light brown complexion, brown eyes and an arrogance to boot, he could have made even the most sensible girl lose her mind; but I was having none of it. I looked over at Cynthia and clearly, he had won her attention.

'I'm Kian. You know . . . Kian Bajo?' he said, and hummed a tune I had never heard. Cynthia also looked clueless but nodded for him to carry on. She was clearly encouraging him and he continued to talk non-stop about himself and his mission to conquer the music industry in Nigeria. Even with my nose stuck in a magazine, he didn't get the hint and only paused after an awkward long wait to ask for our names. Cynthia replied and also offered mine. I smirked and turned back to the magazine.

'So what are you going to do in Lagos, Miss Badu?'

I turned to look him in the eye, astounded by the effrontery.

Cynthia's expression said that she too wanted to know. So I offered 'Work,' and raised my eyebrows as if to ask, *anything else?*

He got the message and turned to Cynthia. I tried to block out what they were saying, but their enthusiasm was hard to ignore. I closed the magazine and joined in, mostly listening but offering my opinions here and there. He was a musician (an unsuccessful one, I concluded, given the way he was bigging himself up) going to the mega city to break into the fast-growing afrobeat industry.

'My cousin is a top manager you know, he's hooking me up

real good!' he enthused, just as the speaker announced the flight to Lagos was beginning to board. 'Eh, let's add each other on Instagram yeah? Maybe we could even link up one of these days. I'll invite you to my concert or something,' Kian said with a grin, before winking at me.

I rolled my eyes and handed my phone to Cynthia. She searched for her profile and clicked the follow button, but before I could take my phone back, Kian took it off her and typed in his too. I let him be and made a mental note to delete it later. *What an interesting fellow*, I thought sarcastically as he fixed his cap on his tapered haircut and swaggered off in front of us.

CHAPTER 2

Cynthia

We took off an hour later than we should have. At that point, I had begun to get irritated and upset all over again at my parents for forcing me to go on the trip. I later learned that the delay had been caused by some passengers who had exceeded the cabin limit. Their extra bags had to be towed away to join the rest of the checked-in luggage. True to form, they had protested, but there was nothing to be done. The rules were there for a reason.

'Chai! Only Nigerians will hear "one hand luggage" and will still enter with two!' the man next to me quipped.

'Yeah, only Nigerians,' I sighed.

He continued to go on about the country and shared information I couldn't care less about. I wasn't in the mood to be friendly. I wanted to be left alone to contemplate how I'd survive a whole year in Nigeria. It didn't make sense. Why would my parents leave only to send me back? What were they trying to prove? It would be an experience of a lifetime, Dad had said, trying to sweeten what he knew was a blow.

The man beside me was still talking. He smiled, revealing yellow teeth. I wished he wouldn't lean in so close. *What is it with these people and personal space?*

'So what do you think about our new president?' the man asked.

'The prime minister you mean?' I fired back, thinking of 10 Downing Street.

'Ah, the president of your country. Abi are you not Nigerian?'

I told him that I didn't follow much of what happened in Nigeria. The most I knew of was whenever Dad came back home happy that the exchange rate had increased in his favour. It still baffled me every time he sent money to his relatives. Could they not work as other people did? If only they knew how hard he worked, they wouldn't call so often about one issue or the other.

'Well, you should know these things. No matter how far we travel, home is home o!'

I nodded in agreement and looked at the empty row in front of ours. I wish he would leave and let me be.

'So, any boyfriend? A fine girl like you can't be single!' A common question from Nigerian men like this one who got too familiar too quickly.

'I'm not single,' I lied.

'Forget that one, I don't mind, I can be your side guy.' He replied and winked.

'I'm not even staying long in Lagos, I'll be heading to Abuja soon,' I said, trying to let him off easy, but he was adamant that he could fly to see me at any time – all I needed to do was give him my number.

'I'll give it to you if you let me sleep, I'm tired.'

'Really? OK,' he said and hurried to the seat in front.

Some hours later, I was awakened by a sharp voice. The man was complaining about his meal. I collected my food tray from the Italian air hostess, smiled and exaggerated my thank you to make up for his behaviour. I didn't want her thinking we were all rude; it took one Nigerian to mar the rest of us.

'Can you imagine, how can a flight to Lagos run out of chicken? Chiiiicken!' he posed as soon as the air hostess had left.

'Some people are vegetarians you know?' I said, even though I'd have also preferred a meat option.

'Abeg, we're Africans, we love meat. Which one is vegetarian? If it was a flight to Paris or Spain, I would have said OK, but a flight to Lagos? Ha, I'm never flying with them again, rubbish!'

I couldn't help but laugh at the passion in his voice. He looked at me and grinned, again, revealing his grotesque teeth. I turned swiftly of my meal, wondering if he ever brushed, and how he had feigned ignorance to his teeth's demise.

Hours later, as the plane was landing, came another incident

I would go on to recount in the days to come. One minute I was seated with my seatbelt fastened, as per the captain's instructions, finishing off the movie I was watching, and the next I was assaulted with a thundering round of applause as the tyres hit the tarmac. I looked around at what seemed like a meeting of a cult – clapping, cheering and thanks being given to God. I looked ahead, five rows to my left, and saw Osayuki on the aisle seat with head tilted back, her big afro a halo adorning her pretty features, mock clapping and laughing, enjoying the show of it all. *What madness is yet to unfold?* I wondered, as the captain's voice came through the speakers, drowning the noise.

Later, as I walked towards immigration, someone rested a hand on my shoulder from behind. 'Please can I have your number now?' I turned to see that it was the man from the plane.

'I don't have a sim yet,' I said, irritated, moving to the side to let his hand drop.

'Are you on BB?' he pressed.

'No,' I replied, trying not to roll my eyes. *Who even used Blackberries anymore?*

'OK, just give me your London number.'

'I'm here for a year though, I don't see the point!' I said, exasperated and walked away.

I didn't look back. The very last thing I wanted to do was give this man my phone number.

'Don't look so mad. You're in Lagos now, there will be more,' Osayuki teased as I joined her in the queue to pass through immigration.

Three hours later, we had finally retrieved our luggage. It had taken us an hour to go through immigration, then another two to collect all of our belongings. *Did anything ever work in this country?*

'I don't know why you'd want to live here, but good luck!' I said and hugged her goodbye.

'Enjoy your week in Lagos, and have a great service year in Abuja!' she replied as she pushed her trolley towards the exit and into the night.

CHAPTER 3

Osayuki

I was hit by the humidity as soon as I stepped out. I wasn't expecting it to be so suffocating. I knew it was going to be hot, but this was an unwelcome surprise. I tried to remember if it had felt this way growing up in Lagos fifteen years ago, but my memory failed.

I tried to avoid the onslaught of touts who offered to help with the trolley. Mum had warned me to be wary of them and wait until I saw her sister, Aunty Rosemary. I looked around, trying to see if anything remained familiar. I breathed in deeply. Even the air had changed. I looked around at the chaos. Men holding placards with names scribbled on them awaited their clients; some who had been gone for a long while, others perhaps only on vacation, and others still who were moving here from abroad. There had been a few of them on the plane. I had looked at the man opposite my aisle and wondered what he had thought of the jubilation when the plane landed.

'Osayuki!'

In London, no one called my name with the right accent except for my mum, so I turned to the direction of the voice. Sauntering towards me in a bejewelled kaftan was my beaming aunt. She looked gracious as ever and didn't seem to have aged since I saw her five years ago, when she had visited our north London home. A year apart in age from Mum, she shared the same honey-brown complexion, five-foot-five-inch frame and pretty smile. Anyone would mistake them for twins, except that where Aunty Rosemary was chubby, Mum was slender; where she was voluptuous, Mum was lithe; and while Aunty Rosemary was loud and outspoken, Mum was quiet and introspective.

'Aunty!' I screamed, and held her in a tight embrace.

If she wasn't my mum's only sibling, I would have declared her my favourite aunty. She playfully pinched my cheeks and looked me over.

'You're still skinny. That you get from your mother, but *this*,' she said, brushing my arm in reference to the colour of my skin, 'is all Victor!'

We smiled broadly, still holding hands, the remembrance of my sweet yet steadfast late father moving across our faces. We embraced again before she led me to where her car was parked. She told me we would have to be quick because she had left the driver parked where they shouldn't be and didn't want to risk a fine. I laughed, knowing that if anyone would break the rules, it'd be my aunt, but she mischievously added she wasn't the only one. It was Lagos after all. 'When the car park is so far nko. Who likes stress?' she said and laughed.

In the car, she introduced me to Mr Nelson who, she divulged, would be in charge of seeing that I got to my appointments. Then she looked at me and sighed. I thought I knew what she was about to ask when she leaned over and patted my knee. I realised that Mum had already told her the sordid details. She said she knew just what I needed, and coming to Lagos was a great idea. I rolled my eyes and laughed. Ever since I finished university four years ago, Aunty Rosemary had been on my case to walk down the aisle. If I didn't know better, she seemed as though she was intending to leave me in peace, but I knew she had other things in mind, and my broken heart wasn't going to deter her from whatever she had planned.

It's funny the turns life takes. Only a month ago, I had been ready to give up moving back to Lagos, but here I was, in a crazy town, sitting beside an even crazier aunt. I'd have laughed if the turn of events that had led me here hadn't been so painful. If there was any place to heal, Lagos was it. The city had its way of spitting out the weak. It had no guises nor care to dote on the aggrieved. Things happen, you move on. That's exactly what Aunty Rosemary said I needed. I didn't like to think of what she could have meant, but I smiled, shaking off the repulsive thought of becoming involved with anyone.

It hadn't always been this way. There was a time when all I wanted was to find 'the one' and live as happily as could be. I wasn't looking for a fairytale, but I was fresh out of university and hoping to conquer the world with a partner by my side. Most of the men I had met were either not interested in a committed relationship or too arrogant. Sometimes they were both, which particularly irked me. But everything changed one Saturday morning on a trip to the bank.

It was a cold morning, and no sooner than I'd left the house it had started to rain. I didn't have an umbrella, so I ran the rest of the way, grateful for the shelter and heat when I got in. As I reached the front of the short queue, I was still trying to brush off the rain drops on my coat when I heard a deep voice say, 'How can I help you, miss?' I paused, raising my head to be confronted with Nick, the voice's owner. God was he handsome! I forgot what I was about to say as my eyes held his. He smiled questioningly. I looked down at his badge: Nick Kwame Asante. *Born on a Saturday*, I thought, translating the meaning of his Ghanaian middle name. He was certainly easy on the eye, his light brown eyes and complexion a stark contrast against mine. It was something his mother would mention when I first met her. But it hadn't bothered me that he had been raised by a white mother and hadn't known much about his Ghanaian roots. Travelling through West Africa had been one of the many things we had promised to do together.

I had left the bank that day with an appointment with him for the following week to talk about opening a business account I didn't need. That's how it had all started, on a cold, rainy Saturday morning. We had three wonderful years together, but in one day, Nick ripped it all apart. I no longer wanted any memories of him. I cried hard for the first few weeks after our breakup, but I was done crying now. Blocking him on all platforms and deleting his number was the first step. Packing my bags and accepting the job offer in Lagos was the second. I was no longer interested in finding a life partner. I was looking forward to conquering the world all on my own, and Lagos was going to be my fresh start.

I looked away from Aunty Rosemary and leaned close to the window, my eyes searching into the night, wondering what life in Lagos was going to bring.

CHAPTER 4

Kian

That same night in a different part of town, Kian was coming to terms with the reality of what he had thrown himself into. He was no longer in London, the only city he had ever known, or under the ever-protective gaze of his mother. He was in his motherland, a place that had become the city of his dreams ever since his cousin, Adewale, had planted the idea in his head some months ago. His mother had been vehemently opposed to the idea of him moving to Lagos, saying that perhaps it was time he looked for a more fulfilling career. Kian was twenty-five years old and she had grown weary of taking care of him and helping him pay his bills. Yet when she had seen how seriously he had taken his dream, and that he had been saving for the trip, she had relented, grudgingly offering her blessings and extending her last fortitude to give him a chance at making something of his life. 'Ọlakitan, after this, no more,' she had said, fearful for her only child.

Although his flight had been delayed, and it had taken longer than expected to retrieve his belongings, there was still no sign of his cousin, who was coming to pick him up. On his way out of the airport, he was suddenly flanked by a man who pulled him aside and requested to search his belongings. Kian had been astonished at first, but relaxed when he realised some other passengers had also been pulled aside by casually dressed officials and were being searched.

Finally out of the semi-air-conditioned building, he was immediately assaulted by a cacophony of sounds. People were all over the place. Some standing and waiting, others in a hurry to unknown destinations. He wasn't expecting the air to be so pungent and humid.

He looked around, trying to find a familiar face. All that greeted him in return were blank stares and questioning smiles. A man approached and offered his mobile phone, guessing that Kian needed to reach whomever he had been waiting for. After three rings, Adewale answered and informed him he was right around the corner, and was only being delayed by the traffic leading up to the airport. Kian breathed a sigh of relief and handed the phone back to the stranger. The man waited. Not sure what else to do, he dipped his hand into his pocket and dug out a pound coin.

Uneasy at being alone, he chewed nervously on his fingernails as he watched the grinning man saunter away with his tip. Twenty minutes later, Adewale arrived in what could only have been described as a worn-out Toyota Corolla, honking loudly to draw Kian's attention. As Kian approached the vehicle, his older cousin, whom he had last seen when he was five years old, jumped out of the car and hurried towards Kian, shouting salutations and locking him in an embrace. Kian saw no resemblance in his face. It seemed an unremarkable face – one that could easily be forgotten. Adewale's only saving graces were his white teeth and wide grin, which lit up his face until he stopped smiling.

'Welcome to Lasgidi. We're about to run this town!' Adewale declared with relish. 'Sorry I'm late o, don't mind me. The traffic was mad, you know how it is na,' he continued.

Kian laughed along and shifted on the springy chair, failing to make himself comfortable as they sped into the night. Now in his cousin's company, he finally began to feel at ease and looked out, trying to make out his surroundings. But the night was too dark and the street lights too dim.

'So how's everyone and your mum?' Adewale asked.

'Mum's good. Not happy I'm here, but she'll be fine. Things are good man. I can't wait to get things going!' Kian responded with bravado.

The boys carried on in their fervour, boosting each other's esteem for the journey to come. Kian noticed Adewale's dishevelled state and asked if everything was OK with him and his family. Adewale said everyone was fine and that things were right on track. As they approached the family home, everywhere was dark, but for a single street lamp lighting the way. Kian hadn't been sure of what to expect, but he was surprised nonetheless as they drove further into the street. Yes, he had heard of the big houses that life in Lagos afforded some, but his mother had also told him the common immigration story of why his grandfather had left Nigeria to the UK in the first place, to seek a better life. He had known that little tale was her way of discouraging him, but had ignored the warning in her voice.

At the end of the road, Adewale drove slowly into the last house after the gate was pried open by a gateman.

'Oga dey house?' he spat out to the gateman as he drove in slowly, making sure his Toyota Corolla wasn't further grazed by the rusty gate.

'E dey inside,' the young man replied, before walking off in the darkness to wherever he had been before their arrival.

'Go on, I'll meet you inside,' Adewale said to Kian.

Kian walked into the house. Unable to see beyond his nose, he stood by the doorway, unsure of where it led to. He heard a man call out just as the lights came on, accompanied by a roaring sound he later found out was a generator.

'You're the spitting image of your mother!' his uncle said as he patted him on the shoulder, leaving his hand there so long that Kian felt uneasy at the familiarity. He had little memory of his uncle although he had heard so much about him; his mother's oldest sibling who had moved back to Lagos. He couldn't yet say how much his uncle's dreams had panned out, but from what he could see, the house looked good enough.

'So, I hope you'll talk some sense into your cousin about joining my business. I'm opening another branch of my store. It's going to be a chain store. Perhaps you can also learn a thing or two while you're here,' Mr Babatunde said to his nephew.

'Daddy, Kian didn't come all the way from London to come and sit in your store. He's going to be a star. Lagos ain't ready!' Adewale boasted.

'Ahh. Olakitan yi? Oniranu. Ki le leyin sin?' his uncle lamented.

Kian smiled when his uncle mentioned his first name, but was unsure as he watched Adewale's jaw tighten. He wished his mother had bothered to teach him the language. He realised his uncle was displeased with what Adewale had said so buoyantly; that much he could gather.

'Anyway, boys, the offer is still on the table. Whenever you're ready, I'll be happy to show you around.'

'Don't worry Uncle, we'll be fine,' Kian replied as Adewale waved his hand and beckoned him to follow.

When they got to his room, Adewale informed him that they were to stay at his father's only for the night. He revealed that he was renting an apartment elsewhere in town until he could build or buy his own house once they hit it big. In their culture, to be fully independent and free, one had to assume total financial independence from one's parents. Nothing like Kian was used to, Adewale was quick to add. Kian nodded with slight embarrassment, because given all of his bravado, he was still very much dependent on his mother.

CHAPTER 5

Osayuki

The weekend had gone by like a breeze. I was awakened with a start by the alarm clock next to the bedside table, and the soft hum of the AC reminding me where I was. I looked at the room I now called mine. It looked nothing like the room I had spent weeks trying to get just right in London. I had been excited when I finally moved away from home a year after graduation and had spent hours tirelessly jazzing up the flat to my taste. Even though the studio apartment in Camden had been smaller than I would have liked, and was more expensive than the place I had rented at university, I had loved every inch of it because it was mine. It was thanks to my hard work that it was beautifully furnished, and that every nook and cranny remained warm in the cold winter nights. I had been proud to have landed a dream job in fashion PR and then, later on, styling, when my manager left and the opportunity presented itself.

I looked at the room Aunty Rosemary had declared mine. I enjoyed the coolness of the white marble floor beneath my feet every time I got out of bed and all the comforts her luxurious tastes could afford. Yet, even though the room was almost as big as my studio flat, it didn't make me miss my old place any less. I missed having all the colourful and eclectic things I had collected over the years around me, and even simple pleasures like putting on the whistling kettle I had bought at a quirky shop in Shoreditch, which reminded me of my time growing up in Lagos. I had hated the cold but waking up warm underneath my double duvet, clinging onto a hot water bottle, was always comforting. Even the little chimes that would ring out from the mini bells I had strung on the dreamcatcher above my bed were reassuring. I wanted the familiar confines of my little bubble, but I knew it was no good. It was best that I was elsewhere, rather than crying myself to sleep every night. Everything still reminded me too much of what I'd rather forget. It was time to move on.

Sliding into my work shoes, I walked down the stairs and joined Aunty Rosemary at the dining table next to the kitchen. Juliet, the house help whom I had been introduced to the night I had arrived, was busy pottering away in the kitchen, but came out to greet me with a curtsy as soon as I entered. Embarrassed, I returned her salutation and asked to have whatever my aunty was eating. She curtsied again and left. I turned to see Aunty Rosemary looking at me earnestly. I was nervous about my first day at work and she could tell. 'They will love you . . .' she had begun, swallowing the remainder of what she had been about to say. I hoped she was right.

'I told Juliet to make you a packed lunch. I don't want you having a runny stomach on my watch!'

'Aunty, I'm sure I'll be fine. I'm not a JJC o!' I laughed. JJC stood for Johnny Just Come. It was a term reserved for people who were new at doing something, new to a place or plain ignorant about a situation. Even though I had left for London at ten years old, I was no JJC. On my way out, I picked up the last remaining agbalumo from the previous day. It was clear Aunty Rosemary missed her children and was ready to spoil me in their place while they were away. She had told Juliet to prepare my favourite dishes and had stocked the fridge with fruit. Biting into an agbalumo the day I arrived, I had gasped with joy – growing up it had been one of my favourite things to eat. I had almost forgotten what it tasted like, but I remembered ten years ago when Aunty Rosemary had brought some with her when she visited to attend Mum's wedding to Bob. She'd done the same again five years later, when she came over for my graduation. Her visits always seemed to be bang on five years apart – we had laughed about the 'five-year curse', joking that another monumental event needed to happen sooner to get her back to London with my favourite fruit in hand. Mum had looked at

Nick suggestively then, but who would have predicted that I'd be the one running back to the continent, a year shy of five years?

Getting into the car with Mr Nelson, I ate the sweet skin encapsulating the seed then proceeded to the agbalumo's juicy, fleshy innards and wondered if I could still make chewing gum out of its outer skin. I remembered how I would chew it extra carefully to churn it into gum, avoiding the otherwise mushy mess. Looking up, I waved goodbye to Aunty Rosemary as her car pulled away from ours, heading to one of her luxurious spas on another part of the island. I looked at Mr Nelson in the driver's seat and told him where I needed to be, and prayed that my correspondent at the office had been exaggerating about the likelihood of getting stuck in traffic at that hour of the morning.

My commute to work in London was very different from this. I certainly hadn't been driven by a private chauffeur. Every morning, I'd jump on the Northern line to Moorgate, where I'd then change to either the Circle or Metropolitan line, whichever came first, to get to my company's head office at Liverpool Street. We were a small team of ten in that office, but we worked well together, meticulously ensuring that our independent fashion label could compete with the best in Europe. I had initially been employed as the Assistant PR after I graduated, but when Melissa, the Head of PR and Communications, abandoned her role to travel the world with her boyfriend, I had to step up, taking more responsibility. It eventually got me promoted, and then more involved in styling projects. I wondered what working in Lagos would be like and if things really worked at a slower pace like Mum had said.

CHAPTER 6

Osayuki

At ten minutes to nine, Mr Nelson rolled the car to a stop. There had been traffic but thankfully, I had left just enough time to save face on my first day at the office. I closed the Instagram app on my iPad where I had been scrolling through images that Cynthia had posted about her first weekend in Lagos, and looked up to see what seemed like a house. I thanked Mr Nelson and told him that I'd call later in the day to inform him when to pick me up. Turning my back on the sleek saloon car I had been allocated, I took in the architecture of the house. It was a two-storey building with a brownish-orange gate that stood ajar. I walked through and peered into the mini security house just by the gate. There was no gateman or security guard in sight, so I proceeded towards the building. It was painted in an off-white colour and surrounded by flowery hedges. I saw ixora and bougainvillea flowers, and was immediately transported back to my childhood, recalling those innocent years when I hadn't a care in the world. I had loved playing in our communal backyard. We had moved to the area after Daddy had lost his job. The other children and I would pluck the flowers and other leaves growing around us. We would then gather at our favourite spot with empty tins in hand as pots and pans. We'd fetch water from the well in the backyard, gather branches, support them with stones and place the tin that contained the flowers, leaves and other bounties on our makeshift stove. We'd then stir the contents and pretend to cook.

I saw another flower around the hedge and realised I didn't know its name. It was peculiar some of the things I had over-looked growing up in Lagos, especially given my current love for nature. Then, just to the right of the building, adjacent to the entrance, I spotted a rose apple tree. That tree – it had been the bane of my childhood. I had hated their pink bell-shaped fruit, but the school children who would stop by our gate and beg to be allowed inside to pluck them thought otherwise. This was before Daddy had lost his job and we still lived in our own house. Mum had tasked me with the responsibility of letting them in and seeing to it that the gate was secured properly once they had gone. If we weren't going to eat it, it was best to give it to those who would, she said, and so it was that I had to wait around until they had taken their share before I could return to my homework or games.

I smiled at the memories and walked up to the receptionist inside. The reception had a huge company logo – 'House of Martha' – embossed in gold on the lilac-painted wall. I introduced myself and sank into the plump black PU leather seat next to the desk, waiting for Mrs Martha Phillips. She was to be my new boss, and this would be the first time I'd formally met her. Before now, I had only spoken to her on Skype when I had had my final interview for the job. I looked around – I couldn't wait to get started. I could feel the warmth and energy of the place. I felt that I would be right at home at House of Martha.

At nine on the dot, I heard the clicking of heels coming towards the reception. *So much for Nigerian time*, I thought as Mrs Phillips walked towards me with a welcoming smile. Her charisma was all-encompassing and I could already tell I would enjoy working with her. She was a tall, dark-complexioned and averagely built woman, sexy in her own way. I watched the ringlets of her weave bounce around her face as she led me through the building. The strands stopped just above her jaw line, giving the illusion of chubby cheeks. I complimented her brocade wrap dress and was informed that it was from her latest collection, yet to be released. In our interview, I had been struck by her determination to ensure her company kept up with the times. She had told me she needed the perfect PR lead to help rebrand her fashion house, to win over the millennial audience and take it to international heights.

I followed Mrs Phillips through the building. The ground floor was home to the canteen and social area, two meeting rooms, a small studio and the reception area. The first floor was where the account managers, HR and the rest of the legal, communications and administrative team were based. On our way to the second floor, the gathering buzz told me this was the hub of the company. In one room were cabinets full of fabrics and patterns. In another, several sewing machines made an orchestra of sounds while next door, a model was being fitted. I was excited by the flurry of activity and couldn't wait to get settled and find my way around. The head office back in London had only been for the corporate side of the business, since all creative and design work was carried out in Cambridge where the director was based. This was different. I could tell that I'd love it here.

After the tour, I was introduced to the other two PR assistants that I was to work with to rebrand House of Martha. I smiled and shook hands with Adaora, the executive assistant who was my second in command. She returned a stiff smile. We were of a similar build, but while my muscle tone gave away a love for sports and exercise, her lanky frame was a result of a fast metabolism. In her wedge heels, she was almost the same height as me. I held her gaze and didn't like what I found there. Her otherwise pretty features were marked with signs of bleaching. I turned to glance at Mercy, the second assistant, who offered an apologetic smile and led me to my office. Mrs Phillips hurried off to continue with her day's schedule, believing to have left me in the capable hands of her loyal employees.

CHAPTER 7

Cynthia

Another midday spent lounging in bed counting sheep. What has my life turned into? Just why was I here? The week spent living it up in Lagos was beginning to feel like a blur. I had begun to think that coming to Nigeria wasn't all that bad, but that was starting to look like wishful thinking. Aunty Ndidi, my dad's younger sister, had taken time off work to show me around and make me feel at home. My homesickness had quickly worn off as she took me to all the trendy places in Lagos. She had declined to take me to Boogie's, supposedly the best club in town, because she didn't want to miss Sunday service the next morning, but seeing I was disappointed, had asked her friend Sophia to take me instead. It was the best night I had had all year.

Here I was now in a lavish house in the capital city, Abuja, a long way from the hustle and bustle of Lagos. It was way prettier here than where Aunty Ndidi lived, but I felt bitter. The short burst of thrill she had injected into my life when I had arrived was finally wearing off. Lying in bed in the cold, air-conditioned room, bedecked with the finest chiffon curtains, premium mahogany furnishings and a rug as soft as a baby's bottom should have made me thankful that I didn't have to experience the true hardships of the majority of Nigerian citizens. Instead, I just felt fed up.

My younger brother Alex had reminded me how lucky I was when I had called to rant about my boredom the day after I had arrived in Abuja. He had always been the most thoughtful of my two siblings and the one I was closest to. He had been the one to console me when I had been irate that evening in December when my parents had first told me of their decision to send me to Abuja. Whenever my brothers and I had been very naughty growing up, Dad had joked about packing us off to experience African life. Mum would complain that, in her day, we would have never gotten away with such behaviour. Who could have thought that my father's threat was going to catch up with me all these years later? If I had known some sort of plan had been brewing, perhaps I would have done something about it. Unaware of the future consequences, I had left my first job after university just two months in. Dad had only looked at me with disappointment and shrugged. Mum, on the other hand, had been upset and sternly reminded me that I was no longer a child, that my time was ticking. I should have known better and stuck with the job until I found something more to my liking. Then came the fateful evening.

My parents were loud people, but I had noticed them speaking in hushed tones that night. It had unnerved me. Call it a sixth sense or whatever, but I had wondered why they were whispering, since I was certain that they weren't aware of my eavesdropping.

Then I heard my name and realised that, whatever it was, there was going to be an uncomfortable discussion. Pressing my ear firmly to the door, I closed my eyes and focused, but I could hardly make out what they were saying.

'If that's what you want, then tell her yourself,' Mum had said flatly, in the tone of voice she used when she wasn't keen on something.

'Nkechi, you have to support me on this. It has to come from the both of us,' my dad pleaded.

'Ehn, shebi you want her to go, call her na. Are you not the head of the house?' Mum retorted.

It became quiet, and I sensed I would be called in at any moment. I turned around and, as quietly as I could, made my way towards the stairs that led to my bedroom on the top floor of the house. But just before I entered, I heard my name.

'Cynthia!'

I threw myself onto the bed.

'Cynthia!'

I counted to three.

'Cynthia! Ahn ahn, is Cynthia not in this house?' my father bellowed from the bottom of the stairs.

'I'm coming!' I shouted, and slowly made my way down again and into the living room.

As I sat down on the sofa opposite my parents, I feigned a yawn and stretched my arms as if I had been taking a nap.

'Yes, Dad?' I said.

'How many times do I have to call you before you answer ehn?' he started. 'Anyway, we've called you here to discuss some important matter.'

He looked at Mum for support, but she had a blank expression; she had clearly decided to sit it out.

Her husband wished his wife had chosen a better time to be stubborn. Her unwillingness to see things his way was going to make it even more difficult, but he continued.

'Now that you've finished university, we can't have you just sitting at home. We've decided that you'll go to my brother's place in Abuja . . . you'll do NYSC while you're there.'

I had been gobsmacked. I couldn't believe what I had heard. I had only been aware of the National Youth Service Corps programme in passing. My Nigerian friends at university had to undergo it after their undergraduate studies, but I had never considered that I might have to do it. It was a year-long mandatory programme for all graduates, set up by the Nigerian government more than forty years ago. The year comprised of an initial three weeks' orientation period in a camp, before the graduates, known as corpers, were dispersed to work for the remaining eleven months, in various public and governmental sectors. During this time, they were to contribute to the communities within their deployed states as a means of serving the country. But I didn't live in Nigeria. *So what was this nonsense with my dad wanting to send me there?*

'Dad. *Dad.* You must be joking! I can't *serve*. I don't even live in the country. Are you serious?' I exclaimed.

'Whether you live there or not, we want you to go. It will teach you discipline and you'll be fine with Peter,' Dad maintained.

'Mum, is Dad serious? Are you not going to say anything? I can't go to Nigeria!'

'Cynthia, your father has spoken. He thinks it will do you some good,' my mum said with a measured tone.

'What good? I just finished uni, I need to start building a career. I don't even know anyone there, how can you do this to me?' I was enraged, yet still stunned, hoping it was all a bad joke to shake me up.

'What job are you looking for? You lie in bed every day, and type on your computer like a typewriter or put on makeup like a masquerade. Cynthia, you have to go o. I think we've spoilt you enough in this house. It's time for you to face the real world. Ahn ahn, enough is enough!' Dad concluded.

I was in tears. I had seen that my father wasn't kidding and my mother's silence was telling. I just couldn't believe it.

'It's called a cut crease by the way and I'm not going anywhere. I'm an adult you know!'

I had stormed out and tried to hide the tears that had slowly begun to cloud my vision. I brushed them off and ran up the stairs two at a time. When I got in bed, I furiously typed on my phone, sending my best friend Veronica a message.

My dad has gone mad, I'm finished.

CHAPTER 8

Cynthia

The next morning, in Uncle Peter's house, my buzzing phone woke me up. I knew who it was before I had even reached under my pillow. Phone in hand, 'Mum' glowed across the screen.

'So you're still asleep, Cynthia?' she started, without even saying hello.

'Well, not anymore. It's not like I have anywhere to go,' I replied in a huff.

She spent the next five minutes telling me off for not waking up early to help around my uncle's home, even though they had a housemaid and I wasn't required to do any chores. But of course when I mentioned this she insisted I still ask about helping out with other things my uncle's wife, Aunty Evelyn, might need.

'Mum, is Dad there?' I asked instead.

I wasn't surprised by her hesitation. She knew I was still hell-bent on escaping the torture that was camp orientation next week. She changed the subject swiftly, asking how my flight from Lagos to Abuja had been. Eager for her sympathy, I spared no detail. I reminded her again of how awful the service had been at the airport in Lagos when I had arrived from London, and assured her that travelling to Abuja was no different. If anything, it had been slightly worse. Not only had the flight been delayed without any adequate information to keep us updated, but a female official at the security gate had aggressively insisted I 'do her new year'. She had been so brazen that I had been momentarily confused as to whether this request for money was mandatory rather than an under-the-table beg. She had only relented when I told her I was a graduate going to undertake the national service. Only then had she grinned and shouted, 'Ah you for talk say you be corper. Welcome dear, we need more people like you to return from obodoyibo!'

'As if! Can you imagine the cheek?' I exclaimed and waited.

But her response had been paltry. She replied that it was to be expected and I needn't worry myself about such things. People like the security woman had to eat somehow in a country where most people were underpaid. She then proceeded to say that it was good for me to see how well off I was. There was no winning with Mum. Not only had I been sentenced to the godforsaken country they had left, I was also being told to sit tight and shut up. *What is this life?* I thought.

The call ended on a sour note. I was upset that my parents were refusing to come to their senses and Mum was cross about my nonchalant attitude towards helping Aunty Evelyn around the house. I didn't see why this was a problem. Aunty Evelyn had a maid who did everything. My cousins weren't babies that needed to be fed or bathed. So what really could I have done? I looked around the room, which was more spacious than mine back at home in east London, and wondered what it would have been like if I had grown up in a house like this, perhaps in Lagos where Dad had lived before he had migrated to England. Or maybe he would have also moved to the capital, where his brother had raised his family and flourished in his businesses. Would this slower-paced, elitist lifestyle I was starting to encounter in Abuja also have been mine? Would I leave for wherever I was driving to with just enough time to get there promptly and not stuck in senseless traffic as was the case in Lagos? Would I be seen as a posh kid who was fattened by her father's money and sent abroad to study at the best universities? Would I be mistaken for one of the 'runs girls' – always up for a good time for the right price – for which Abuja is notorious? Or a junkie who had more money than sense and could afford to be reckless with no lasting conse-quences, knowing that Daddy had connections in the right places? Aunty Ndidi's friend Sophia, who had taken me clubbing, had shared all these possibilities with me on our last night out in Lagos. She had warned me to be careful and not to trust anyone because, with my accent, flair and curvy figure, I'd be like a sweet piece of cake every man in the capital would want to devour.

The afternoon I had arrived at the Nnamdi Azikiwe airport in Abuja, Uncle Peter had been busy at work, so Aunty Evelyn had arrived with her driver Danjuma to pick me up. I hadn't really thought of what to expect. I was still just mad that I had to stay for a whole year in Nigeria, so I wasn't concerned about where I was headed in particular. I had hoped that a capital city would at least be tolerable. When I had asked Aunty Ndidi about Abuja, she had smiled and said it was a great place, but she wasn't sure I'd love it. As the car sped through green lights, undisturbed by the traffic jams I'd seen in Lagos, I was astonished by the view. I could just about see the famous Zuma rock in the far distance. I wondered about the lives of those living in the shanty communities we passed. They were in stark contrast to the mega-buildings and well-kept estates we had seen earlier.

We had passed the National Mosque on the way to Uncle Peter's home and I realised I had been expecting worse of my homeland. The architecture of the grand mosque was astounding, its golden dome basking in the glow of the hot afternoon sun. I had been told that we were in the last days of the harmattan season, and while Aunty Evelyn had drawn her shawl tightly across her shoulder to shield from the 'cold breeze', I felt engulfed by the heat and couldn't wait to get into the air-conditioned house. Perhaps it had been rude when I suggested I'd rather go inside when Aunty Evelyn had tried to show me around the property, and her pride and joy – a well-manicured garden with beautiful blooming flowers, big enough to hold a party of two hundred or more guests. It didn't matter at the time that I had just rolled up to the most spectacular house I had ever seen, like something from MTV's Cribs, and that I was going to be living there. I just needed to get out of that heat.

The white house shone bright like it had just been painted, the orange roof gleamed in the scowling sun and the bougainvillea flowers surrounding the entrance made the whole structure colourful and enchanting. This place was a mansion. But I was mad. I still wanted nothing to do with Nigeria. I didn't want to be there, and putting up a fuss was my little way of having a say in the matter. I didn't care that Aunty Evelyn wasn't the object of my fury. She was a pawn nonetheless.

CHAPTER 9

Cynthia

The day before my three weeks' exile to the NYSC camp, Uncle Peter finally made time to take the family out. He had been so busy the first week I was in Abuja that I only ever saw him late at night when he was having dinner. One day when I had asked why he stayed out so late, even at the weekend, he had grinned and said in a matter of fact way that he liked to be hands on with his two businesses, to ensure his family had the life he never did growing up.

'That's what real men do. They take care of their family.'

I had to stop myself from rolling my eyes. I wondered what the point was of working so hard that he hardly had any time to spend with his family. I chose not to mention the importance of a work-life balance. I knew better than to air my views with my elders. Instead, I said I wished to snag a husband like him in the future, to which he replied: 'Very soon I hope, now that you've finished university.'

I sniggered, but held my tongue. It seemed that every woman's life had a certain and sure course that could never be departed from. You are born, you go to primary school, then secondary school, and by God's grace you make it to university, after which you have to marry and bear children. You always have to remember that your clock is ticking. And while you are doing all this growing up, you are never expected to date. Oh, never, lest you fall pregnant from the mere touch of the opposite sex. But of course, once you are done with university, you are expected to come to your senses and settle down. None of that rubbish the Western women do. And if to the glory of God you make good money, you must remember not to flaunt it because you must be wary of scaring possible suitors away. You always have to remember you are getting too old for the 'market'. Men don't want an 'old cargo', nor do they desire a woman approaching menopause. After all, the most important reason for your existence as a woman is to bear children. That, right there, you can never forget, so you'd better make hay while the sun shines.

I sighed as Uncle Peter drove into Ceddi Plaza, which I had been told was one of the most popular malls in Abuja. I had already been there with Aunty Evelyn the day she had walked into the room and caught me staring at the ceiling daydreaming. I needed something more exciting than window shopping or watching another movie at the cinema. My social life had slowed to a halt since I had stepped into the capital. There were only so many pictures I could post of the house, garden and surroundings. And since I wasn't going out, I didn't waste any of my makeup on creating 'looks of the day' posts on Instagram. Abuja was seriously becoming a drag. Luckily, we had just missed a viewing of the latest teenage-friendly movie in the cinema, so we went straight to have dinner.

I hadn't spent much time with my younger cousins. They left for school each morning before I was up, and had a host of extracurricular activities in the evenings. We had only shared a few moments during dinner, before they retired to their rooms to complete their homework and head off to bed. I made an effort to ask what they enjoyed most in school and learned that the oldest, Onyedikachi, was learning to play the piano, while his younger sister, Adaobi, preferred the flute. I wondered why I found it surprising that a teen in Nigeria would be adept at a musical instrument. There were great artists from the country and the continent; they had obviously learned from somewhere. I guess there was a disconnect between my media-influenced preconceptions of what it was like to live in Nigeria, and the complex realities of real day-to-day life here.

The day out was lovely, even though I hated to admit it. I enjoyed learning more about all the relatives I had heard so much about, but hadn't seen since I was ten years old. I even enjoyed

Uncle Peter's humour. When I said I was full from all the food at dinner, I hoped Uncle Peter was joking when he told me that I had better eat up because, starting from the next day, I'd be begging for a bite to eat.

'Haba, she can eat from mammy market na!' Aunty Evelyn interjected, giving her husband a knowing smile. I didn't understand what they meant exactly, but hoped that the NYSC orientation camp wouldn't be the end of me.

We drove back home in good spirits. After I retired to my room, I lay in bed praying I'd have the strength to cope with whatever was to come.

CHAPTER 10

Cynthia

I thought the heavens had my interests at heart when the morning arrived with an incessant downpour. I hoped the poor weather would mean a delay to my arrival at the camp, but Aunty Evelyn stormed in and said it was best I got there as soon as possible. The earlier I arrived, the better accommodation I could sort out for myself, and the quicker I would acclimatise to the surroundings. I didn't understand why finding accommodation would be a problem, given I was expected, but she had told me to trust her judgement and get going. Uncle Peter had delayed going to work to drop me off personally, as a show of respect to his older brother. It didn't matter to me. The fact I was being made to go made me still begrudge my fate.

The drive to the orientation camp where I and about three thousand or so others were to be *tortured* in the name of patriotism took about forty minutes. Most of it passed in silence. I was lost in my thoughts and so was Uncle Peter. As we approached the gate that would keep us in like captives for the following three weeks, our car joined the queue of other corpers and their families creeping forward in the traffic. The 'gate of Hades' was how one blogger had described it, writing about her experience at the camp.

A week after Dad had first announced that I'd be travelling to Abuja to partake in the NYSC programme, and I had realised that he was serious, I had looked up everything I could to convince my father otherwise, but it had all proved futile. He had made up his mind and said that for once, I had to prove my character and not baulk at a challenge. After watching all the videos, and gathering all the information I could, I still felt unprepared for my stay. For my sake, I had hoped some of those bloggers had been exaggerating and that I wouldn't have to go through all the drills that were to come. I still didn't get the point of it. I thought the whole NYSC deal was a cruel joke, and I certainly wasn't laughing.

After what seemed like an age of slowly edging forwards, I could finally get out of the car. Uncle Peter helped with my luggage while I grabbed the bucket Aunty Evelyn had bought for me, in case of water shortages. We hugged awkwardly and he imparted some final words of wisdom, then waved goodbye as I joined the queue of graduates making their way to the registration on foot. I forced myself not to look back as the gleaming sun made me squint, as we all moved along like sheep to the slaughter.

The camp was exactly as I had seen on the blogs, although standing in it for real, it looked much bigger than I had assumed. I could see rows of bungalows across different areas. They looked quite basic, as if from another era, and I wondered again how I'd survive the three weeks. The road leading to the main grounds was untarred and a long way from the gates. The queue snaked as we all tried to avoid the muddy puddles that had been created by the rain. I looked at the white trainers I had worn and sighed. I knew I'd have no chance of keeping them sparkling white. I groaned. I shouldn't have worn my favourite pair. Ahead, there was a massive field in the middle of the buildings with patches of worn grass and red sand. I could definitely kiss goodbye to my trainers if all the stories of daily drills and marching I had read were to be believed. I shuffled on as the queue moved forward. Aunty Evelyn had been right. Even with the earlier downpour, the camp was already buzzing with lots of activity and filling with people who were either excited, disorientated like I was, or simply morose.

I could see several policemen ahead of the queue searching each entrant's bag for contraband, while asking if they had their call-up letter. Once we were through the security check, we were directed to a tent to continue the registration process.

'Aunty buy bucket!'

'Aunty, aunty, you need passport photo?'

'Call me for recharge of any phone battery!'

Overzealous vendors and service boys accosted us as we made our way across the field. I didn't know why I would need anyone to help with charging my phone, but I summoned the boy who looked to be similar in age to my older brother Nathan, and collected the piece of paper he had scribbled his phone number on. This was Nigeria after all. Power outages could occur at any time of the day – even, I imagined, on a government property.

I stole a look at the boy as he walked off to approach other potential customers. I wondered how he came to offer such services when he should have been out there working a proper job. It made me think of Nathan – I wondered what he was up to and if he was thinking of me. He was twenty-three years old, which made him two years older than me, but the way he would nag me, you'd think he was much older. He was the proud son of a father who was equally proud to call him son. Nathan had flourished after his graduation and had been able to move out a few months after starting his job on a graduate scheme at one of London's investment banks. He never tired of teasing me about how I seemed to lack our Igbo money-making genes. We had been close once, but with our combined six years away at university, the distance and my laissez-faire attitude towards life had chipped away at the bond we once shared.

Reaching a tent, we were informed of the day's proceedings and pointed in the direction of where we needed to go to continue the registration process, depending on whether we had studied in Nigeria or completed university abroad. But before any of that, we were told to go and find a bed in the dormitory. At this, the crowd, already anxious, quickly dispersed, following a female officer to a building to collect our mattresses.

CHAPTER 11

Cynthia

When I entered the dormitory, I was surprised to see the other girls scurrying around the large room. I immediately joined in and tried to find a bed I'd be as comfortable as possible in, given the circumstances. If I was to survive the next three weeks, I was ready to do as the Romans did, or in this case, the Nigerians. I found an unoccupied bunk close to a ceiling fan and claimed the top bunk as mine. I dumped my handbag on the two thin mattresses I had stacked together and looked around as I began to take in my surroundings. Rows and rows of single iron bunk beds were crammed next to each other. We were going to be packed like sardines.

I looked up and saw a cobweb on the wall above my bunk, which did nothing to ease my anxiety. The journey had hardly begun and I already couldn't wait for it to be over. I heaved myself up on my bed and watched as more people trooped in and ran around, trying to claim a bed for themselves.

'Hi, I'm Yetunde from Ogun State,' said the girl who had placed her things on the opposite bunk to mine.

'Hello, I'm Cynthia. I'm from—'

Before I could finish my introduction, she murmured, with hands over her mouth, 'You have an accent,' and giggled. Yetunde had a round-shaped face with a single tribal mark on both cheeks. I noticed that the half-inch lines didn't detract from her pretty face and wondered if she ever regretted the existence of this particular Yoruba tradition. She was a skinny, dark-complexioned girl with long fingernails, which were already harbouring grime. I looked at my own baby-blue acrylics and withdrew my extended arm. 'Yeah,' I said dryly.

Yetunde seemed to know what to do, so I followed her lead and began working on the mosquito net Aunty Evelyn had packed for me, using long pieces of wood strung to the sides of the bunk's frame to create a makeshift insect-free haven. When we were done, we walked out together, but stopped abruptly as soon as we caught sight of what was going on at the gateway ahead. The corpers at the gate had their luggage on their heads and were doing frog jumps to the sound of a commandant's whistle. If it wasn't so pitiful I would have bounded over in a fit of laughter, but the idea that it could have easily been me over there sobered whatever humour I would usually have felt. *Just what was the point in putting them through such an ordeal?* I hated this place and the quicker the days came and went, the faster I could be done and retreat to somewhere more sane. The list of things I was planning to bitch about that night to Veronica was getting longer. My new roommate was laughing, so I excused myself and headed towards the registration tent for international students.

CHAPTER 12

Cynthia

The queue hadn't looked that long, but after an hour in it I was getting seriously irritated. It was another hour again before it was my turn to process my documents. At that point it was clear that the officer at the table was just as irritated, so I braced myself for the worst, having read about how the officials loved to shout and tease corpers. Thankfully, I was in luck. My registration was done without any hiccups and I was handed my platoon number and meal ticket. When it was time to collect my uniform, I reiterated the sizes I had written on the application form, but I needn't have bothered. Whatever size I had stipulated did not matter to the NYSC officials. I looked at the T-shirts that were clearly twice my size, the boots that were way too big for my size 38 feet, and sighed. After refusing to leave with such ill-fitting items, I was told to wait at the side in the hope that the next batch of uniforms would have something in my size. But after half an hour awkwardly waiting, all I had managed was to exchange my boots for a size 39. I gave up and headed back to my dormitory.

Where had the whole day gone? It didn't seem that long ago that I had arrived, but a glance at my watch told otherwise. When I got back to the dormitory, there were no more empty beds on my side of the room and I couldn't see if there were any left at the other end. The dormitory was a very lengthy bungalow and the stream of people who came in and then sullenly walked out with their belongings and mattress told me there were no more available beds. I looked at the other suitcase that now leaned against my bunk, making the already narrow space even tighter, and wondered who I'd be sharing my bunk with.

An hour later, Yetunde walked in looking unlike her earlier chirpy self. Obviously, the queue for home students had been much longer than mine and unlike me, she hadn't been able to change any of her oversized uniform. It seemed ridiculous that we had been asked for our sizes and yet nothing had been done to accommodate us. I looked at the tired girl with pity and offered her some water, which she drank in one big gulp.

'Ah, I was thirsty,' she said, wiping her mouth as a bugle went off.

We were being summoned to gather at the parade ground to listen to the camp director's opening remarks. When we got to the open field, we were welcomed to the camp, told the camp rules, and told to read the orientation booklet as soon as the meeting was over. The director then went on and on about all the other things we were expected to do and the activities we were to complete during the three-week period. Then, after what felt like an hour of unnecessary chatter, an army officer took to the stage and began his act.

'When I say WEE, you say WAA!' he screamed into a megaphone.

'Wee!' he started.

'Waa!' we boomed back in chorus.

'Wee!'

'Waa!'

'Come on, louder! Wee waa wee!' he screamed in a singalong voice.

Yetunde and I, and the other roommates who had followed us out, looked at each other and giggled. *What madness*, I thought and rolled my eyes. But who cared? I was tired, sweaty and hungry. All I wanted was for it to be over. So I joined in and shouted in unison with my fellow corpers:

'Waa wee waa!'

That night, my new friends and I abandoned the dining hall after seeing what had been served. The beans were suspiciously runny, and I definitely wasn't going to touch the garri they had rationed for each table. Disappointed, we headed to mammy market, a makeshift market within the camp selling everything and offering every service a corper or staff member could need. We made ourselves comfortable at a food seller's tent and helped ourselves to jollof rice, plantain and other delicious foods we craved. For the duration of our stay, mammy market would be our favourite place to hang out. We could eat barbequed chicken, suya, fried rice, egusi soup, ayamase, yam porridge and any other food that didn't look like it had the potential to upset our stomachs, unlike the food from the camp's kitchen. You could also find someone there to wash your clothes for 50 naira per item – Veronica had been as astonished as I was when I told her that it was equivalent to 11 pence. I definitely wasn't going to be doing laundry while I was there.

We were also able to recharge our phone batteries at the market, since our dormitory wasn't fitted with enough sockets. I needed to be synced to the outside world at all times. Keeping up to date with friends on Instagram or Snapchat offered a sense of relief, although it sent me half insane seeing what I was missing out on. At least the nightly hangouts at mammy market with new friends, full of banter and gossip about who was doing what or where each one of us had come from, made camp almost bearable.

Still, those brief moments didn't make the 4.30 a.m. starts any more tolerable, nor the bathrooms any cleaner. They didn't make the yelling from the soldiers any softer, nor the stern officials any kinder. In fact, I was simply surviving. At one point, a girl eight beds away from me had fallen ill and had to leave camp in order to get better medical care. I envied her. I even wished for sickness, or any other thing, in order to leave that hell of a place. Yet, I remained.

CHAPTER 13

Cynthia

The first night at the camp it had been almost impossible to sleep. The two mattresses stacked together were still so thin that I could feel the bunk rails pressing into my skin. The chatter of roommates sounded like eleven-year-olds at boarding school and drifting off to sleep was difficult. At 10 p.m. the lights went out, which quietened the room. But it seemed like almost as soon as I'd fallen asleep, I was suddenly awoken again by the sound of the loud bugle.

I glanced at my phone. It was 4.30 a.m. *Why in God's name were we being awoken at such an hour?* I slowly got out of bed and was reaching for my shower things when my bunkmate Mirabel told me not to bother. After first spotting her suitcase, I had met her the night before on our way to mammy market. She had said she was originally from Port Harcourt, one of the oil-rich states in Nigeria, although she had studied in Lagos State. I envied her and asked why she hadn't chosen to carry out her service year in Lagos. She explained that no one had a choice about where they could serve. Mirabel was an ordinary-looking girl with smooth, brown skin like the back of a coconut. But the makeup she wore did nothing for her face. The application was awful and her choice of eyeshadow was ghastly. But she was warm and friendly, always looking out for me and offering to help me run errands, so I took to her easily, hoping that she'd come to learn a thing or two from me before our camp orientation was over.

That first morning, Mirabel had said frankly that if I wanted to take my bath before the first sessions, I would have to wake up earlier than 4.30 a.m. So I pushed the bucket back underneath the bunk and grudgingly changed into my all-white regalia. We hurried out of the dormitory and joined fellow corpers heading to the parade ground like ghosts on the move. Some were wide awake, others were rubbing sleep-deprived eyes.

Yetunde, Mirabel and I made it to the assembly but were so far at the back that it was impossible to hear the official clearly. He droned on and on until I found myself bored and sleepy. My legs felt weak, so I squatted like some others around me, and begged for the torture to end. After four hours of more talk and singing the national anthem – as well as the NYSC anthem (which we were made to learn) – the early morning ritual concluded. I was elated to be free again, until we were told to gather together with our various platoons and follow the prompts of our platoon leader. I sighed and waved goodbye to my friends who were in different groups, then joined the two hundred-odd people that I was to work with to try and win various competitions for cooking, drama, cultural dance, Mr & Mrs NYSC, volleyball, football and the like. Why we needed to engage in such activities was beyond me. *Was it just me, or weren't we through with secondary school?* I was told it fostered teambuilding and all that rubbish, but it felt like a waste of time to me. *But who was I to voice my opinions?* The soldiers made sure we knew we had none.

On the third day, we had our swearing-in parade. Suited in our full NYSC uniform (consisting of a white T-shirt, long-sleeve khaki shirt and trousers, white long john socks in the national stripes, jungle boots and cap), we took the oath and sang along to the NYSC anthem like the newly inaugurated patriots we were supposed to be.

By the fourth day, I was terribly uneasy. I had managed to steer clear of the toilets and had taken to having my bath under the cover of night like my friends who had introduced me to the idea. We would wake at 2.30 a.m., and with bucket in hand, fetch water from the taps and head off to the back of our building, which, luckily, was covered by bushes at one end. There, we would soap and sponge in record-breaking time, then stand and shield each other using a long ankara fabric, which was commonly called a wrapper, while the others did the same. How I managed this feat surprised even me and no less my mother when I told her about it.

On that fourth day, an embarrassing episode occurred that made me reconsider my tactic of avoiding the toilets at all costs. Although they were cleaned every day, somehow they became grimy again within seconds – I tried to stay away as much as possible. On that particular day, I had avoided the toilet for a while, which meant my time was coming sooner or later, especially after eating beans and plantains the night before. I was with my platoon going through the motions of the daily morning exercises when the havoc began. We had formed a circle and were running anti-clockwise when my stomach groaned. Some gas let loose. I had never been so embarrassed in my life. I glanced at the corpers closest to me to see if they had gotten 'wind' of what had just happened. Of course they had, and their pitying looks made me wish I could sink into the red earth. Mortified, I continued with the exercise and just as we rounded off, I was pulled aside by the girl who had been behind me.

If anyone had told me that I would experience my first 'shot put' lesson at orientation camp, I would have laughed in their face and been disgusted by the idea of it, but that afternoon, I was a living example of adapting to one's environment. The girl, whose name I never asked, led me to the other side of camp where it was dense with vegetation. She showed me I needed to take cover behind a tree, poop into a plastic bag, then fling it as far away as possible into the bowels of the forest. That, I was told, was 'shot put'.

Afterwards, while we took turns washing our hands with water collected in an Eva bottle, I swore to banish the memory forever. I could only imagine Veronica's face if I told her about it when I returned to London. She would have never let me hear the end of it.

Days went by, but the routine stayed the same. We woke to the loud sound of the bugle, we assembled for a four-hour lecture covering supposedly essential things we needed to learn, we gathered in our platoons and endured morning exercises and drills, and we partook in a skills acquisition scheme (I joined the makeup class but found it pointless once I realised I was better at contouring than the beauty expert herself). In the evenings, we abandoned our meal tickets and made the makeshift restaurants of mammy market our home, we joined evening parades, and took part in a whole host of practice sessions for the inter-platoon competitions. But none of it mattered. After several days, I had mapped a routine for myself and found loopholes to avoid the draining morning exercises and rehearsal marches.

CHAPTER 14

Cynthia

By the second week, I was still no closer to getting over the fact that I was stuck at that camp. I couldn't 'embrace it for what it was', as Yetunde had suggested, frustrated with me. Although I had got on well with the other corpers on my side of the dorm, and had befriended a few others in my platoon, Yetunde and Mirabel were my favourite companions. I mostly spent time with either or both of them at mammy market, or in my room skipping the drudgery of lectures and rehearsals. I used my reclaimed time to create makeup looks for Instagram instead. I couldn't let my followers know that I was actually suffering in Nigeria.

On the tenth day, we were reimbursed two thousand five hundred naira, a paltry five pounds forty-two pence, for our travel expenses to the camp. Everyone was happy to have the extra cash and wasted no time in heading to mammy market. That night I learned that most people in my friendship group had wanted to serve in Lagos because it was the place to be and some were already hatching plans and hoping to fake illnesses just to be redeployed there. Of course, this was widely known by the officials, so refusals were common unless one had strong connections or irrefutable proof for reasons to be redeployed. I had initially not given this much thought, but after I had seen Instagram pictures of Osayuki living it up in Lagos, holding cocktails and looking gorgeous at beach-side bars on Lagos Island, I decided that if I was to stay a whole year in Nigeria, it would have to be in Lagos. I had already met Aunty Evelyn's close friends. They were all married with children, and no match for Aunty Ndidi's fun and hip friends back in Lagos. I knew that life in Abuja would be boring and regimented if I was to stay with Uncle Peter and his family, so it had to be Lagos. While Aunty Ndidi had a no-nonsense attitude, I also knew that she'd pretty much leave me to my own devices. I began hatching a plan.

The next afternoon, I bounded off to mammy market to charge my phone after congregating with my platoon. So far I had successfully shied away from signing up for any of the competitions, and when I was pushed to sign up for the cultural dance my platoon had been assigned for the carnival day, I strongly declined. I would rather not prance around in cultural wear and pretend I was having a great time. I was still sour from having to be there, and openly enjoying any part of it was to betray my stance. It didn't matter that my dad couldn't see what I was up to. I wanted no part in camp activities because when I called home to bemoan my predicament, I wanted the words to sting. There could be no trace of pleasure.

I began to set my plan in motion that afternoon, which was as hot as all the others that had preceded it. I collected my phone from the boy I had paid to get it recharged, stepped out of the canopy and dialled my dad's number. He picked up on the second ring, and I cut straight to the chase. I reminded him of every single complaint, like the fact I was being bitten by mosquitoes despite my protective net, the despicable toilets, inedible food and how, in general, I hated being there. I finished off by informing him that if he expected me to continue with the service year, then I had to redeploy to Lagos. He listened in silence as I spoke and when I was done, the silence continued.

'Dad, are you there?' I asked, puzzled, wondering if the connection had gone bad.

'Cynthia, you won't kill me. Why do you want to go to Lagos now?' he heaved.

Valid question. I hadn't planned a comprehensive response, but sprang into action and bargained hard. I told him that I was mentally unstable in the capital and that I had no friends there. At least in Lagos, Aunty Ndidi and her friends were closer in age and I related better to them. 'Or don't you want me to be happy? At least I should have a say on where I'm located,' I concluded.

Somehow, my melodramatic narrative seemed to do the trick and I could hear his voice softening and his mind changing as he started to respond. He paused. Then he started again. Then he paused. I pleaded that it was no different if I served in Lagos, but at least there, I'd be happier.

What I failed to mention was that although Uncle Peter possessed all the comforts I could want, they couldn't outshine the time I had spent in Lagos. I couldn't tell him that the one week I had spent with Uncle Peter's family had given me a glimpse into how boring it'd be if I stayed there for a year. In Lagos, I could stay with Aunty Ndidi and party with her friends. Lagos was beckoning, and I was falling for its charm.

My dad reluctantly accepted my plea. Excited by his concession, I squealed in delight, sent my regards to my mother and brothers and hung up. When I turned around, I was startled to see a guy leaning on the canopy, eating corn and ube and staring at me. Not giving it much thought, I looked away and started walking back towards my dormitory. He quickly followed and started a conversation.

'So you're one of those "I can't wait to redeploy" girls?' he remarked, flinging the cob of corn to the floor, nonchalantly.

'I beg your pardon?' I replied in distaste, looking at where the cob had landed.

'What is it about Lagos you love so much? It's overrated in my opinion. I've lived in Lagos all my life and it's nice to try somewhere else.'

'I'm sorry, do I know you?' I asked flippantly and kept walking.

'Na wa o! So I'm that invisible? OK, what platoon are you in?'

'How does that matter?' I countered.

'Ah, only Nigerians will answer a question with a question!' He laughed and I noticed he had nice teeth. I wished he'd just leave me alone and return to wherever he stumbled out from, but I replied: 'Four, so?'

'I'm in four too,' he said with a flourish.

I stopped and looked at him closely. His dimpled smile softened his pronounced features. At about five foot eleven, he was only five inches taller than me. With arms now folded against his chest, I could make out the flex of muscles underneath his long-sleeved T-shirt and wondered if he was one of the guys I had seen behind the boys' dormitory lifting blocks of cement as free weights.

'Oh, sorry. I don't think I've ever seen you,' I responded with an apologetic smile.

'Maybe because you're never at rehearsals. Why do you hate it so much?' he asked.

'What's there to like?' I countered.

'Haba! I enjoy some things and it's our country at the end of the day . . .'

'And that's why we should be under these conditions? Please tell me, what do we actually gain by being here?' I asked, waving my hand around and then stopping to look at him with one hand on my waist, waiting for his answer.

'We're learning to be disciplined for the task at hand!' he said with a grin.

I could tell he was being sarcastic. I put down my verbal weapons and continued walking. We finally exchanged names. His was Munachi. I wondered why I hadn't noticed him before.

We continued to talk as I walked back to my dormitory, and by the time we got to the building, he had offered several reasons why it was better to serve in Abuja than in Lagos. Whatever he had said didn't register. I laughed and told him not to bother. My mind was set on redeploying. He seemed harmless, so when he asked, I gave him my phone number.

'I hope I'll see you tomorrow morning?' he asked as I turned to leave.

I waved goodbye.

CHAPTER 15

Cynthia

The next couple of days, whenever we were free, Munachi and I would meet with our other friends at mammy market. We quickly became firm friends and by the end of the second week he had managed to coerce me to resume attending the platoon meetings. However, taking part in the morning drill exercises was still out of the question. I had been lucky so far, in that the army officer who patrolled the dorms to catch any errant corpers lurking there had never made it to my end of the room. Although this wasn't down to luck alone. Originally, there hadn't been enough bunks for every corper, so the officials had *imaginatively* decided they could fit in more bunks into the middle of the room. This meant that as she moved around the room, the female officer was squashed tighter than a bacon butty and couldn't be bothered to go all the way to my end of the dorm.

It continued this way until I got so bored of hiding out alone that the thought of Munachi and his jokes sent me out to attend the damn drill. I snuck out and narrowly escaped being seen by an official from the Man O'War unit who usually disciplined any latecomers. I had heard of corpers who had to endure hours of sitting in the field under the hot sun or doing punishment frog-jump drills for being late or committing an error of judgement.

That morning, during our platoon exercise, a female member had collapsed out of exhaustion. It turned out that for the rest of our time in camp, she was told to lay off any exerting physical activity. This meant that the group that was to compete in the cultural dance category was missing a member. They asked for a volunteer and Munachi had looked at me. I mouthed 'hell no'. The flash of disappointment that ran across his face, while other members urged me to participate in at least one activity, gave me a change of heart. I didn't care much about the competition, but I didn't like the thought of my new friend being disappointed in me. So I accepted and cheered myself up with the fact that I was going to get my redeployment. I could let this little defeat slide.

Uncle Peter had called me the night before and had clearly been annoyed at my insistence to redeploy to Lagos. My dad had obviously called him to ask the favour that he make it happen. We had argued, I had insisted and he had finally relented, but not before stating that he wouldn't be able to keep an eye on me in Lagos so I should have a rethink. But I didn't get what all the fuss was about. I had been away at university for three years and I had been fine. Besides, I was an adult and had the right to decide where I wanted to be.

'Things are different here, this is not London o,' Uncle Peter had said. I could imagine him pulling at one ear while making his remark, a common expression used by Nigerian elders to tell those who were younger to listen to their wisdom carefully; but I didn't budge.

Later that afternoon, before my first rehearsal with the cultural dance group, Munachi accompanied me to submit my redeployment form. I was ecstatic.

CHAPTER 16

Cynthia

For the rest of the second week, I joined the cultural dance group for rehearsals and learned the choreography we'd be performing. At first it had been a struggle, but after a couple of lengthy rehearsals, I was beginning to get the hang of it. By participating more in my platoon's activities, as the days rolled by, I was enjoying my time at the camp more than ever before. Munachi's ability to see the light in most things helped, and that weekend he surprised me. I had just returned from Sunday church service with Yetunde and Mirabel when I received a text message from him. We were allowed to wear our own clothes until 4 p.m. on Sundays, but I usually didn't because after the first Sunday at camp, I had realised that the clothes I had brought with me were either inappropriate or too precious to soil in the dusty environment. But Munachi told me to change into what I could for the surprise. By this time, my friends had already started making fun of how quickly I had taken to the boy I had only met earlier that week. They teased that it was only a boy that could coerce me to do what they had been telling me to since the start of our orientation and I couldn't deny that there was a truth to it. That afternoon, I joined him under the ebelebo tree by the pathway that led to the main gates, as he had requested. I was still trying to guess what his surprise could be when he showed me the passes he had secured for us. Every corper knew that it was almost impossible to leave the grounds except for an emergency, health reasons or if one knew their way around key officials. It turned out that Munachi had found out how to do the latter, from another corper in his dormitory, and had gone to great lengths to arrange a day out for me.

I was excited and pondered on how strange it was that being in a confined environment could make such an inconsequential gesture matter so much. Without thinking, I grabbed him into a hug then pulled away awkwardly. His brown eyes gleamed as he laughed at me. We walked side by side to the gate and brandished our signed passes when the official stationed there yelled at us to ask what business we had coming up to him. Five minutes later and one thousand naira short, we were free. Outside, I put my hands up to my sides and closed my eyes. I raised my head to the sky, and sighed. It felt good.

An hour later, we were sat under a mango tree next to Jabi Lake with the food we had bought from a fast food restaurant. I was surprised by the expanse of the park and realised I had never thought such a calming and public green space was possible in the country. Munachi had laughed when he saw my look of surprise.

'You better stay here. You won't find this one in Lagos o.' He nudged my shoulder and teased.

And for a second, I wished I hadn't already handed in my redeployment papers, but the feeling didn't last. Although I was seeing things in a different light and loving the moment, I still yearned for the freedom and rebellious rage Lagos would provide. Abuja just seemed so routine and boring in comparison. We ate in silence and let all the stress from the past few weeks in camp drift away in the cool breeze. When I finally looked at Munachi again, he held out his hand and we got up and walked the circumference of the park, stopping a few times to take pictures by the lake. I was happy that he had thought to organise such an outing, even though we were on a short leash and borrowed time. On our way back to camp, we talked about our differing childhoods and what we missed most.

'I used to be such a tomboy . . .' I started. Munachi gave me a disbelieving look. 'Seriously!' I said. 'Of course, this was before I fell in love with makeup. Anyway, when my brothers and I would get back from school, we'd play football and rescue mission games on our PlayStation until our parents got back from work.

Then they'd change the channel or send us to our rooms to do our homework.'

'Ehen . . . action girl!' Munachi teased while boxing the air and making silly fighting sounds. 'You were lucky o. There was nothing like that for my two brothers and me. We had to do so much homework as soon as we got back from school, unless we wanted to get flogged the next day in class. And as for games, we loved playing football with the other children in our compound whenever our father was late home from work. In fact, if our father had caught us playing football during the week ehn, he would have flogged our buttocks!' He continued: 'We always had our youngest brother on the lookout sha and I think he knew and always tried to catch us! But we had our coded signal that we'd make whenever we saw him approaching and we'd run through the back entrance in the compound and rush back home before he could ever catch us. Those were the days,' he said and grinned, strong feelings of nostalgia across his face.

'Are you still close to your brothers?' I asked.

'I try to be.' He shrugged. 'We manage to call each other whenever we can, but you know how it is now everyone is growing up and doing their own thing.'

I understood exactly what he meant and wished things had never changed between my brothers and me, especially Nathan, who I didn't speak to as often anymore. We kept on talking and trading childhood memories as we made our way back to camp.

'Wait o. Did you ever play boju boju?' Munachi suddenly asked, excited.

'Nope, I've never heard of that,' I replied.

'It's this game where one person covers their face and sings out to the others who have to hide while answering to the prompts of the song. The person covering their eyes isn't allowed to open them until the others tell them to. Then they can start looking and whoever the person catches first will be next to cover their face while everyone else hides,' he explained.

'Isn't that the same as hide and seek?' I asked, just as he started to sing:

Boju boju

O

Oloro nbọ

O

Ẹpara mọ

O

Ṣe ki n ṣi?

Ṣi sin ṣi

Ẹni to loro ba mu a pa jẹ

O

He explained: 'The song is basically saying Oloro, the chief masquerader, is coming so everyone has to hide. The Oloro later asks "Ṣe ki n ṣi?", which means 'Can I open my eyes now?' but yes, I guess it was our hide and seek. The Yoruba children in our compound taught us the song. It was always so much fun catching the little children trying to hide.' He burst out laughing.

I joined in, laughing at his terrible singing voice. It had been a very special day, and by the time we got back to camp, I felt we had a genuine connection. It was strange that only the week before, I hadn't known his name, but by chance, we were bonding over our childhood memories and shared experience of the regimented NYSC orientation.

When we got back to the camp, we quickly changed into our camp uniform and joined our friends who were having dinner at mammy market. They teased us, but we laughed it off. I did wonder how Munachi felt about me though. By the time he walked me back to my dormitory, the sun had fallen and though I hoped that he wouldn't try to make a move, I secretly wondered what I'd do if he did.

'See you tomorrow,' he said and slowly walked off, looking back once to wave. I was glad. I was tired of my every interaction with boys being sexual or alluding to romance. I respected him for it.

CHAPTER 17

Cynthia

The third week moved so fast that I found myself wondering where time had gone. Whoever said 'time flies when you're having fun' was right. During those first days of being at camp, I had begged for time to pass quickly, but by the last week, I caught myself wishing the end wasn't drawing so near. That week, my platoon had finally undertaken one of the biggest challenges of the orientation – the Man O'War drill. We had crawled under barbed wire, walked through a muddy trench, climbed over a rope fence, crossed a single rope bridge, completed a tug of war against each other and completed a host of other trials that any army man would be proud of accomplishing. It had been a tough exercise to say the least, but I was proud to have soldiered on and pushed myself to the end. For the first time in a long while, I was enjoying being out of my comfort zone. Munachi and my other platoon members had cheered me on when I reached the last assault course, before finally joining them on the finish line. The purpose of those morning exercise activities finally became clear. If I hadn't joined in the week earlier, I doubted I would have been able to make it. Perhaps I would even have still been hiding in the dorm, missing the whole thing. With the sense of accomplishment I now felt, I realised what a shame that would have been.

Two days later, it was finally time for the carnival day parade. The night before was tense and the anticipation could be felt even after lights out. I could hear people whispering into phones, reminding their mates not to forget things needed for the following day; or others tossing and turning in bed, unable to relax. I was no different. My platoon had decided to split our dance performance into three sections to demonstrate the cultural diversity of the three major tribes in Nigeria. The girl whom I had replaced had been in the Igbo set of the performance and I was proud to be representing the tribe I was from. It had been fun, but taxing, learning all the steps, but I had stuck with it, even letting Munachi take a video of me to send to my mum. She had once told me that she used to dance at cultural gatherings when she was growing up as a child in her village. When I sent her the video, she had replied, 'My Ada, see how beautiful you dance!' I felt so proud seeing those words. There was something about the sway of hips and the movement of shoulders in the traditional dance that made me feel so beautiful and connected to my roots. Veronica, on the other hand, had simply commented '#DanceQueen', accompanied by a series of laughing emojis, when I posted the video on Instagram. I sensed Osayuki understood though – 'Love it!' she had commented, adding a queen emoji.

On the morning of carnival day, everyone gathered on the parade ground. Canopies had been set up for the officials and other staff members to sit shielded from the blazing sun while judging the performances from all nine platoons. Each platoon had been assigned a different theme related to Nigerian culture – a drama depicting a polygamous home, for example, or a demonstration of the country's colonial history. In my platoon's dance group, I took charge of the makeup and body markings, having previously researched and illustrated how we would present ourselves to the judges in keeping with the tribespeople we were dancing as. We had all contributed between five hundred and one thousand naira each so that the platoon lead and some other members could go outside of the camp to get all the costumes and necessary materials.

With Munachi standing ready as one of the drummers, it was finally time for us to perform in front of the officials. We gave it our all. We had uli symbols drawn with mascara all over our arms and legs, since we couldn't get the plant from which the dye is made. We had pieces of yellow-and-red-patterned ankara fabric tied across our chests and around our waists. We wore strings of thick red beads on our ankles and wrists. In addition, the three guys in my set held a white horsetail staff, which they waved in the air in rhythm to the beat of the drums. I'd never moved my body so fast, and I don't think I have since. By the time we were done, I was sweating profusely and my heart was thumping as if it was about to jump out of my chest. We had put on a great show and were hopeful of winning the best performance prize.

On the penultimate evening at camp, a representative of the state governor was invited to welcome us on to the programme and thank us for dutifully accepting to serve the country for a year. He also talked about the norms of the region and the northern culture. For the first time since I had attended the evening lectures, the hall was absolutely still. We were all transfixed by his charisma and inspired by his views on culture, leadership and life. By the end of the night, I was so moved that I felt prouder of my heritage than ever before. The night was still young and after his speech, we all left to prepare for the cooking competition and bonfire to take place that night.

Everyone was looking forward to the night, expecting that it would crown our experience beautifully. It did not disappoint. The whole camp was abuzz and I could feel the positive energy of everyone around. After the cooking competition, in which my platoon came fifth, the bonfire began. The captain of each platoon walked forward with a flaming torch. They each gave a speech about what they had learned since the start of the orientation, what they hoped to achieve during the service year and what values they'd return home with. There were some long-winded speeches that became a bore, and some humorous ones that tinged the night with excitement. After the last captain had given his speech, the head official stoked the flame and the bonfire blazed. Everyone began to cheer. A speaker, which I hadn't noticed earlier, crackled into life and 'Eh aladji, aladji aladji', DJ Ramatoulaye's hit song, burst into the air. As if it had been orchestrated, everyone started dancing and cheering. It was by far my best night at camp.

As usual, I was in the company of Munachi, Mirabel and

Yetunde, who was lovestruck and dancing closely with her camp crush. Corpers were dispersed everywhere, some in groups, chatting, drinking and laughing and others in twos, out of range, falling in love or perhaps in lust. A good number of us carried on dancing even when the fire began to dwindle, and our 10 p.m. curfew came around.

CHAPTER 18

Cynthia

The last day came around too quickly and the atmosphere was solemn. It seemed like almost everyone was sad the orientation phase had come to an end. However, there were others who were glad to be rid of the place and some officials who made it known that they were also happy to be rid of us. I found myself feeling conflicted. For the most part, I had undoubtedly hated being there, but I had enjoyed some of the activities, and meeting my camp besties and Munachi had taken some of the sting out of the experience. It didn't rid me of my disgust for the pathetic conditions we had lived in, or soothe my mosquito bites. But in their own way, my friends had helped ease the horrid experience.

Before we left for the parade ground, my roommates and I gathered round and recounted our experiences, laughing at the absurd moments (tempered by the bad ones). We hugged each other and, in the usual Nigerian way, prayed that each of us get posted to our preferred governmental ministry or private company, rather than being allocated to teach at a government school. We looked at those we suspected had swindled their way to getting their preferred location and giggled. I wasn't any better. I hoped Uncle Peter's connections had worked in my favour and that my posting letter would contain a redeployment confirmation to Lagos. I was sad at the realisation that it'd probably be the last time I'd ever see Mirabel, Yetunde or Munachi. I pushed the emotion aside and followed the rest of the girls out of the room to attend the final parade march where the competition awards would be announced and the army officials would commemorate the whole event with their own march.

Hours later, we were required to stand in lines according to our platoon numbers. I stood with Munachi, waiting for our platoon officer to begin handing out the posting letters.

'Do you think you'll be redeployed?' Munachi asked tentatively.

'I hope so,' I replied guiltily, shielding my face from the glaring sun with my right hand.

'Will you miss me?' he asked in a lowered tone, his left hand now over his face too.

'Of course. If we had met earlier, maybe I wouldn't have asked to be redeployed. Let's see what happens,' I replied sincerely.

'Of course you'll get it.'

I didn't know why he felt so sure I would or what he would think of my family if I did, but I didn't like the uneasiness I felt or why I was suddenly hoping Uncle Peter's influence might not be as strong as I originally thought. Munachi probably also felt the tension in the air and swiftly changed the subject. We talked about how we still couldn't believe our platoon hadn't won the carnival day parade after all the effort we had put into our costumes and the performance. I thought of how I had given my all to master the choreography I had learned in only a little over a week. I had only put in all that effort to impress Munachi after all he had done to help improve my camp experience. I didn't want to disappoint him. It was strange how I had suddenly grown to rely on his friendship. And although there had been insinuations by our mates, we had remained only friends. I found our brief friendship more special as it was left untainted by any romantic declaration that would have complicated things, especially because I was possibly going away. Even if I wasn't, I only had a year in the country since I was sure that I wasn't going to stick around after the NYSC programme was over.

When my number was called out, I walked to the front of the line and collected my letter from the soldier who I felt had looked at me a little too intensely. *But who cared?* It was almost over, and to turn my back on the officials who had been rude and unnecessarily snarky was a welcome relief. I stood against a wall with peeling paint and held my breath as I opened the folded sheet of paper to reveal where my fate lay for the next eleven months. I breathed out and laughed; a small win. I was returning to Lagos. Munachi walked over to meet me, smiling. He had been right, I was going to get what I wanted. At that moment, it didn't matter what had been done to facilitate my redeployment, I suddenly felt alive and realised that even though I would miss my new friends, I really wanted to be in Lagos.

I looked at Munachi and the two other friends I was going to miss dearly. I thanked them for making my time at the orientation camp as good as it had been. I had managed to hold back the tears when we sang the NYSC anthem for the last time, but as we hugged each other and said our final farewells, I surprised myself – a tear ran down my cheek. Before I could raise my hand, Munachi's wiped it away.

'Don't forget me o,' he said crestfallen.

I heard the gentle plea in his voice. 'I won't,' I murmured and smiled reassuringly.

'And don't take this NYSC thing too seriously o. I know that Nigeria is not an easy place to live. In fact, if I get visa now now, me sef will run!' he exclaimed with humour, making us laugh. I squeezed his arm and promised not to.

'OK OK! Enough of this. You lot, make sure you call me if you're ever in Lagos for a visit,' I said, wagging my index finger at him in particular.

The three of them walked me out of the gate. We stood in silence before having our last group hug. I left them and continued walking forward until I saw Aunty Evelyn's head sticking out of the window of a car. I looked back at them still huddled together and waved, before jumping into the back seat of Uncle Peter's car. I greeted Aunty Evelyn and waited for Danjuma to put my suitcase and bucket away in the boot. When he got in and started driving, I continued to wave, even as the distance between us grew. When I could no longer make them out, I relaxed my head on the headrest and closed my eyes. It had been the longest three weeks of my life, but it now seemed to have come to an end so abruptly. Just as suddenly as I had passed through the gate of Hades, I was finally departing out of it. I couldn't wait to get back to the house, properly scrub up and feel wholly like myself again. There was so much I needed to catch up on with Veronica, back in London, who had finally started a job in fashion and was excited to be starting the career she had talked about so much since our A level days in college.

CHAPTER 19

Cynthia

On the way back to the house, I was still elated from the whole ordeal and everything I had experienced in the three weeks I'd been gone. I was excited to share everything with Aunty Evelyn, but she didn't seem too interested or in the mood for conversation. I figured she was probably having a bad day and retreated to my room. I relived the last couple of days' events and was still surprised that I had been able to complete the Man O'War drill and even competed in the carnival day competition. Although the others had been upset that we came in third place, I was simply impressed that I had followed it through and enjoyed the process. My thoughts drifted to Munachi, and I was grateful for the day we met at mammy market. I felt that our chance meeting hadn't been a coincidence after all, but indeed a blessing. Thanks to him I was beginning to see things in a different light and was for the first time optimistic about my year in Nigeria. It still didn't quite make sense, but Munachi had a certain way of looking at things and I guessed he was right. Even if I didn't know it at the time, perhaps there was a reason for my being in Nigeria and I just needed to keep going until it became clear; and if it didn't, he had said he was sure that it would be worth it anyway. I hoped he was right. Being sullen or upset all the time wasn't going to change the fact that I was there. I actually had a lot more to lose than gain that way. So I promised myself to have a better outlook on life when I returned to Lagos.

Before going to bed that night, I decided to go thank Uncle Peter for handling my redeployment application and apologise for being difficult. I was about to knock on his bedroom door when I overheard the conversation he was having with his wife.

By the sounds of things, she had only found out that I'd be moving to Lagos while I was talking excitedly on our way back.

'But what can I do? He's my older brother . . .' I heard Uncle Peter say.

'So that's why we should close our mouths and not talk? She's too spoilt. At her age I knew what I was doing,' Aunty Evelyn remarked. I could just imagine her broad nose flaring in anger.

'Haba Evelyn, you know how he helped us with the loan when we had nothing, it's the least we can do to pay him back. Let's leave her, she'll learn,' Uncle Peter said in that tone that meant that the situation was no longer up for discussion.

'And must you say that every time your brother needs our help? He gave us money and so? Is he the first person to help his own family? I don't even know which one is my own inside. If Cynthia thinks she's better off at Ndidi's place, let her go then. She'll learn!'

I couldn't believe they were arguing over my going to Lagos. I didn't understand why they needed to control where I was located. *What did it matter if I was in Abuja or Lagos as long as I was doing the bloody thing?* I turned away and retreated to my room in defiant mood. Before I drifted off to sleep, I looked at Osayuki's Instagram feed again to catch up and wondered if I'd ever bump into her in one of the trendy places she frequented on the island. She seemed so cool.

CHAPTER 20

Osayuki

I sat by the window at my favourite cafe off Admiralty Road with my new friend Wendy, scrolling through my phone distractedly. She was excitedly filling me in on the upcoming events she said I had to attend in order to be part of the Lagos 'in-crowd', especially as an 'IJGB'. The week I met her, I had learned that an IJGB stood for 'I Just Got Back', a term used for returnees like me who were either visiting the country or could be heard talking about how they had 'just got back'. I had laughed because it was so true. Only minutes before she had explained the term to me, the lady sitting at the opposite table had complimented my handbag and asked where it was from, to which I had replied 'London'. But when she probed to find out who the retailer was, I had coolly responded, 'Oh no, I just got back from London.' Wendy had given me a knowing smile and I realised I had probably said the phrase more times than I could remember since I had returned.

Wendy was a five-foot-eight boisterous woman from Delta State who had lived in Lagos most of her life. She was only two years older than me and made sure I never forgot the measly fact. 'If you had older brothers or sisters when you were growing up, you would have known that even if it is only one year that I use to senior you, it is something!' she had first chided me, as she insisted she had the right to the first pick of the clothing samples Mrs Phillips had given us to wear at one of our socialite parties.

I knew she had only been joking, but I also knew that the Nigerian culture of respecting your elders was the bane of many a younger sibling's childhood. Before I had moved to London, I had seen my then best friend Kelechi taunt her younger sister whenever an adult wasn't around and she wanted to get her way. We had been primary school friends but had since lost touch – it had been the era before mobile phones or social media. I sometimes wondered if I'd even recognise her if she walked past.

I put my phone away and looked up at Wendy. I had been reading an Instagram post by Cynthia on her NYSC experience. Her posts so far had been either sarcastic, or about her makeup. I was quite sympathetic – I was happy that undertaking the programme hadn't been a prerequisite for my job. 'Shey you're listening to me?' Wendy rapped on the table with her long French nails, continuing before I even answered. She was hell-bent on not giving up her personal mission to make me one of Lagos' social elite. I laughed at her determination and wondered how she was able to cram so many events into a week and not get tired at work. Although I had attended a few of these events with her, I was still insistent on making them infrequent because it seemed they were mainly catalysts for gossip or meeting potential boyfriends, and I was interested in neither. I remembered the first day we had met during my lunch break when I had gone to the fro-yo store beside our office. It had been a week after I started at House of Martha. I had placed my order at the counter and was waiting to be served when I heard a loud voice.

'You must be the new Head of PR!' she had squealed and extended a well-manicured hand.

'Wow, that obvious?' I had replied as we shook.

'Your *virgin* hair is a dead giveaway,' she had drawled, before grinning and pointing to my natural afro.

'I see,' I had responded slowly, not knowing what to make of her or the assertion.

'I'm guessing you're not so popular with your colleagues. Just don't worry yourself with their own palaver,' she had remarked while leading the way to a table.

Her comment had surprised me, but it began to make sense as we ate our frozen treats and continued our conversation. Through Wendy, I learned that Adaora, my executive assistant,

had been gunning for my job. She had worked at House of
Martha for three years, and when the Head of PR position was
advertised, she had applied believing it would naturally go to her.
When I had initially declined the offer, it looked like she was
going to get the job, until I sent another email two days later
apologising and confirming the position. She had been livid, and
even without us meeting had formed a strong dislike for me. It
seemed my skin complexion made it even worse. I had begun to
pick up that Adaora and her closest confidant Mercy, the Junior
PR Assistant, were prone to gossip.

As for Wendy, she went whichever way the wind blew in order
to keep up to date with happenings in the company. I found out
that she had studied accounting and finance in the UK and was
the Accounts Manager at House of Martha. She had been holi-
daying in Paris the first week of my arrival, but it had taken no
time for Adaora and Mercy's gossip to reach her ears. That I
was 'dark as charcoal with virgin hair', as Adaora had put it,
made her missed opportunity even more of an insult. To her, the
position should have at least been given to a fair-complexioned
woman. I had been stunned at the revelation and greatly disturbed
by the reasoning behind such a belief, but Wendy had assured
me that it wasn't so much of an unusual mentality in Lagos,
where lots of women bleached their skin to get a job or the man
of their dreams. In Lagos, it was 'the fairer the better', and the
realisation made me sad for the plight of those who bore the
brunt of such outlandish beliefs; not that a different form of this
colourism didn't occur in London as well. Colourism was a big
issue amongst Black people everywhere in the diaspora, but I
had never thought a variant would take shape in Africa too. Even
after years away, I still felt Nigerian, but since my return, I had
begun to learn things I had never known about the city of my
childhood. A lot of things remained the same, but the things that
had changed, or perhaps the things I had never been privy to as
a child, were inconceivable.

I looked at Wendy quizzically. She wanted me to attend a beach
party the weekend after next, which she claimed I couldn't afford

to miss. I was unable to wiggle my way out of it, so I relented and promised to go. I would at least look forward to it more than the wedding my aunty had insisted I attend this coming weekend. She had already unsuccessfully invited me to two others but finally put her foot down and said I must accompany her to this latest one. She reminded me that soon enough she'd be travelling to join her husband in America and she'd be out of my hair, so we had to spend as much time as we could together before her departure. She thought I didn't know what she was up to, but Wendy had let me know that weddings were the place to be for singletons looking to get hitched. So since Aunty Rosemary was set on being a matchmaker, I decided to let her win for once. I had reckoned that attending one wedding wouldn't make a difference. The messy breakup with Nick had put me off men completely as far as I was concerned.

CHAPTER 21

Osayuki

On the day of the wedding, I began to regret accepting my aunty's invitation. The night before had been so hot that I was forced to leave the AC on, but come morning, the sky looked like Armageddon was about to happen. I drew the curtain open slightly and peered out from my bedroom window to see clouds gathering. The sky was the weirdest grey I had ever seen; even foggy England couldn't compare. I hoped Aunty Rosemary would cancel our outing, but an hour later, when I finally got out of bed and went to see if she was awake, she said the plan hadn't changed and at the worst, we'd only be missing the church ceremony. She reminded me that the reception was always the main event and my tummy growled at the thought of jollof rice. We had all grown up to know that party jollof was the best type of rice because of how it was prepared, in a huge pot over firewood.

After breakfast, we began to get ready. An hour later, the makeup artist Aunty Rosemary had hired arrived and began to work her magic. I declined getting mine professionally done, but relented when it came to wearing a gele – I had never worn one, so I decided to embrace my culture wholeheartedly.

Aunty Rosemary had bought some ankara fabric allocated to the friends of the groom's mother and had had it tailor-made to show off her full figure. She had bought just enough for herself weeks before my arrival, so I had to look for something in my closet that would fit the gold-coloured gele I was wearing. After rummaging through my closet, I found a long midnight-blue slip dress with a slit on the right side. I paired it with my gold Aquazzura heels and a teardrop diamond necklace my mum had given me for my birthday in December. I grinned in the mirror at my reflection with the gele. I looked like one of the beautiful women I had seen on Bella Naija Weddings.

Just as Aunty Rosemary had hoped, by the time we left home, the bad weather had cleared and if not for the pothole-ridden roads, which had collected the rainwater like a calabash does soup, no one would have been any the wiser that there had been a torrential downpour earlier. If I hadn't known better, I'd have thought that the traffic-free roads were due to the weather. But the maddening queues at filling stations across the city evidenced that only those who still had fuel, or whose cars were surviving on their last legs, could enter the motorway. The fact that an oil-rich country like Nigeria could suffer a weeks-long fuel scarcity was appalling. As we sped easily along roads that otherwise would have been jam-packed with okada bike riders, private vehicles, and danfos and molues – the yellow air-polluting public buses Lagos is well known for – I couldn't help but wonder how the twenty-million-plus people who resided in Africa's Big Apple were able to make do. We whizzed past a fuel station that had a sign saying it was 'closed', yet was obviously selling what little fuel it had to the droves of cars that had to creep forward one inch at a time to get to the pumps. I saw citizens from every background there. It didn't matter whether you were in a public bus, a luxurious car, on foot with a jerry can in hand or pushing a motorbike, everyone had to wait in line. What's more, fuel was being sold at staggering prices, far different from those advertised. I couldn't help but feel pity for the small retailers, market sellers and citizens of an underclass who were forced to live such a hand-to-mouth existence. *Nigeria is changing* – that had been the idea that led to my return. But was it really? I recalled my experience of getting a taxi one Friday recently, when my driver had spent so much on what little fuel he had that he was forced to inflate my fare. When I'd tried to bargain with him, he'd explained his predicament in such stark terms that I ended up giving him a tip. It saddened me as much as it angered me, but what could I do?

'With God all things are possible,' went the popular Nigerian phrase. I, however, begged to differ.

CHAPTER 22

Osayuki

When we got to the venue, we were quickly ushered to our seats and informed that the bride and groom had just arrived and were about to dance into the reception. Lagosians were obviously used to the temperamental weather in the rainy season because the hall was already packed with guests spectacularly dressed in the colours chosen by the families of the bride and groom. The rain had clearly not been a deterrent.

Just like Aunty Rosemary and me, the groom's female family and friends who sat around us had tied gold-coloured geles on their heads and some, mostly the older women, had an ipẹlẹ across proud shoulders. The men sported a similar-coloured hat, known as fila by the Yoruba people. To our right sat the bride's family and guests in red geles, ipẹlẹs and filas. The whole ceremony was bedecked in these colours – red and gold – which made it a glorious sight. Each family's sub-group had also picked out ankara fabrics to be custom made by a tailor of their choosing. So the bride's friends who didn't make the bridal train had their own ankara fabric and so did the mother's friends, and extended family groups. It seemed like only the groom's and both fathers' friends hadn't jumped on the ankara bandwagon. It was no surprise that men didn't bother themselves with such a tiresome task as going to the Lagos Island market to hand pick a material, then sell it to their friends who would then get it tailor made for the occasion. They just didn't bother themselves with such frivolous affairs. Everyone knew a wedding was for the bride and her mother. However, the men saw themselves as the big spenders and as such, the important figures of the day. They let their women think what they like and everyone went home happy.

The MC announced the entrance of the newly married couple and everyone turned towards the back of the hall to watch their first dance. The bridesmaids, beautifully clad in red silk dresses, and the groomsmen, in dapper black suits with gold-coloured pocket squares, lined the passageway and danced in rhythm as they cheered the newly married couple forward. Following this, there were lots of cheers from the guests and picture-taking from both the cameramen and well-wishers, who wanted to capture every moment. The bride was dressed in a regal off-shoulder wedding gown with lace sleeves. She was hands down the belle of the ball and her groom, no less of a beau, had a proud smile plastered on his face. I looked at both of them with admiration and a longing for what could have been. Not too long ago, I too had been dreaming of my big day, but it had been taken away in one strike. I shook the thought away, clapped in tune to the song and smiled as the well-matched couple proceeded to the front of the hall, not missing a step.

After the couple had danced for a while and had taken their seat, mounted on the stage facing the guests, the MC moved on to the next item on the agenda. He started to tease us as our attention was diverted by the delicious aroma of jollof rice and chicken in the air, making its way from serving trays to dinner tables. After another couple of minutes trying to coerce the half-interested crowd, the MC gave up his ruse and welcomed the live band to the stage. Minutes later, I saw him with a plate of pounded yam and vegetable soup. I gestured and laughed with Aunty Rosemary as we spooned jollof rice into our mouths. I hadn't bothered with a knife and fork, after being scolded by the elderly woman to my right who sat too close. Proper Nigerians, she said, ate rice with spoons or even with fingers in the confines of their homes, and none of that oyinbo nonsense that caused sensible adults to eat with forks in their left hand. Everyone knew that using the right hand was the proper way. Whether it was to give things or collect them, wave, give a handshake or eat, the right hand was the right way. I was told that, after all, Jesus had said he sits 'at the right hand of the Father', never once mentioning the left as an equal proposition.

CHAPTER 23

Osayuki

When the MC resumed his duties and called for the couple and their families to take to the stage and dance, Aunty Rosemary didn't waste any time in pulling me up with her, but I didn't mind. I had secretly been desperate to dance. Perhaps it had been my toe-tapping and head-shaking that had given me away, or perhaps it was her youthful exuberance, but either way we were straight up to join everyone on the dancefloor.

Family members and guests danced alongside the bride and, as is customary at Nigerian weddings, the couple were literally showered with freshly minted notes. For those who especially wanted to show off, the spray of American dollar bills wasn't uncommon. Aunty Rosemary and I waited our turn then moved forward and threw the fifty- and hundred-naira notes she had collected at the bank the previous day. We danced, and then danced some more, even after we had run out of cash and my feet hurt from the gold strappy heels. But, eventually, I had to tell Aunty Rosemary that I was going to sit down for a while. Not only were my feet *really* hurting now, but the tightly wound gele that I had managed to endure all day was becoming too much. I walked to the back of the hall, sat down at an empty table, took off my shoes and sighed as I drank from a bottle of cold water that had been left unopened. I proceeded to untie the gele and then finger-combed my twist-out hairstyle.

'Wow,' I heard from behind me. I turned to see who the interloper was. Walking towards me was a dashing young man with the broadest smile. I was stunned and found myself unable to respond as he introduced himself as Afolabi, a childhood friend of the bride. He was good-looking and, annoyingly, the type of person who carried themselves with the pride of knowing it. He grabbed a white plastic chair, arranged it to face me, then sat down and made himself comfortable without asking if it was OK to join me.

He had mesmerising eyes, a full beard and sexy lips. I wished I hadn't noticed all this. His lavishly embroidered agbada was a muted red, in keeping with the bride's family's chosen colour. Somehow, I could tell that underneath all those layers of fabric, his wide-sleeved robe and trousers, he was all muscle. I regained my voice and hesitantly offered my name.

'You're a good dancer,' he responded.

I was startled. *How long had he been watching me?*

'Oh trust me, every sane man in this room has noticed you,' he said, seeing my quizzical look.

I looked at the gele in my lap and teased out the creases, trying to suppress my laughter.

'It's true,' he continued. 'So who are you here for, the bride or groom?'

'My aunty's a friend of the groom's family. My gele should have been a giveaway. You clearly weren't looking well enough,' I responded.

'Oh yeah? Well it was your dance moves that blew me away . . . and some other things . . .'

We both erupted with laughter, and when I turned to look him in the eye, I saw rich brown eyes that twinkled in an indescribable way and held my gaze. He was still smiling and I noticed that his mouth was adorned by dimples on either side. I quickly caught my wandering eyes and looked away.

'You're not smooth,' I said and giggled.

'And here I was, thinking I got game!'

We carried on chatting and he was surprised to find out that the hair on my head was all mine. So I began to talk about my love for natural hair and why I stopped using chemical relaxers to straighten it. I felt like I had talked a bit too much, as was mostly the case with topics I was passionate about, but he didn't seem to mind and said it all sounded interesting when I apologised.

'It's nice. I like it,' he said; and although I didn't care what anyone else thought about my hair, I somehow liked that he had said it.

'So what other music do you enjoy?' Afolabi asked. 'I already know you like afrobeats from the way you were dancing.'

'I love quite a few genres, but Sade is my favourite artist!' I replied.

'Let me guess, your favourite is "Sweetest Taboo"?'

'No,' I laughed. '"By Your Side" actually, but I'm currently in love with "Pearls". There's something so haunting and beautiful about it that resonates with me.' I looked up from fiddling with the gele again.

'Hmm, I'll have to listen to it then,' he replied with a wink.

I turned away from his gaze just as the MC cleared his throat in the microphone and announced that the song about to play was chosen by the bride for her groom. Everyone clapped and waited. Then, as if I had had a premonition, on came Sade's 'By Your Side'. I looked at Afolabi in surprise.

'This must be fate,' he said. 'Come on, let's dance!'

CHAPTER 24

Osayuki

I was taken aback and stared at his outstretched hand. I nervously shook my head. There was no way I was dancing with this deceptively charming man. He insisted and, as I felt too self-conscious while he stood and waited, hands still outstretched, I gave in. I brushed his hand away and stood up by myself, leading the way. As we passed my table, I saw that Aunty Rosemary was back in her seat and she winked at me when she saw Afolabi in tow. I cringed internally, knowing very well what she was probably thinking as I walked to the dancefloor. It didn't matter though; I had already made a promise to myself that I intended on keeping.

Afolabi held out his hand again and this time, I put mine in his and followed his lead. I put a distance between our bodies, but as we danced, rocking to the rhythm of the song, what gap there was was breached as we moulded into each other's curves, dancing as one. I was transported to another time when I had been quick to laugh and love. A time when nothing else in the damn world mattered. A time when my laughter could be heard from afar like the ringing bells of a Catholic church; and the spring in my step was like that of a two-year-old, set free in the park to roam and explore.

Still lost in my reverie, I made the mistake of looking up at Afolabi. I caught him staring intensely. I laughed nervously and broke the embrace as I became self-conscious that we were dancing very closely. He chuckled and reminded me what a good dancer I was. I thanked him and teased that I would never have thought that he was such a good dancer. He assured me that there were lots of things about him I didn't know and that he'd like to share, but I waved the comment away. As far as I was concerned, the chances of another encounter were next to none. As the song came to an end, he asked if we could exchange numbers. I declined, and he begged. I declined again, and he teased: 'What are you worried about?'

'Nothing,' I said a little too quickly. 'I'll give it to you if we ever meet again.'

I didn't care to hear his response and had only said it because I didn't think we would ever see each other again. I was adamant to remain a singleton. I walked away quickly with shaky legs, feeling like everyone in the room had witnessed the embarrassing interaction. At my seat, I avoided looking at Aunty Rosemary's face. How was it possible that my mind was in one state but my body in another? I didn't care why I felt a shortening of breath and a tingling when he had been near some minutes ago. It was an uprising I was ready to quash with balled fists. But that didn't stop me from stealing a few glances at him on the other side of the room.

When Aunty Rosemary said it was time to leave, I wondered if he'd run up to me and make one last plea in the 'have no shame' fashion that was customary to Nigerian men. But he didn't – and I caught myself wishing he had.

CHAPTER 25

Osayuki

The following week, I found my thoughts wandering to Afolabi. I had initially withheld that particular piece of information from Wendy when she had asked how the wedding had been. But by Wednesday, she had managed to pry it out of me after she had caught me looking wistful. The thing is, I had also been thinking a great deal about Nick since that weekend. Because I didn't want to tell her that I had been thinking about him and how his betrayal still affected me, I told her about Afolabi instead, guessing that morsel of gossip would be juicy enough. As expected, she hung on my every word and when I finished narrating, she asked what I had been unable to answer myself.

'So what will you do if you *do* see him again?'

It was a silly thing to have said at the time. I had simply wanted to get rid of him. Now, confronted with the possibility, I didn't know how I'd react. I said as much and decided to leave it to how I felt in the moment if it happened.

For the rest of that week, all Wendy talked about was the beach party happening that Saturday. It was a good distraction – as was my continued immersion in the Lagos high life. On a weekday, Wendy and I would get lunch at our favourite restaurant, on the same street as House of Martha, then indulge in gossip about what the elite of Lagos were up to: which governor was fattening their already bulging wallet, which married man had gotten another woman pregnant, which celebrities were drawn into a bitter Twitter battle, or which socialite was jetting around non-stop on the account of her assumed sugar daddy. Like a sponge, I was soaking it all in. To keep up with the Joneses of Lagos, I had to be in the know, and with a job in PR, I had to be in with the right crowd. Where I was seen and whom I was partying with didn't matter if it didn't end up on Bella Naija or in the pages of *Genevieve*. The company I kept was my network and, thus, my net worth, irrespective of whether I went to bed at night on Lagos Island or the mainland. But of course everyone knew the island was where things happened, and just like how zones in London mattered, the divide between those living on the island and the mainland also did. Luckily for me, Aunty Rosemary's house was on the island, in the coveted suburb of Victoria Island.

On the Saturday, Wendy picked me up for the party and by noon, we were en route to one of the harbours at Victoria Island. From there, we would board a hired speed boat to Tarkwa Bay, a twenty-minute ride away. When we got to the departure point at the harbour, we realised we were the last to arrive. After the introductions, we sped off in a group of fifteen. I sat in the company of Wendy and her friends, who had also invited more friends. My mind drifted to another beach I had visited before I moved to England. I had been about to turn ten and was adamant that I celebrate my first decade at Bar Beach. Dad had been against the idea, but I had always been strong-willed, and when it became clear that I wasn't going to give up easily, Mum had told him to allow me go. At the time, they had known our migration was imminent and my mother later told me that she had pleaded I go since it was going to be my last chance to go. Although Dad was overprotective, he had given way. I still remember that day. I had been full of excitement from the moment I woke up until we arrived at the beach. I had invited two of my friends from the neighbourhood and one from school. Their parents had come along too and the grown-ups watched us from afar while we played ten ten and built sand castles. We didn't know how to swim then and had been warned not to venture far into the sea. When we had tired from running around, Mum had brought out the coolers filled with the food she had woken up early to prepare. My stomach had rumbled as the delicious aroma of jollof rice, fried rice, moi moi and chicken filled the air. We all ate to our hearts' content and I slept all the way back home. It was my favourite childhood birthday.

Since my return to Nigeria, I had learned that Bar Beach was no longer the place I remembered. It had been filled with sand for the Eko Atlantic City project, a planned city on land reclaimed from the Atlantic Ocean. A lot of things were changing around Lagos, some for the good, but I couldn't help but wonder how building this new coastal city, estimated to cost six billion dollars, was going to help the plight of the millions who lived in abject poverty. The juxtaposition of the new Atlantic City with the rest of Lagos State was grotesque. While the majority of people lived with blackouts, unsanitary neighbourhoods, bad roads, congestion, pollution and the like, the new city promised its own twenty-four-hour power supply, clean drinking water, a world-class school, well-manicured gardens and a comfortable suburban lifestyle. It was obvious that only the rich would be able to afford this 'prime real estate of West Africa'. The islanders were already far removed from what life was really like for the mainland inhabitants, and with another nouveau riche society on the horizon, what hope did the average Lagosian really have?

Some miles away from the burgeoning new development was Makoko, a floating slum left untouched – a stark contrast. Didn't the government and powers-that-be know that Makoko was in much greater need of development? Questions like this plagued my thoughts, until I was brought out of my reverie by the sight of the shore.

CHAPTER 26

Osayuki

From a distance, the beach had looked serene, but as we approached, it was evidently full of life. I saw other fun-loving Lagosians who had already taken residence under tents or were splashing around in the sea, playing a game of volleyball or football, or frolicking in the sand, chasing children and loved ones. When we disembarked, we were greeted by the sound of a popular afrobeat tune booming from a nearby hut. I could feel the electricity in the air and I was ready to unwind and let the cool breeze take away the pressures that had been mounting within me. We left the men in the group to deal with the entrance fees while we offloaded our food and drinks, and busied ourselves with renting beach huts and chairs. When everything was sorted and everyone had settled, we played board and card games, ate jollof rice and suya, and drank and danced like we were having the time of our lives – which we were.

Wendy rallied the few who had been sitting trying to read and cajoled them into joining those dancing or splashing around in the sea. She was in her element and so was I. I danced with new friends, soaked in the sea water, and then raced back to our beach hut for some snacks. There was something about being by the sea that seemed to soothe my worries. I shed my self-consciousness and pushed away the stress of the previous week. One of my favourite songs came on, and I jumped up in a frenzy to dance with one of the guys in our group. I was thrusting my hands in the air and swaying my hips from side to side, when I felt a warm hand on my shoulder. I turned around and was startled to be staring at a familiar pair of deep brown, twinkling eyes. With his hand still on my shoulder, Afolabi grinned.

I glanced around in shock. *What were the chances we'd meet again so soon?* I tried to compose myself and play it cool, but I was jittery on the inside. Before I could collect myself, Wendy was by my side, introducing herself and welcoming him to join the party. I shook my head and said I believed he had friends waiting for him. But Wendy had realised he was the guy from the wedding I had told her about, and she insisted. To my relief, he declined, saying instead that he would like to speak with me alone. I tried to refuse, but Wendy waved me off and before I knew it, one foot was slowly making its way in front of the other.

'So we meet again,' Afolabi started, grinning.

'I guess. A coincidence huh?' I replied flatly, avoiding his eyes, but feeling giddy on the inside.

'Fate I dare say,' he said with resolve.

We laughed as we walked off towards the other side of the beach, away from the blaring music and noise to where it was truly tranquil. We walked for a while in silence and I could feel the air charge and the adrenaline course through my veins as I began to wonder what he was thinking.

'I haven't been able to stop thinking about you since last week,' he said, as if reading my mind. 'I hoped I'd see you again.'

'Interesting,' I said, turning away to hide the smile that had crept onto my face.

'No, I'm serious. I now believe in fate! I would never have imagined seeing you here. I left my friends to take a stroll on this side of the beach to clear my head, and there you were with your beautiful hair.'

'You're quite the drama queen,' I joked.

'Only when it comes to you,' he said playfully, poking me on my waist.

I stopped walking and sat cross-legged on the sand. Afolabi joined me and we watched the waves lapping at the shore. The silence made me nervous and I tried to make small talk.

'So, Mr Fate – what do you do for a living?' I asked. He told me he worked in a bank. It unnerved me for a second, but I took it in my stride, knowing that not every male bank employee in the world had a dick for a brain like my ex.

'Have you always lived in Lagos?' I continued.

'Yes, and I love it here. I can travel all over the world but Lagos will always be home. What about you? Are you just here for a visit or back for good?' he asked while staring at me intensely.

Eager to keep talking, I began to tell him how I had come to work for Mrs Martha Phillips.

CHAPTER 27

Osayuki

I explained to Afolabi that I had wondered for years what it would be like to return home to Nigeria. Although Aunty Rosemary had begged me to come for a visit when her children were back home for the holidays from their studies in America, I had never seriously thought of putting a plan into action. And when Mum had said that Nick had become too comfortable and that some time away from him would ensure he missed me and force him to put a ring on my finger, I dismissed it. But one day I had been browsing my favourite fashion website when I found an article spotlighting the young Lagos Fashion and Design Week designers exhibiting their collections at the International Fashion Showcase. My curiosity had been piqued, and that was when it all began. I started to follow the African fashion industry more closely, often trawling the internet for the latest news. Then I spotted it: a vacancy for a fashion job in Lagos. The ad had called for experienced PR officers of Nigerian origin in the diaspora to apply for the role of Head of PR at House of Martha – they were looking for someone who could take the lead in rebranding the company.

I had been excited at first, but my enthusiasm had quickly abated when I realised it would mean leaving my family and, in particular, Nick. What's more, I had spent more than a decade integrating into the new society I now called home. Tales of power blackouts, rife unemployment and blatant sexism didn't help either. I tried to forget about the advert I had seen, but the dream of returning to my other home, where my fond memories of my late father were formed, lingered on. With two days to the deadline, I put aside my reservations and applied. I told no one.

That had been a week before the December holidays. Christmas came and went and I received no email in my inbox. I soon forgot that I had applied altogether, until Nick saw the email alert while he was using my laptop on New Year's Eve. I instantly felt terrible that I hadn't told him. I had tried to explain, pleadingly, that it had only been a silly experiment one night while I was bored. Thankfully, he had remained calm. He was my Nick after all. He understood my whimsical ways and even suggested I reply to see how far I'd go in the interview process. While we were in good spirits, and high on the turning of the new year, I drafted a response to formally accept the invitation for an interview.

I was giddy with 'what ifs', wondering what would happen if I were to succeed, but I pushed those thoughts away, leaving the decision to be made if and when it presented itself. A week into the new year, I received another email telling me that the interview was scheduled for the following afternoon, over Skype. I was pissed off at the short notice, and felt cornered and unprepared. But I pulled myself together. I knew my stuff. I had worked in the industry since I graduated from university and had climbed ladders swiftly. The interview would be a piece of cake, I told myself. If international coverage was what they were seeking, I had a lot to offer. I talked myself up in my head and, by the next afternoon, had come away from the interview filled with admiration for Mrs Phillips, who had carried it out in person.

I watched now, sitting on the beach, as Afolabi listened keenly to my story, uttering interjections where appropriate to show that he was following my every word. I became aware that I had uncrossed my legs and wrapped my arms around them.

'To cut a long story short,' I continued, 'I was offered the position and had a tough decision about whether to move back here. I had this feeling that it was something that I had to do. Not just for the job, you know? I feel like I can contribute and should give back, using the knowledge and skills I've gained while I've been away. It took me a while to realise it, but Nigeria is also home.'

I turned my gaze from the sea to him. I saw an expression I couldn't decipher and wondered what he thought of everything I had said. And again, as if he had read my mind at that moment, he said that he agreed with me.

'Nigeria is honoured to have you!' he boomed and leaned back on his hands to watch me.

I felt too shy to look back at him. I laughed. But what my laughter hid was the next part of the story – the betrayal that shook my world, the defining event that truly led to my acceptance of the job.

It had been a terribly cold day in January, with snow forecast in London for the evening. Just two days before, I had made the difficult decision to turn down the job at House of Martha, because when it came down to it, I just couldn't see myself without Nick. We were so good together, or so I had thought, and I couldn't start a new life if he wasn't part of it. Nick was half Ghanaian, but had no strong ties to his African roots. I couldn't ask him to move to Nigeria with me. And anyway, one of his new year's resolutions had been to take evening classes to learn how to code in order to pursue his entrepreneurship dreams. I was proud of him and happy that he had finally started taking the initiative to be more ambitious – I had started getting worried that my career was ascending steadily while his remained stagnant at the bank.

That night I had decided to make beef pepper soup, one of my specialities, to get us through the chilly night. After rejecting the job offer I had been sullen for the past couple of days, so I wanted to surprise him and show how much he meant to me. I had taken the spices for the soup to work with me and stopped at a butcher on the way to his place in Finsbury Park to get the fresh beef. I had been in a wonderful mood. As it was a Friday, I was looking forward to staying over and spending all weekend with him. He was out at an evening class, so I entered his shared flat with the spare key I had owned for almost three years. The heating was on, which was unusual. Nick and his flatmate rarely used it because of the cost – it was one of the reasons I preferred us spending time at my place instead of his. His light had been on too – also unusual – so I set my groceries on the kitchen counter and went to his room to turn it off.

That was when I saw what I would never be able to unsee.

Nick was not at his evening class, as I had been made to believe. He was in his room, and he wasn't alone.

I didn't care about the woman I had seen him cheating on me with. I had never met her before. But seeing Nick pulling on her dead weave from behind while they had sex had been a horrible scene to stumble upon. Still, she was nothing to me and could have been anyone. I wasn't going to be the woman who would lash out at the stranger, ignoring whose responsibility it was to stay faithful. It was Nick who had betrayed me and set fire to our love. I felt the world that we had built around us crumbling down and I fled in a flurry of tears. By the time I got home, I was in a full rage and couldn't believe what he'd done to me. But before I told anyone, before I sat and cried, I knew what I had to do. Without even proofreading what I had beaten out of my keyboard, I hit send to House of Martha. And just like that, a new chapter in my life began.

CHAPTER 28

Osayuki

After the unburdening that came with telling (most of) my story, I felt vulnerable. I told Afolabi that it was only fair he now tell me something about himself. What I really wanted to know was why this man I hardly knew had left the company of his friends to sit with me. I wanted to know what he wanted, because I had learned the hard way that most of them wanted the same thing, until they didn't anymore. He started by telling me that he was neither married nor did he have any children, but was curious about someone he had recently met. The first part was reassuring – I had come to learn that neither marriage nor kids deterred men in Lagos from chasing after women they had no business entangling themselves with. I ignored the second part of his comment and waited for him to continue. He talked about his family and his only other sibling who was studying in New York, how he missed her presence in their home where he still lived with his widowed mother. I hadn't been expecting such revelations and was glad that he was able to express his feelings. I liked his openness and the ease with which we were able to communicate – that we were trading histories and experiences like friends lost to time seemed unusual for two relative strangers.

We continued to share our experiences and had completely lost track of time until my phone rang and Wendy said that it was time for us to head back home. She said the party was drawing to a close and Afolabi's friends had joined ours after they had walked by to look for him. I relayed her message to Afolabi and we headed back to meet our friends.

'When I got home last Saturday, I listened to "Pearls", you know,' Afolabi said as he helped me up.

'You did?' I asked, surprised.

'Yeah, and I see why you described it as haunting. But I wonder why you say it resonates with you?'

I smiled and avoided the question, but he persisted.

'Running from a troubled past?'

I knew he was probably teasing again, but I sensed curiosity too. I ignored both.

'Anyway, it was nice seeing you again,' I remarked.

'Not so fast. You owe me your number! You thought I'd forget?' Afolabi stopped and grabbed my arm, forcing me to turn back to look at him.

I laughed nervously but, finally faced with the reality of my proposal, I had no other choice than to honour the deal – or so I told myself when we parted ways and my number was saved on his mobile.

On the way back, I purposefully sat away from Wendy. I knew she'd pry, so I made sure that all I had to do was return her cheeky winks with knowing smiles of my own. Everyone else seemed tired from the day's activities and leaned against each other as the boat raced back to Victoria Island. Once again, I let my mind wander through the events of the day till it reached the exchange between Afolabi and me. I had tried to make it clear I wasn't interested in anything physical and for his sake, I hoped he had got the hint. He was a very good-looking man and I reckoned that the list of women vying for his attention in the city was enough to keep him preoccupied.

CHAPTER 29

Osayuki

Monday arrived, and I went back to work as normal. After more than two months of living in Lagos, I was still as irritated as ever by the incessant traffic. Whether I was travelling to work or to an event, in the morning or at night, the roads were a nightmare. I thanked God for the comfort of Aunty Rosemary's car and the gift of Mr Nelson, who drove me to work and then back home, but it was still frustrating. I had heard tales of being stuck in traffic for two hours just to go a few miles, and I wondered how everyone didn't explode from the sheer frustration of Lagos life. But like them, I was determined to persevere.

Afolabi began to be bothersome. He called on Monday, and although his name appearing on my phone lit up my face, I ignored the call. He tried again on Tuesday, and twice more on Wednesday. I carried on ignoring him until Thursday, when I was sat in another traffic jam on my way home. The fuel shortage was still going on and every drop we had was precious, so I had told Mr Nelson to turn off the AC. To distract myself from the skin-lashing heat, I answered Afolabi on the fourth ring.

He sounded surprised. He stuttered, then composed himself and asked how I was doing. It was clear that I had been ignoring his calls, but he said nothing about it and instead asked if he could take me on a date. I was already irritable due to the heat, and his incessant calls, and in no mood to mince words. I was about to give him a verbal thrashing, but he didn't give me the chance. Cutting straight to the chase, he recited the address of where he wanted us to meet and no sooner had he finished, he ended the call. I stared at my phone, baffled at what had just occurred. He was a rogue. I laughed at his nerve and put the phone back in my bag.

I spent the majority of the next day trying to call Afolabi, but I was unable to get through to him. It seemed like the joke was on me. Unbelievably, *he* was now ignoring *my* calls. I was exasperated, but I was having a taste of my own medicine. I got on with work: replied to the emails that needed replying to, contacted the people who needed contacting, edited the copy that needed editing and finished the week with a team meeting. Even once the working day was over, there had still been no response from Afolabi. I left for home bothered and upset.

The next morning, I woke up to a message from him. He apologised for the silence and pleaded that I didn't cancel the date – it was 'too late', he said. I read the message in awe of his determination. I caved. *One meal won't hurt*, I thought. But I had already planned a lazy weekend with Aunty Rosemary to spend time together before she left on her trip. I felt like I was ditching her and apologised that I was going out for lunch, but when she found out who I was meeting, she couldn't wait to get me out of the door. Her mission was to get me hitched to a Nigerian man. I remembered that, in order to cheer me up the night I had arrived from London, she had exclaimed with passion that Nick's departure from my life had been a 'good riddance'. 'That boy was so selfish! You'd have ended up doing everything if you had married him . . . I don't even know why I'm surprised. I heard that's how these Ghanaian men behave o,' she had exclaimed, to which I had said nothing, holding my hand over my mouth in astonishment.

Sitting in a taxi on the way to the restaurant – Mr Nelson had taken the day off – I frantically sent a text to say I'd be late. Not because of the traffic, which, thankfully, had been light that afternoon, but because I had spent longer than planned picking an outfit. I had been deciding whether to go with my culotte pants and an off-shoulder top that would expose collarbones that I was proud of, or a colourful layered maxi dress that would show off my gym-toned arms. Or skin-tight jeans and a cool-but-casual top to indicate a measure of indifference to the whole thing. I tried all three over and over again until I finally decided on the maxi dress. I reckoned that another meeting with Mr Twinkling Eyes deserved my best dress.

The date went better than I had imagined. Afolabi was both attentive and intriguing. He had the ability to pull me in, his eyes begging me to unravel the mysteries of his mind. And even though I really didn't want to, I found myself besotted. We talked like old friends, the conversation and laughter flowing easily. We traded stories of childhood experiences, dreams, realisations and epiphanies of adulthood. I learned about the tempestuous relationship he had with a father caught in old traditions, and of how his father's death had knitted his family more closely together. He talked fondly of his younger sister, and inspirationally about his aging mother. I talked about my family, of having to grow up with the advantages as well as painful realities of being an only child, my move to the UK and the insanity of having to come to terms with self and identity in a new world. I surprisingly found myself sharing my doubts and fears. I told him of the sudden death of my father, whom my mother and I had solely depended on – how, three years after the upheaval of settling in the UK, Mum had had to step in and play a role she had never been required to before. I talked about my step-father Bob, and how he'd been a blessing even though I hadn't thought so at the start. I had been a confused teenager battling with the storms of puberty when my father had died, and was finally coming to terms with it three years later when Mum announced she was engaged to the white man who had become her companion while she worked at the local library. He had been there for research, she had lent a helping hand, and as they say, the rest had been history.

We ate, drank, talked and laughed and after it all, I was pleased to have spent a wonderful day with the unlikeliest person. As the date drew to its end, the tension in the air was palpable. I wondered what was next and began to rehearse my cue to leave, but he beat me to it. He made his intentions known, and said I couldn't deny there was a chemistry between us. He wanted to see me again.

'I'm sure you say that to all the ladies you pick up at weddings. I know what happens in Lagos!' I protested.

'Osayuki, I wouldn't say I'm proud of my past, but I've grown a lot and I'm better. I know what I want.'

I snorted – from experience, I knew better. I had once thought I was in love, but I could no longer trust such feelings. I told him I wasn't ready, nor was I interested. We decided we would just be friends.

CHAPTER 30

Osayuki

A week later, I found myself bored. I had waved goodbye to Aunty Rosemary, who had gone to join her family in America. It was Saturday, and having been desperate for some time alone, I suddenly found I wanted it no longer. I wandered around the empty house and listened to my voice echo as I sang along to the music on my iPhone. Not knowing what else to do, I decided it was time to get my hair braided. My natural hair was struggling to cope with the Lagos humidity. I needed a more protective style. I called Wendy to accompany me to a salon but she had already made other plans. I looked at the message I had received from Afolabi, asking to meet up again, and sighed. But suddenly, I had a wonderful idea – it was about time that I had an adventure in the city of my birth. Since my arrival, I had lived, worked and partied on the island, never stepping foot on the mainland. Thinking about it, I found it interesting that one could live in the same city with millions of others and easily never cross paths with the majority of them. I had laughed when Mr Nelson had said one day that all that was needed on Lagos Island was an international airport and none of the islanders would ever need to tread on the mainland. But that had become my reality.

Growing up, I had heard a lot about Yaba market, but had never experienced it. It was probably the most popular market in the city, where all sorts of wares were on sale. I had always been too young to venture there alone and my protective father had ensured that my mum never took me on her market runs whenever she went. *So what better time than now*, I thought as I got my bag ready, leaving a note to Juliet to say I'd be out for a while getting my hair braided at the market. I could imagine her reading it, aghast. She was always astounded when I talked about things I'd like to experience or places I wanted to see. She didn't understand why an *ajebutter* – a 'posh' lady like me – would want to visit unrefined places like the market. After all, she was there to run such errands on my behalf. Putting myself in her position, I understood her attitude and wasn't surprised by how she viewed the world. Housemaids like her were used to being summoned at the snap of a finger, and were always expected to be at the beck and call of their ogas and madams, who offered their housemaids some of the opportunities their own families couldn't. Such ogas and madams weren't expected to lift a finger, even if it was to get the remote control when it was only an inch away from them. So to imagine them going down the street to buy an item that had suddenly run out in the pantry, or travelling to the market on a hot day, was an abomination; but I planned to challenge such views. Since my return, I realised that I was in a peculiar position where I didn't personally have the economic capital to command the status I enjoyed in Lagos, but where it had been ascribed to me as an extension of having been raised abroad, having a foreign accent, living in a coveted estate in Lagos Island and by all of the excesses Aunty Rosemary's money could provide. I was suddenly part of the elite crowd of Lagos socialites, afforded privileges I would never have experienced in London as a lower-middle-class professional working her way up the career ladder.

I had promised myself that, one day, I'd take public transport on my own and travel the streets of Lagos, but finally confronted with the opportunity to do so, I chickened out and pushed it to another day. Instead, I flagged down a yellow taxi outside the estate's gates and jumped inside. The driver was an old man who I quickly learned loved to talk. I had planned to take in the sights around me as the worn-out car navigated the bridge that connected Lagos Island to the mainland, but the baba – which was what most older men were referred to as

– had other plans for my time. As was often the case in such situations, we began to talk about the economic climate and the failings of the president who had recently been elected. If there was one thing that had quickly become clear since my return, talking about the failings of the government in Lagos was like talking about the weather in London. Two strangers could easily become companions over their shared hatred for the government and all that it stood for. To begin talking about the inadequacies of NEPA, for example, was to invite everyone within earshot to the conversation. Such conversations defied age, tribe or religion. It was the one burden every Nigerian shared.

The baba talked all the way from Victoria Island to Yaba. Even when I stopped offering interjections and asking encouraging questions, he continued. As we finally got to the market, I tuned him out and traded his raspy voice for the feral chimes of my surroundings. The voices of sellers calling out to prospective buyers mingled with car horns, screeching tyres, the music blasting out of booming speakers, and the gruff voices of street thugs and male sellers who felt the need to catcall almost every woman who passed. These sounds made up the pulsating heart-beat of the market. Combined with the blur of colour and motion, and with the tropical heat, it was enough to send anyone in its vicinity slightly mad. People were quick to snap, quick to insult, quick to haggle, quick to bluff and quick to move on. You simply did not stand still. The market was a revolving door with no sympathy for those lacking street smarts. Any thought of window shopping was out of the question.

As baba parked by a kerb along the street, I momentarily became timid and contemplated asking him to turn back and deposit me where he had picked me up. But I willed myself to be steadfast. I was in my country and whether I had been gone for long or not, I was determined to belong. Yaba market wasn't going to be my undoing. I paid for the fare and got out while thanking the driver, who didn't care for my salutations. He looked ahead of me at the oncoming traffic to the right and turned into the one-way road, daring anyone to try to cut him off. They blared their horns and spat out insults, but baba simply shouted that they should learn to respect their elders. Soon enough, he was on his way and the passenger who he had carried just moments ago was already a distant memory.

CHAPTER 31

Osayuki

I was out of my depth and had no plan. I looked around like a lost child in search of its mother but no one came calling. I had no idea how to find where the hair braiders were located, but knowing that the sight of my unwoven hair would draw them out, I kept walking. After fifteen minutes of walking around stalls, throngs of people moving in every direction and cars careening through tight and already crowded streets, I was ready to call off my adventure, when I heard the question:

'Aunty, you wan make your hair?'

I looked towards the direction of the voice and saw a slim, big-breasted woman staring at my hair. I nodded and followed as she led me through another street, and then through densely packed shops, back to the area I had been dropped off in. I had been totally oblivious before. Just by the old railway tracks stood her hair shop, made of wood and with a tin roof. It was next to several others, a few of which consisted only of a couple of chairs placed underneath trees. In my new hairdresser's space were two other women, who were attaching purple kanekalon braiding extensions to a woman's thinning relaxed hair. I looked at the customer. Her wrists and neck were clad in gold jewellery and her nails were well manicured nails, with rhinestone accessories. I wondered why some paid such care and attention to other parts of their body, but simply slapped on a wig, weave or braids when it came to their hair.

The shop owner called me over and gestured for me to loosen my bun so she could see what she'd be working with. When I did, she didn't look impressed, so I asked how much it would cost.

'Aunty shey you go relax am?' she asked after biting into a roasted plantain she had picked up from an old newspaper. Unsurprisingly, she didn't wipe her hands before collecting more extensions from her assistant to continue installing the braids.

I was also astounded by the sheer audacity of her question. If she had known how long it had taken for me to finally love and embrace my natural hair, and the daily prejudices I withstood, would she have dared to ask me if I would chemically straighten my hair? I quelled my anger and concluded it was a fight for another day, and left in a huff. Approaching the second shop away from her, I hoped the same thing wouldn't happen. I described what I wanted done and waited for the woman's response. She looked at my hair and then at me, from my head to my toes, and then offered a price. I almost doubled over but composed myself. *If these women think I'm a JJC, then they're mistaken.* No one was going to overcharge me; I knew a thing or two about haggling.

'Aunty, but you know say your hair long. Oya tell me, how much you wan pay?' she asked quizzically.

There was no use. Her initial asking price of ten thousand naira had already revealed that there was no way she'd come down to my maximum of three thousand. I walked away again, as she called out behind me: 'No one go gree for that amount o. My own cheap pass sef, go na, you go see!'

I hadn't come this far only to go back home defeated. *Was it really this difficult to get your hair braided for a fair price, or was I just unlucky?* I looked around and saw other women staring. I was contemplating whom to approach next when I heard my name. I doubted anyone in the market knew me and wondered if it was a coincidence, but when I saw a figure coming up towards me, I was astonished. Cynthia, the girl I had met three months ago, was suddenly stood in front of me, one hand on her hip and the other cradling a phone. She didn't look any different, bar the slight tan she seemed to have acquired since we had first met.

'Wow, what are you doing here? I thought you were still in Abuja?' I asked, puzzled.

'Yeah, I was, but I came back here at the beginning of the month. It's a long story. How are you and what are you doing here?' Cynthia asked.

'I'm good. Trying to get my hair done once these women stop trying to rip me off or asking if I'll relax it!' I explained in frustration.

'Wow, that bad? My aunty is over there making hers, maybe she can help you talk to the girls over there,' she said, and pointed towards some figures underneath the canopy of a tree.

We walked over to the iroko tree where her aunty was seated on a plastic chair, her hair half done. Aunty Ndidi was a single woman who carried herself with an air of elegance that made her look younger than her thirty-five years. At five foot ten, she was taller than both Cynthia and me, but with a skin complexion akin to Cynthia's. She was of a similar build to me though, and somehow I could sense that she had a no nonsense attitude, which befitted her managerial role at one of Nigeria's oldest banks. Cynthia made the introductions and I bent my knees slightly to greet her, as was customary. I described the awful experience I had had and Aunty Ndidi asked the lead braider if her girls would be able to do mine. The woman, who had been listening, turned to look at me squarely.

'No problem, attachment na easy thing! So how much you go pay?'

I was getting tired of hearing that question. Seeing a glint in her eyes, I matched it with mine.

'Two K,' I remarked.

'Ehn!' she exclaimed. 'Just give me four K I go do am fine fine for you.'

'Four K for what? Madam abeg take your time o, so how much I dey pay?!' Aunty Ndidi interjected before I could respond.

I was tired of haggling and reckoned an extra thousand wouldn't render me poor, so I conceded, knowing full well that a local could pay less than half the amount I was about to settle for.

'OK, I'll give you three K and that's it,' I said with finality.

'Thank you aunty no worry we go do am well for you. You be customer na!' she replied, understanding that she wasn't going to get any more out of me.

I looked at Aunty Ndidi and Cynthia and smiled ruefully; I knew very well I had been outpriced. But when I thought about it, I couldn't be too angry at the women. The life they led wasn't an easy one and that extra one thousand naira meant a lot more to them than it did to me. I was still a little annoyed that they had swindled the unsuspecting returnee, but losing out on the equivalent of £2.17 was hardly going to mean I starved.

I was offered a chair. Cynthia sat opposite me. She began to tell me about all she had gone through at the NYSC camp in Abuja, and how she had plotted redeploying to Lagos. But it was clear that she still hated the programme, as she told me quietly, aware her aunt was only a few metres away. I told her about what had happened to me since we had left the airport that night in February, and we bonded over our experiences of trying to settle in Lagos.

As we chatted, the lives of those around us in the market carried on as normal. The young woman whose hips swayed from side to side in her skinny jeans was quick to swat away any stray hands that tried to smack her on the buttocks – after years of growing up in Lagos and visiting Yaba market, she knew all too well that her protruding backside was a target for the unwanted admiration of entitled men. The older woman buying her weekly vegetables had learned that in a country where respect was of the utmost importance, receiving it at her age was conditional on whether she was sporting a wedding ring or in the company of a man. And the boy who walked too closely to another in a busy street filled with traders could expect to be assumed a thief, and shouted at: 'No touch my pocket!'

All these things and many more every Lagosian had learned. Meanwhile, the goings on at the market never skipped a beat – the blaring of music mixed with the calls of traders, the vocal bartering of seller and buyer, the pidgin of both the illiterate and the literate, the screeching tyres of okada riders, the battered cars and police vans that drove through, the humidity, the heat, the dust. It was a truly mad place.

Just on the opposite side of the market stood the recently built shopping complex that promised a vision of the future. To some, it represented modernity and civilisation. But to the poorest of the market traders, it was what they feared the most; a future that, with a single swipe, could snuff out the light of their already dying candle.

CHAPTER 32

Cynthia

I was about to snooze the alarm for the third time when Aunty Ndidi burst into my room, shouting that I'd better get up and get ready if I was going to get to the school on time. Although happy I had been redeployed to Lagos, I'd been annoyed to find out that I'd been posted to teach at a primary school. On my first day, everyone at the school had been excited that I was joining them. I had tried to be pleasant, but my demeanour hid the truth. The kids in the class that I'd be teaching had clung to me like baby birds after the principal announced that I was from England and would be teaching them the 'Queen's English'. I had swallowed my laughter, wondering if he realised how different my accent was to the Queen's. Didn't they understand that just as Nigeria had regional dialects and even tribal accents, so did the British?

I looked out at the dreary sky through the window, guarded by a mosquito net, and yet again couldn't believe that rain could fall so heavily. It had rained all through the night and didn't seem to be letting up. I covered my face with the ankara wrapper Aunty Ndidi had given me as a blanket and groaned.

'Look, you better get up. We're in rainy season so get used to it. You can't be late for work. That's what being an adult is, or you think I also don't want to lie in bed?' Aunty Ndidi stared sternly at me with both hands on her hips.

Still on the bed, I watched as she walked out of the room and wondered where the fun Ndidi had gone. No longer was she the aunt that wanted to show me around town and take me to beer parlours to eat nkwobi and pepper soup. Gone were the trips to the cinema, shopping mall, lounge bars and clubs. These days, she was either working, nagging me, or attending a church event in the hope of finding a 'God-fearing' man to marry. Since her friend had got married and moved out of the room I now inhabited, she had made it her resolution to find a suitor of her own. Her socialising days had proved futile, so she had moved on to the church instead. I had so far declined her invitation to attend midweek services with her, but evading Sunday service had been out of the question. So every Sunday, while she laid out her best clothes, I sat at the foot of my bed and tonged my hair – providing there was electricity – then meticulously applied my makeup. Since I wasn't going out much, I was determined to make a fanfare of it whenever I did. At first she had complained about the amount of time I spent on my appearance, but with time, she had slowly started to request my help. First it had been to fill in her sparse eyebrows, then it had moved to eyeshadow, and before I knew it, I was applying a full face of makeup for her every Sunday. But I didn't mind – I enjoyed it just as much as she enjoyed the transformation when she looked in the mirror an hour later.

I arrived just in time for the start of my class at the school. I had once again missed the Monday morning assembly, where praise and worship songs were offered to God, irrespective of whether each student or staff member was a Christian. My shoes were drenched from the rain and to say that I was in a bad mood would have been an understatement. I wanted to be any other place but there. I needed time to recoup, so I decided to set another impromptu English test. The principal had placed a notepad containing the syllabus in my hands on my first day and had made it clear that how I wanted to teach the kids was up to me. But as was the custom, impromptu tests were expected to keep the children on their toes. He also told me that how I chose to discipline those who failed was at my discretion, and I had shuddered when he pointed at a tree in the playground where I could 'pluck' a cane from.

I hurried into the class and told the children that they had twenty-five minutes to revise the last set of words I had taught them, and then walked off to the staff room. There was a small space in the corner of the room that had been allocated to me and Harmony, the other corper who had been posted to the school. By the time I got to the room, almost all the other teachers were out in their classrooms. But Harmony, whom I didn't know very well, was at her desk marking some papers. She was twenty-three years old and petite, probably no more than five foot four. She had pretty features and mostly styled her hair in a puffy bun with all the kinks springing out from the elastic band she tied it with. She carried herself in a way that suggested she never wielded her beauty as a weapon in a society obsessed with fair skin. A week after I had first started, I heard the social studies teacher refer to her as 'yellow pepper', a term used to describe someone of very light complexion. She had hissed at him and kept walking.

As I approached, she shifted her gaze and offered a quick greeting, but her eyes lingered. I responded and tried to ignore her expression; it looked like that of someone who wanted to say something but didn't quite know how to start. I sat down and took out a heap of papers I had already graded, pretending to be busy. I was wasting time – when I returned to my class, all I'd need to do was spend the remaining time calling out the words to be spelled and gathering the test papers.

CHAPTER 33

Cynthia

In the staff room, I raised my eyes from the papers to find Harmony watching me.

'You didn't come back after your CDS yesterday?' she asked. A rhetorical question I assumed, since she already knew the answer. The community development service was an NYSC initiative where we were allocated to different governmental or non-governmental bodies. These included organisations like the Red Cross, Lagos State Traffic Management and various health centres. For our CDS sessions, we had to attend weekly meetings to discuss how to develop our host communities according to our body's goals. I had chosen the tourism body and had revelled in how easy it had been to convince my group that I be in charge of an Instagram account dedicated to illustrating an evolving Lagos. I'd argued that, after the BBC's documentary *Welcome To Lagos* had painted the city in a negative light, more positive coverage was needed to attract tourists. In truth, the idea meant that I could have a day off in the week, since I could make posts to the Instagram account from anywhere once the weekly meeting was concluded early in the day.

I closed my folder of papers slowly, enjoying the satisfaction of giving a delayed response to Harmony. 'Yeah I didn't. It isn't compulsory right?' I replied.

'No, but it's good for you to come back. Teaching the next generation is a great privilege, or don't you think so?' Harmony posed.

I looked at her bushy eyebrows and wondered why she was challenging me. Of course she was right, but it was a privilege I hadn't asked for.

'Yeah, but not everyone wants to teach and not everyone *can* teach, you know? I mean, I'm not even trained or qualified, so why would they post me to a school?'

'Ehhn, it may be true, but I believe you were sent here for a reason. God places us where we're needed . . . and the children always miss you. Every Wednesday they ask me if you'll come back after your meeting.'

'Really, my class?' I asked dumbfounded.

'Why do you sound surprised? You may not know it, but I think you're actually good. At least, when you decide to be. You just need to accept that you're here now. You know I've heard of other corpers that get posted to places where they don't even really do anything. All they do every day is run one errand or the other for their managers. At least here, you're teaching children who look up to you and you can instil in them good values.'

'Sure, but I didn't go to uni to become a teacher. I didn't sign up for this,' I explained.

'No one did, but that's our country my dear and we have to do what we can and hope for the best.'

I rolled my eyes at 'hope for the best' and wondered what hope had done so far for Nigeria. I nodded my head in mock agreement and left when my alarm went off. But as I walked away from the staff room to the class where my students were waiting, several conversations I had had since my service year started began replaying in my head, like a rewound cassette tape. I remembered how I had hated the three weeks at orientation camp until I met Munachi, and then my promise to him to take everything in my stride and be the best version of myself. I wondered, as I thought of the conversation I had just had, whether I was keeping my promise. If a timid girl like Harmony had taken it upon herself to call me out, then perhaps I wasn't.

When I got to the class, my entrance was greeted with immediate silence from the group of children who had only moments before been yapping away like an untamed herd. Their response to authority figures was in stark contrast to what I'd experienced at school in London. Sadly I had been one of those kids who talked back, but now, standing at the front of a class myself, I realised how tough it must have been for my teachers. Childhood was certainly one of those times where ignorance had been bliss.

I looked across the room, each child looking back at me expectantly, and I promised there and then to do better by them. I truly hoped I would.

CHAPTER 34

Cynthia

Ever since our chance meeting at the market, Osayuki and I had kept in touch on WhatsApp. That Friday evening, I was headed to hers in Victoria Island for a much-needed drink and a chat. It felt like ages since I'd had a conversation with someone who could understand my point of view about living in Nigeria. So far, most people had told me to make the best of my situation, but to find someone with whom I could wallow in pity at the stress of everyday life here was a welcome respite.

When I got to Osayuki's beautiful home, I was welcomed in by a maid who quickly disappeared, only to reappear with a tray of wine and glasses. I looked around the living room as Osayuki played gregarious hostess and served the drinks, telling the blushing maid she wasn't needed. It was a beautifully decorated space, with her aunt's family portraits hung on several walls around the room. If the sheer size of the house from the outside, with its manicured garden, didn't give away the status of its owners, the expensively furnished interior certainly did.

'So how've you been and how's teaching going?' Osayuki asked.

'I'm OK I guess, but sometimes I feel like I've been dropped into a bad dream. I just want to scream "get me out of here!"' I replied candidly.

'Yeah, I understand how you can feel that way. Nigeria is a lot to get used to even for someone who has lived here before,' she conceded.

'I don't understand why you'd come back willingly. They better be paying you loads at that company!' I remarked.

'The pay is alright, but home is home I guess. I'm just rolling with the punches. But I can imagine how hard it must be for you . . .'

I laughed, but I could tell Osayuki's concern was genuine. She wasn't the type to ask a question for the sake of idle talk. She moved back onto the couch, folded her legs underneath her like a Buddhist ready to meditate, and waited. I felt like she knew what was on my mind and the tenderness in her eyes made me feel safe enough to share. I told her that since my talk with Harmony, I had been caught in a cycle of self-doubt and scape-goating. I obviously hated my predicament but I had got on the flight to Lagos willingly, so why did I still blame everyone but myself for the actions that led me here? I concluded that, at some point far back, I had stopped thinking for myself and instead started to behave as I thought others expected of me. Teaching at the school reminded me too much of things I'd rather forget, like how I'd been bullied in Year 6 when, unlike most of my classmates, my progression into puberty had kicked into full force. The same boys who had teased me for having a 'back off' then lauded the Coke-bottle figure that had been the bane of my adolescence. In those days, I had wanted to shrink and be invisible.

I saw the look in Osayuki's eyes after my mini confessional and felt reassured that it was OK to be open with her. Perhaps it was because she didn't have any real history with me. She took the last gulp of wine in her glass, and in the gentle manner that I would become used to, assured me that I had a right to feel the way I did, but also encouraged me to make a change if I wanted to feel better about my 'exile', as I called it. Then, to lighten the mood, she talked about her job, joking about the incompetence of her team members. We laughed at a particular incident that had happened a few days before, and then her phone rang.

I laughed again as she tried to bury the sound of the phone under a red cushion with gold trimming. It eventually stopped, but then immediately started to ring again. I was intrigued – it didn't seem like her to ignore a call, especially when I'd said I didn't mind if she answered. I had seen the expression that had passed across her face at the first ring, and suspected it was someone she'd like to speak to, but was avoiding for some reason.

'Come on, pick it up already! I know it's a guy,' I teased.

CHAPTER 35

Osayuki

It was Afolabi on the line. I wished that he hadn't called, but I was also happy to hear his voice. I listened as he spoke and tried not to laugh as Cynthia made silly faces at me. He told me that, after much persuasion from his mother, he was going to be having a big bash for his thirtieth birthday. He hoped that I'd be able to make it. I let the words settle for a minute and pictured him on the other end of the phone. I turned away from Cynthia's curious gaze and tentatively replied that I'd attend. I realised the thought of meeting his mother, whom he was so fond of, had already got me nervous.

'So that's why you didn't want to pick up?' Cynthia teased once I had hung up.

I laughed off her indirect question, but she wouldn't let it go. As she correctly said, I'd only moments ago advised her that she should stop holding back and make the best of her experience in Lagos – so what was stopping *me* from enjoying the company of someone I clearly liked?

'Oh no, we're just friends. I'm not ready for a relationship!' I interjected, a little too quickly.

She waited for more, and feeling like it was only fair I shared my thoughts as she had, I revealed that the breakup with my ex was still quite recent and although I wasn't going to crucify all men for his deeds, I was certainly not ready to jump back into the dating scene just yet. But, I told her, still perhaps a little giddy from the call, I liked him more than I had hoped – and even when I willed myself to see him as only a friend, my heart disregarded my instruction.

'Well, then it's my turn to offer some advice,' Cynthia began.

Just as I had advised her to fully embrace life in Lagos, she said, then I must do so too, by going to the party and having a great time no matter what happened with Afolabi. Nothing was set in stone, after all.

'Anyway, you're not the only one having boy drama,' she continued. 'I have a date tomorrow and I hope it goes better than the last! Seriously, guys in Nigeria can be craaazy!' she squealed, and I nodded in agreement. I couldn't wait to hear all about her dates. Cynthia seemed like the kind of woman who knew exactly what she wanted from men and what she wasn't going to accept. From what I had heard, it was the kind of attitude she needed if she was hoping to successfully date in Lagos. It was going to be a fun year getting to know her better. I could already feel it. I refilled our wine glasses and made a toast: 'To an adventurous year!' we said excitedly, as we clinked glasses.

CHAPTER 36

Kian

Kian looked at the mirror above his bathroom sink. He could hardly believe that it was his reflection staring back at him. It had been three months since he arrived in Lagos, yet he was still no closer to his dream. All his ideas of making it big and returning home to London as a superstar seemed as real as a unicorn. He walked into the parlour and sat on the couch that doubled up as his bed, pondering why life was determined to make a mockery out of him. After weeks of partying with his cousin Adewale, and being introduced to supposed industry insiders (but being refused entry to the VIP areas), he had quickly realised that Adewale had drawn him over from the other side of the world on the basis of a pipe dream. His cousin was certainly not the calibre of manager that he had made out he was. He was just trying to climb the ranks of the showbiz industry like anyone else, and had latched onto Kian to do so. Adewale had been a runner on several shows and music videos and had worked backstage at a few events, but the 'industry contacts' he had alluded to having were thin on the ground.

At first, Kian had believed Adewale simply wanted him to enjoy the thrills of Lagos before buckling down to work in the studio. But when Kian had expressed his desire to get down to serious work after two weeks of partying at his expense, proposing they set up meetings with industry professionals, he had been met with evasion. Kian had gradually begun to realise the extent of his cousin's deceit, but it was a visit to a producer's home studio, that Adewale had set up, that really confirmed it. Three weeks after his arrival in Lagos, Kian had finally pinned Adewale down and insisted he set up a meeting with the famous producer that he had seen his cousin in a picture with. It was the same picture, on Adewale's Instagram, that had first prompted Kian all those months ago to get in touch with his cousin in Lagos about his music contacts. The weeks that followed, both men decided to give their partnership a go and thus his ambition to move to Lagos to pursue his lifelong dream of becoming an international star was born.

After days of wondering if Adewale would come through, Kian finally received the good news that they were scheduled to visit the producer at his studio. His dreams of a hit collaboration might just be about to come true – he could already see himself on stage under the bright lights.

The day of their appointment arrived and Kian was excited that things were finally coming together. He had worn a black T-shirt and his best ripped skinny jeans, with a gold belt. He also had his favourite necklaces and rings on, and had visited Adewale's barber for a fresh fade and trim. At 1 p.m., the cousins arrived at the sprawling house in a gated estate in Lekki, only to be told by the security guard that they would be unable to see his boss. Adewale had appeared to be annoyed and had requested that he go in and speak to someone else who would confirm their appointment. The guard had grudgingly gone inside only to return ten minutes later with the same news. His oga wasn't expecting them and had ordered he returned to his duties. Kian had been stunned, and Adewale confused. Adewale had got out his mobile phone and furiously keyed in a number, but on the other end of the line, no one responded. Kian was embarrassed and suggested that they leave, but as they were about to, the guard offered a suggestion. He told the cousins that just like them, other young artists turned up at the producer's house hoping that he would work with them or listen to their mixtapes. Sometimes, if they were lucky or perhaps if the artist was truly blessed, his oga would roll down his window while driving out and collect their CDs.

Adewale jumped at the idea, but Kian was hesitant. However, after his cousin pleaded that they had come so far and shouldn't return home without trying, Kian had given in. The security guard had said that the producer was due to leave at any minute, but it wasn't until half an hour later that they saw his car proceeding out of the car park to the gate. The cousins had nervously shifted from one foot to the other in anticipation. As the car slowly made its way through the opened gates, Adewale lightly tapped on the window with his other hand raised in the air, ready to greet the driver within. But with a loud rev of the engine, the car pulled away from him. Mouth agape, Adewale looked away from the car to Kian, and then back again at the car, which had sped off, leaving them in a cloud of dust.

CHAPTER 37

Kian

That unfortunate event had greatly disturbed Kian, and he began to wonder if his dreams of stardom had been too grand. He had been mad at Adewale, but what could he do? He was already in Lagos and thought it best to make the most of what life had handed him. He couldn't just return to London; the shame would be too much to bear. He had left with a personal promise of only coming back when he could do right by his mother. Returning after a defeat was to prove his father right – that he, Adekitan Adebanjo, was worthless. He had no recollection of the father who had abandoned him and his mother before he was even a year old, so he despised him for all that he was and all that he had never been. He had secretly wished that his father would reach out to him on his eighteenth birthday, but when he didn't, his resentment grew deeper. He had vowed to shame his deserting father and prove him wrong with his success. He would watch as the old man crawled out of wherever he was hiding to latch onto his newly famous son, and he vowed that he wouldn't show a sliver of mercy for all that the man had made them go through. He hated him even more for how his mother had had to suffer alone, at the hands of an unkind society. She was the most hardworking woman he had ever known and it was up to him to treat her like the queen that she was. All he had ever wanted to do was to make her proud. He needed to restore her dignity and laugh in the face of those in the community who had thought that her life was ruined after getting pregnant out of wedlock. His conception almost tore his mum and her family apart, but when they had found out about his father leaving a few months after Kian's birth, they had ended their feud and rallied around her.

Kian's heart ached for all that he knew he could do for her but was yet to. After years of supporting his dreams, he had slowly begun to see the light in her eyes dim whenever he talked about music, but he didn't blame her. All she had ever wanted was the best for him. So when Adewale begged Kian to forgive him for his lies, and vowed to start afresh to achieve their dreams, a pact was made. They would hustle till their blood ran dry, or at least Kian's money. They would do everything in their power to make their partnership a success. Kian would rise to be the artist that they both knew he could be and Adewale would be right by his side championing him all the way. It was Lagos after all, where, with enough determination, even a slum kid could make it big in the music industry. If the recent successes of impoverished young artists was anything to go by, Kian felt that he was already ahead of the game.

'Guy, are you ready?' Adewale asked.

Kian was brought out of his reverie and realised he had zoned out on the chair. He got up and followed Adewale out of their shared one-bedroom apartment. They were headed to meet with a new producer they had been introduced to who went by the name Beaterbox. 'Just like a chatterbox you know? But Beaterbox for my beats,' the producer had explained on their first meeting. After working on two singles with another producer who had gradually grown expensive and then had refused to work with them when Kian had commented on his lateness, they had been lucky to find Beaterbox.

Kian had been worried about his slowly diminishing finances, but luckily Beaterbox had struck them a deal. If Kian only worked in the studio overnight or during the less busy hours, Beaterbox would let him pay in instalments. With no other options, Kian had agreed to the terms. But as the weeks rolled by, he had quickly realised that what Beaterbox hadn't mentioned was that he'd also be an errand boy. Determined to achieve his goals, Kian swallowed his pride and did the producer's bidding.

He sometimes caught himself wondering what the girls he had met at the airport, all those weeks ago, were up to. Were they faring well or finding it as hard as he was to settle in Lagos? The one with the Badu hair had unfollowed him, but he still peeked at her feed whenever he remembered to and she seemed to be living the socialite lifestyle. The one with the wicked bod was all about her makeup and groaning about NYSC. He wasn't sure what he'd do if he was to ever see them again, but knew they couldn't learn of his struggles if they ever crossed paths again.

CHAPTER 38

Kian

Beaterbox's studio was situated in Festac Town at the southern part of the mainland. It was an area that had produced one of Afrobeat's greatest musicians and was still living off that old glory. The studio itself occupied the ground level of a duplex whose first floor was empty except for the landlord's old furniture that remained, gathering dust. At the front gate of the building, Beaterbox had a mini blackboard resting on the open gate. It read: *Beaterbox Studios. Where stars are made.* On the veranda was a three-seater couch that leaned on a wall streaked by green algae. Behind it was a tinted sliding door for guests. The recording studio had been created without much fanfare. Its walls were decorated with images of the town's Afrobeat star and several others, but besides those, it was fitted with only the bare essentials. It was devoid of any sense of luxury, in contradiction to its owner's sense of self-importance.

When Kian got to the studio, another artist was still in session. Kian was asked to wait his turn even though he had been scheduled to begin. He looked at his Emporio Armani watch and sighed. He walked out and Adewale followed closely behind. Cursing under his breath, Kian wished Beaterbox didn't have to be so arrogant just because he was doing them a favour.

An hour later, the other artist left the premises and they were called in. Kian stormed into the studio and went directly to the booth, ignoring Beaterbox's feigned apology. They had been working on a new sample song for some days, but Beaterbox had insisted that something felt off. 'Unoriginal,' he had quipped when he thought Kian wasn't listening.

'Again from the top! You've got to feel it man, forget this your fine boy swag o. Make dem know who you be. You suppose feel the beat na!' Beaterbox barked.

'Yeah, feel the beat!' Adewale mimicked.

Kian put the headphones back on and put his mouth as close to the microphone as the pop filter would allow. He closed his eyes and gave it all that he had.

After twenty minutes of recording, Adewale said he needed to head out to handle some business. Kian hoped that whatever business it was, he'd come back smiling. As soon as Adewale left, Beaterbox's sidekick also vacated the room and Kian was called out of the booth. Beaterbox had something on his mind. Something so precious he needed to talk to Kian alone.

'You know that girl that is always greeting you at the bukka?' Beaterbox began, pointing to the right to indicate the eatery next door to his building.

'You mean Eunice?' Kian asked blankly, staring at a pimple on the producer's jaw that looked ripe enough to burst.

'Yesss, Eunice,' Beaterbox replied, nudging Kian on the knee. 'I like her.'

'Raah, I feel you man. Go on then, I've got no business there,' Kian responded with a grin.

'Ahn ahn, you know she has eyes for only you. You'll help me get her,' Beaterbox remarked.

Determined not to be anyone's side man, Kian tried to talk his way out of it, playing on Beaterbox's ego by saying he wouldn't need any help talking to Eunice. But the producer told him to get back in the booth and have a good think about it. Kian felt trapped, but before he even closed the door behind him and resumed his place in front of the mic, his decision had been made.

Eunice was a courteous and unremarkable girl who always seemed happy to help others. She had deep brown eyes and full lips, with an oval-shaped face. And although he'd noticed her big breasts and slender frame, she was dark-skinned – not the type of girl Kian was interested in. But it didn't matter much anyway. He convinced himself that it was no different from the other girls he had used for his means. He remembered the call he had received from Lulu, who he thought he had only been casually hooking up with until she had called a week after his departure from London, crying that he had broken her heart by not saying goodbye before he left. She'd been a good shag but he should have never let her get as close to him as he had allowed. Without remorse, he had coldly told her that night over the phone to grow up and get on with her plans to go to uni. He said that he knew her type and why she clung so tightly to him. He was unsure how long he'd be away, he told her, and she shouldn't bother waiting for him.

'Live your life!' he had shouted into the mouthpiece, imagining how her freckled face would have crumpled at his words. But he didn't care. He cut the call even as she continued to sob.

When Kian had first laid eyes on Lulu one hot Saturday in August, it had all been dandy. That week was the hottest London had seen for years, and Kian and his boys were hanging out in Lewisham Park. They had been chatting about music, hustling and their female conquests, Kian teasing his friend Dan about his lack of game with women.

The boys were passing a zoot amongst themselves while Kian went over the details of the event he was set to perform at that night. As he talked, he saw two girls walking past them holding ice cream cones. Distracted, he paused to watch the light-skinned one, who had stopped to lick dribbling blue ice cream off her fingers. She had raised her head and caught him staring. Kian held her gaze as she turned and walked towards them, taking in her form and waiting as she sauntered forwards. His boys had also grown quiet, staring as the second girl followed her friend. 'You guys got weed, yeah?' she had asked, looking only at Kian. Both girls sat down and joined them. Kian found out that the name of the one he fancied was Lulu, and her friend was called Comfort. Kian and Lulu had got chatting, and before they all left, he'd invited her to his gig. Ever since he'd got a small amount of exposure in the underground scene, Kian always got his way with the ladies.

CHAPTER 39

Kian

Kian had begun to see clearly what he had overlooked for weeks. Because he had been uninterested in Eunice, he had failed to see that she had a crush on him. She was simply the girl who worked at the place next door and up until then, he had assumed her friendliness towards him was just her way of being proper.

In the days that followed, now that she had become another means to reach his goal, he began to take more notice of Eunice. He paid closer attention when she came over to the studio to deliver food that had been ordered and he also made an effort to linger at the bukka when he wasn't in session. He was quick to return her greetings and asked her more questions about herself – questions that, until now, he'd had no interest in knowing the answers to. When she spoke, he listened. When she looked tired, he was quick to offer a compliment. When she attempted to make him laugh, he laughed immediately. The more time he invested in getting to know her, the more he quite liked her – she was a nice enough girl in her own peculiar way. He could see why Beaterbox was interested in her, because unlike the other girls who served at the bukka, Eunice alone was able to counter his cockiness with wit. She failed to be taken in by his charms and no matter how often he had left her with tips, she remained unimpressed.

Within a couple of weeks, Kian had developed an easy rapport with Eunice, but was yet to successfully broach the subject of Beaterbox with her. Whenever Kian had tried to gauge whether she was interested in him, the producer's name was met with a disapproving response. Kian was faced with the daunting task of asking her directly. Beaterbox had run out of patience; he was holding out on mastering Kian's song, since Kian was also yet to pay up fully. The favour that he had promised to deliver was all that he had to go on with, so that Friday, he decided to seal the deal.

On his way to the studio, he first stopped over at the bukka to get some drinks. When he saw Eunice, he told her that he had a surprise for her that evening and she should come look for him during her break. At 9 p.m., he was told she was waiting for him outside. Walking up to her, he could see that she had made an effort. She had a pink tinted lip gloss on and had changed from her palm oil-smeared dress to skinny jeans and a yellow blouse that complimented her skin tone. He told her he wanted to head to the new Domino's on the street next to theirs to buy her a pizza – what Lagos girl didn't like free pizza?

On the way back, he had managed to convince her to come into the studio to listen to his new track. Feeling honoured, Eunice obliged – it was the first time that she'd ever entered the inner part of the studio. Kian offered her a seat and proceeded to play the track that he had finished working on. As she sank her teeth into a pizza slice and nodded in rhythm to the song, Kian told her what had inspired it and how instrumental Beaterbox had been in the process. Right on cue, as they had planned, the producer walked into the studio. Eunice was clearly startled as she had thought they were alone. She tried to get up to leave, but Kian insisted that she stayed before quickly leaving, giving her no time to argue. On his way home, he hoped the plan would work and Beaterbox would seal the deal.

CHAPTER 40
Kian

That weekend, Kian steered clear of the studio and by the time the new week arrived he still felt uneasy about returning. He was worried his plan with Eunice had been a bad idea. By the Wednesday, after being unable to keep on dishing out excuses to Adewale for missing his studio time, he set out to pay a visit to Beaterbox. When he got to the street and walked past the bukka, a feeling of guilt arose, but he forced it aside.

His overnight session working on a bonus track with Beaterbox was awkward. The producer evaded his questions on how his meeting with Eunice had gone, saying he had better things to do than talk about a silly girl with no 'home training' and as a result no respect for men. Kian concluded that it hadn't gone as they had planned and hoped that Beaterbox would get over it soon enough. By the early hours of the morning, he had wrapped up his work for the night and settled down for a few hours' sleep on the couch.

He got up at 8 a.m. and was setting off for home when he was accosted by Eunice, who had been in the process of carrying some cooking materials into the restaurant. She stomped towards him and shouted a series of words in her language that he guessed were of the X-rated variety. He had expected that she might give him a ticking off, but she was livid. He was taken off guard. Until then, he had never imagined that she possessed such strength and all of a sudden he experienced a sharp pang of shame for the part he had played in the whole affair. He finally realised why the other guys at the studio sniggered whenever Beaterbox's female conquests were mentioned.

Eunice was right to be angry with him. She shouted at Kian

that she hadn't been the first victim of Beaterbox's unwanted advances, and that she had been lucky to have had the taser that she always carried in her bag. Being a single young woman in Lagos had taught her to be prepared for all eventualities in life. Kian tried to move closer to her to apologise but she dipped her hand in her bag and shouted that he move away from her. She would never forgive him for the danger he had put her in.

Trying to avoid the stare of the passers-by who had paused to watch their heated conversation, Kian hurried to the other side of the road to hail a taxi. He was in a haze all the way home. When they reached the apartment, he absentmindedly handed a wad of cash to the taxi driver and ran inside, sinking to the floor behind the sofa. He wondered how he could have gone that far to get what he wanted. He remembered how fun it had all been at the start when he and Dan had decided to take their music careers seriously. They had been fresh out of sixth form college and uninterested in going to university. Nothing his mother had said persuaded him otherwise. He had truly believed his fate was written in the stars. Spitting rhymes during break time at college had started off as a joke, a way to goof around with his friends and win the hearts of the ladies who hung on their every word, but soon after winning his first rap battle, he had begun to envision himself on stage. He had begun to truly appreciate the art of it and as he researched the lives of the greats and studied their career progression, he saw himself as the next in line. Then, one day, Dan's uncle had introduced them to a friend of his who had just set up a studio in his flat.

He'd believed that his big break was just around the corner – the world was going to know his name – and he hadn't turned back ever since. But it had been a bumpy road, and after three years, Dan had made peace with the idea that it wasn't going to happen for him and had focused his efforts on a career in the sports retail industry. Kian had persevered, but on days like this he wondered: *is it ever going to work out?*

Kian raised his head and looked around him. He despised what he saw. How was it that he had come to live with Adewale in this shack of an apartment while his uncle's comfortable house was only a couple of miles away? He looked at the worn rug caked with dust and debris and wondered why Adewale failed to do the sweeping whenever it was his turn. The glass louvres on the window were no less dusty and the once pea-sized hole in the mosquito net that had been covered with cotton wool was now as big as a CD. It was no wonder that the hesitant buzzing of mosquitoes kept him sleepless at night and smacking at his body whenever they dug into his flesh. The rest of the flat was just as shabby. The toilet and shower, housed in the same space, were in an awful state. He hated this hell hole. Was this all his fault for coming here in the first place, he wondered? No, he decided, his ego taking over. It was Adewale's fault, and the fault of that famous producer who had so arrogantly driven away from them. Beating at his chest in fury, he yelled that if it wasn't for them all, he'd be a star by now.

CHAPTER 41

Osayuki

The day of Afolabi's birthday party had finally arrived, and I had the feeling that something monumental was going to happen. I could feel it in my heart that it was the day I had to either choose Afolabi or let him go. We'd been speaking on the phone, and there was no denying the connection between us. Although he wanted to see me more, I had come up with excuses for why I couldn't meet up. Afolabi had been patient and accepting about being just friends, but I had begun to sense that the barricade I put up any time I felt he was getting too close was playing with his emotions; and mine too, if I was to be honest. It was time to make a decision. As I stared at my reflection in the mirror, wearing a patterned skater dress with a low-cut back, I couldn't help the huge grin on my face. *Cynthia definitely outdid herself*, I thought looking at my high cheekbones, further defined by my friend's makeup skills. I loved the gold glitter she had lined my eyes with; it made them shine like bright stars on a cloudless night. The makeup wasn't overpowering, but enough to dazzle Afolabi, Cynthia had cheekily suggested. I had laughed as an image of him was conjured in my head and I knew that secretly, I couldn't wait to see him. He had been even more attentive than usual in the past couple of weeks. He'd sent flowers to my home, and when I had been swamped at work with deadlines and impossible colleagues, he had sent lunch from my favourite grill restaurant. I had tried to make out that I didn't want the attention, but he had persevered, and truth be told, I enjoyed it. It had been a while, after all, since a man had treated me this way.

I watched in the mirror as Cynthia fiddled with her white

bodycon dress, which rode up as soon as she took a step, no matter how much she pulled the hem towards her knees. I laughed at her; it was a futile fight. I was happy to have her as a friend and glad that we had stumbled upon each other again that day at the market. It was interesting how similar we were, though in some ways we were different; and except for Wendy, she was the only other person I could call a close friend in Lagos. So far, we had hung out most weekends and when Afolabi's birthday party drew near and Wendy informed me that she'd be unable to attend, Cynthia had gladly obliged even though I had joked that she had no choice in the matter since she had been the one to convince me to attend.

When we got to the party, we were greeted by a maid who ushered us in and led the way towards the back of the house. The party extended from the living room to the backyard where a barbeque was underway.

'Osayuki, the guy is goals. You better not slack!' Cynthia teased, her eyes bulging as we walked through his house.

I toyed with the idea of Afolabi and me together and found myself smiling at the image. I guessed that without even knowing it, my resolve to keep a friendly distance between the both of us had slowly melted away and I found myself hoping that he'd make a move. And then, seconds after I had had the thought, Afolabi materialised in front of us. Before I could gather myself, I was locked in an embrace and drowned in the familiar scent of his cologne. I pulled away a little too quickly and then regretted that I did, but Afolabi was preoccupied by other things. He stared at me with an expression I couldn't yet read and I wondered what was going on in his head. We continued to stare at each other, smiling and not saying a word until Cynthia cleared her throat and stretched out her hand to introduce herself. Realising the faux pas, I reiterated what had been said and watched as they shook hands. After finding his voice, he beamed at me, eyes twinkling like never before, and commented on my new hairstyle and look. He had a way of making me feel special with just a look, and when I also regained my voice, I praised Cynthia for her help and they both laughed as he led us towards his friends and family in the splendid back garden.

The celebration was already in full swing and we tried to fit in, making ourselves comfortable with the other friends we had been introduced to. When Afolabi was called to the centre of the gathering and left my side to be toasted by his best friend, the woman sitting next to me dragged her seat closer to mine to talk to me in confidence. She had the expression of an amebo – someone who loved to know everyone's business and weigh in on matters that didn't concern them. I was concentrating on the speech and could hardly hear her, but after she had repeated herself twice, I managed to ascertain that she wanted to know how I knew Afolabi. She had an expression that looked something like nervous suspicion and I wondered if perhaps she saw me as competition. Afolabi was a good catch and in Lagos, where the number of women who deemed themselves wife material far surpassed the number of single, educated, good-looking and successful bachelors, men like Afolabi were either hitched, playing the field or doing both at the same time. So I didn't blame her. I politely replied that we were just friends, but I couldn't tell what she thought of my assertion. Just then, finishing off his speech, his best friend suddenly looked my way. Holding my gaze, he said he wished Afolabi all the best for the future and hoped he would settle down soon. Everyone laughed, and I felt a host of eyes turn in my direction. I too chuckled, and then stared at the Malta Guinness that I was nursing in my hand.

We cheered as the speech ended, sang happy birthday and watched Afolabi blow out the candles on his cake. Then the chattering and clang of silverware resumed as the guests tucked back into the rice, plantain, yam porridge, moi moi and other delicacies on offer. The woman by my side began telling me how well she knew Afolabi and his family. Apparently, she had known him since primary school, even though they had only reconnected around a year ago when they had met again at another friend's birthday party. She continued to tell me stories I had no interest in hearing; I listened with curious amusement, oohing and ahhing where necessary, until I was thankfully rescued by Afolabi. He wanted to introduce me to his mother, who was about to 'retire to her boudoir and leave the boogying to the youngsters', as she put it. Cynthia, meanwhile, had proved a useless wing woman as she had wandered off to enjoy the company of some other man who had attracted her attention, at least for the time being. I had been nervous to be introduced to Afolabi's mother and hoped for a smooth first meeting as we walked over to where she stood by the door leading into the house. I greeted her with a curtsy, since the last thing I wanted was for his mother to think I was disrespectful. Growing up with my culture rammed down my throat by my mother had taught me that much.

His mother was a tender-looking woman who was gentle in her ways. She embraced me with a fondness I wasn't expecting and, to anyone looking in from the outside, it was clear that she loved her son. *A mama's boy*, I thought as she shooed him away and asked me to follow her up to the second level of the house to help bring down more serviettes and paper plates. I followed silently as she led me through a different section of the house and up the staircase. There was another living room there, where she asked me to wait while she hurried through another set of doors to gather what was needed. I looked at pictures of the family that hung on the wall in the corridor as I slowly walked in the direction that she indicated. At the entrance of the living room, I was greeted by the familiar sound of the Afrobeat song blaring downstairs as a soft breeze made the sheer curtains billow inwards. I walked towards the balcony that overlooked the party in the garden. I spotted Afolabi in the crowd and instinctively smiled. He was seated with a group of friends and they were drinking and chatting as a tray of cake was passed around by a server in a dashiki dress. I stood there daydreaming until I felt a hand tap my shoulder, and turned to see his mother behind me. She looked mysterious, so I smiled at her, wondering how long she had been watching and if she could tell what I had been thinking.

CHAPTER 42

Osayuki

'He has not always been like this you know,' his mother started.

'Hmm,' I responded and then nodded, not quite sure of what, if anything, I should have said.

She continued, telling me how she had thought she had lost her son too after his father's death. Afolabi had not always seen eye to eye with him, but they had always been there for each other and although Afolabi had always acted strong, she knew that his father's passing affected him even more than he himself imagined. One day he was simply Afolabi, then with the break of a new day, he suddenly had to take on his father's responsibilities. She had watched him take up the role and live day to day like nothing else mattered. She had begun to worry about him, but after one long year, something had happened along the way and she had seen him begin to turn a corner. It was as if her prayers were finally being heard, and the last few months had been the happiest she had ever seen him. She searched my face and I quickly lowered my gaze away from hers. I didn't know what she was aiming at, but I didn't want to betray my feelings by letting her through.

She said that she had never heard Afolabi talk so passionately about any woman. Still, I remained quiet. I mean, *how exactly does one reply to such a statement?* Then she added that she had watched how I had looked at him from the balcony. I tried to laugh it off, but stopped when I caught her eye again. I didn't understand what was happening. Was his mother, the most unlikely person I'd have imagined, giving me relationship advice? If I had known her better, perhaps I'd have realised that her request for help had been perfectly orchestrated to get me alone.

But it didn't make sense until she spoke of her love for her late husband and how she prayed every day that both her children would find a soulmate whom they could grow old with. Finally, I understood what it was all about. She was simply a mother trying to ensure her son would be happy.

In some ways, she reminded me of my parents. Daddy had been the best father anyone could have wished for and unlike Afolabi, who got to have his until he was an adult, mine had been taken away from me at a much younger age. We had only been in England for a year when he died. It had been all the more painful because he hadn't even been ill. One day he had been there, offering his daily motivational quotes at breakfast before he left for work, and the next we were called by a member of staff at the hospital where he worked to tell us he was no more. I cried for days and refused to eat. The irony that he was a medical doctor and had suffered such a fate had been too great to bear. Thankfully, I no longer harboured any of the resentment towards God that had festered during those days. I had mourned him for a very long time and as the years rolled by, the heaviness in my chest began to lift. But it almost returned again when Mum had announced that she was engaged to Bob, who I had thought was just a friend from the library where she worked. It had been a long road to acceptance, but Bob Adams had proved himself. He wasn't my father, but he had been the next best thing. Years later, when I had wanted to go out clubbing for the first time and Mum had refused, it had been Bob who had come to my rescue. I had soon realised what things I could go to Mum for and what Bob would help me with. We were an unusual family and we sometimes got weird looks when we were out, but it was a family I'd never trade for another.

CHAPTER 43

Osayuki

Mama Fola continued our conversation. She launched into another story, telling me we must all live to seek that which makes us happy. 'Life's too short,' she kept reiterating, and I couldn't think of any other two people who would understand those words better than the two of us.

'God forbid o, but if I should die tomorrow, at least I'll know that my son is happy!'

'Ahn ahn Mummy, God forbid!' I quipped.

I was charmed by her enthusiasm and we both laughed. I guessed that she had a point. There was no doubt in my mind that I liked Afolabi, and after the discussion with his mother, I felt that I had seen other parts of him through her eyes that I hadn't yet been privy to. In that instant, I made the decision that I knew had been looming. I was no longer willing to let my past have a hold over my future. I had been hurt badly by Nick, but to live ceaselessly with the trauma and isolate myself because of what he'd done was to give him power over my life. If there was anything I was good at, it was navigating my own path, and no one had the power to direct my life unless I granted them the privilege to do so. I deserved happiness, damn it, and that was exactly what I was going to get. I thanked Afolabi's mother and praised her for organising such a lovely party, then saw myself out.

When I returned to the backyard, it felt like I had been gone for longer than I actually had. A few guests had left, while some had moved towards the pool, although no one seemed interested in swimming despite the sweltering temperature. I put the plates and serviettes on the serving table and looked around for Cynthia, but I shouldn't have bothered. She was clearly having a good time, sitting by the pool with both feet in and talking to the same suitor she had been with all evening. I walked over to her to ensure that she hadn't been worried about my whereabouts and Afolabi joined us.

'What did my mother have to say?' he whispered.

'Oh nothing much, she was just telling me some interesting things about you,' I replied with a wink.

'Well, in that case you'll have to tell me all about it!' he said and grabbed my hand, leading the way towards where his friends were dancing to the DJ.

As we danced, I looked into his eyes and wondered if he had put his mother up to it, but it didn't matter. If I was honest, I had known for some time that I'd regret it if I didn't give him a chance.

After an hour, the party began to wind down. Afolabi's friends thanked him for the invite and bade him goodbye. I left him to see his friends off to the front gate and joined Cynthia, who by then had moved away from the pool area back to the cluster of plastic chairs that were placed in the garden. She gave me a knowing look as I sat beside her and we giggled.

'Well, has he asked you yet?' she asked.

'Asked what . . . no, no we're just friends. Remember?' I replied without my previous enthusiasm.

'Just friends and you were dancing like that?'

We laughed again and left unsaid what we both understood. Then she looked at the time and gasped. She said she'd have to be up early for church the next day and needed to head home. So we got our things and looked for Afolabi to say goodbye. When we found him, he insisted that he would drop us home. Despite Cynthia's protestations that her place was a long drive to the mainland, and that he needn't bother, he wouldn't take no for an answer, so we all left in his car.

CHAPTER 44

Osayuki

It was an interesting drive to Aunty Ndidi's apartment in Ikeja. I sat in the front with Afolabi while Cynthia sat behind in the passenger's seat. At first, it was quiet in the car and as his Jeep sped through the night, I could feel a change in the air. I looked straight ahead, avoiding his face, although wondering what was going through his mind and if he had felt the same things I did when we had danced earlier. I looked back at Cynthia but she was busy with her phone – no doubt on social media, the girl was obsessed.

I was about to break the silence when Afolabi beat me to it. He got Cynthia's attention and asked how she was finding NYSC and coping with life in Lagos. As I already knew, she explained that while she finally had begun to enjoy teaching the kids and seeing their faces light up at discovering new things, she wished she didn't have to get up so early in order to beat the morning traffic and road blocks. Afolabi responded to her answers with understanding and interest and I loved that he genuinely seemed to care. And unexpectedly, Cynthia had a lot more to say than I had imagined. As was the case with anyone returning to the motherland with an accent, she had found that the prices of things suddenly increased whenever she opened her mouth. It didn't matter if she had bought the item for a thousand naira less from the other trader down the road just the day before. Other things she had begun to find off-putting were the manner-isms she had found some people put on when they were in her presence, compared to when they were with other born-and-bred citizens. A guy who had never crossed borders would all of a sudden develop an American accent when talking to her, or would engage in profuse swearing and using vulgar words that weren't in the Nigerian lexicon. We all laughed at the example she described and I chipped in to say it wasn't anything unusual. What did she expect from people who had consumed so much Western media since childhood, and who had developed an inferiority complex thanks to the common idea that 'everything foreign is better'? Some people lived by the 'monkey see, monkey do' rule. To them, in order to get her attention, they had to become like her. I had noticed a lot of it in the Nigerian media and entertainment industry. I shared the fact that almost every time I listened to the radio on my way to work, my ears were accosted with a plethora of accents, none of which were Nigerian or even distinctly African. Some would say it was due to all of the Nigerians who had studied or lived abroad returning to influence the industry, but I begged to differ. We all knew that once a person reached early adulthood with a native accent, totally losing it was almost impossible.

'So why all the phoné?' I continued.

Afolabi and Cynthia were listening to me keenly at this point and I told them that I reckoned such people led fake lives, made fake friendships and revelled in ostentatious living; and the age of social media wasn't helping. I had read somewhere that people often took selfies in front of cars or houses that weren't theirs, or went as far as walking into the lobby of an expensive hotel (or perhaps finding a suitor who actually could afford such luxuries), all for the sake of 'the gram'. Lagos was definitely a tough place and in a city where almost every woman was out to prove that she was a 'Lagos Big Girl', the stakes were high when it came to showing you were of a certain economic class. It had been only earlier that month that I had received several calls from friends in London after a documentary titled *Lagos to London: Britain's New Super Rich* had aired. It had detailed the lives of super-wealthy Nigerians who travelled to the UK in luxurious style. Given the economic instability in Nigeria, and the tendency for xenophobia in the UK, the documentary had done little to help the plight of the average immigrant. My friends had wondered if I also lived in such extravagance given that I too was inhabiting prime real estate on Lagos Island.

Afolabi and Cynthia agreed with my reasoning and we all took turns in trading experiences and ideas of how to better the country we all currently called home, even though Cynthia was glad that she'd be leaving at the end of her 'family-imposed exile'. After we dropped her off, we made a U-turn and headed back south to the island. The drive back was quiet, but it was the sort of silence that didn't need filling. Being in each other's company was good enough as we listened to the soulful vocals of Sade – I was glad that he had remembered.

When we got to my house, he parked and turned to look at me. I waited two counts then looked up to hold his gaze. I wondered what would happen and I could feel the butterflies flapping away in my tummy, clearly in tune with what I was feeling. I remembered that I still had his birthday card in my bag and reached for it. When I handed it to him, he held onto my hand and asked the question I'd been waiting for all day. I didn't hesitate, I didn't stutter. With a smile, I said yes, and before I knew it, we shared our first kiss, and I was elevated to somewhere else other than seated in that Jeep. When we finally drew apart, he looked at me lovingly, caressing my cheeks. I was engulfed by his aura and didn't want to leave. And even when the gateman opened the gate and shouted, 'Madam, na you be that?' I squeezed his hand and stayed.

CHAPTER 45

Osayuki

The next couple of weeks were magical. It was like I had been given a new lease of life and nothing else mattered much. The traffic to work was no longer as tiresome as it once was since I spent most of the ride chatting on the phone with Afolabi or gossiping with Wendy. Even Mum had noticed a change in my voice and demanded to know what was going on. I didn't tell her everything but suggested that things were looking up and I wasn't surprised when Aunty Rosemary called an hour later to enquire if I was coping in Lagos while she was away. I kept quiet about my relationship status. I played along like I didn't know Mum had divulged that I was cheerier than I had been when I left London and that Aunty Rosemary should try her luck to see if I'd spill to her instead. She had ended the call telling me to have fun but to be safe – emphasising the word 'safe'.

'God, Aunty Rosemary!' I had screamed into my phone, cringing with embarrassment. I hadn't had sex with Afolabi yet, but it had definitely been on my mind and imagining it had made me giddy with excitement. Afolabi and I spent all the time that we could together and I was beginning to open up more to him. Getting back to my old unguarded self, the way I had been before Nick's transgression, felt great. It was crazy that I had almost denied myself this experience and I was glad that Afolabi had stuck around.

One afternoon, while I was at lunch with Wendy, my phone rang and, seeing my face light up, she guessed it was Afolabi and wrinkled her nose in mockery, muttering: 'Love birds'. He wanted us to go out on a date that night and said that he had everything planned and all I needed to do was get to the location. I loved his spontaneity. It had been missing in my relationship with Nick – after being with him for so long, I had tired of always being the one to set up date nights. I realised now that I should have been more vocal about my needs and expectations.

I told Afolabi that I didn't feel dressed for the occasion, but in his usual fashion, he said I needn't worry because he knew I'd look great in whatever I had on in the office. That evening, he picked me up after work and we headed out. I asked where we were going but he refused to divulge his plans. I gave up asking and waited for the night to unfold.

We stopped at a swanky Chinese restaurant that had just opened in Ikoyi. Last week, I had said that I missed Mr Wu's takeaway restaurant, which had been around the corner from my apartment in Camden. I had only said it in jest when he had asked what I missed most about London, but sitting there at the restaurant, eating chicken lo mein and spare ribs doused with barbecue sauce, I was so happy to be eating Chinese food for the first time since I had moved back to Lagos.

And the night didn't end there. When we were done stuffing our bellies, we got into the car and I soon realised we were on Awolowo Road, which wasn't in the direction of my home.

'We're almost there,' he said as he brushed my hand.

When we got to the destination, still in Ikoyi, he led me into the lounge area of Hassana, a boutique hotel buzzing with fellow young professionals. I had heard about the open mic night there, but had never been. Hassana was a distinctive place, fusing a sense of style, art and aspects of northern culture to evoke a spirit that was hip, modern and very neo-African. Already promising myself a return with my girlfriends for a night out, I was mesmerised by the aesthetics of the place. We walked into the dimly lit room, the floor paved with small colourful marbles and the walls bedecked with portraits of striking faces and landscapes from the northern states. A big raffia fan hung on the wall above where the live band had set up and behind the main stage was a big mirror that reflected the audience, seated in the middle of the room. The two long couches at the other end of the lounge were already taken, so we proceeded to find seats and Afolabi greeted some people he knew along the way. From his demeanour, it was clear that he was a regular. When he placed his hand on the small of my back, I realised that it was our first time officially out as a couple in the presence of others.

When the lounge was fully packed and the night's event was about to start, the host made a final call for anyone wanting to sign up to perform. Afolabi stood up. I wondered what he was up to as he walked up and wrote down his name, winking at me cheekily from across the room.

The first person was called to the floor and the live band played along to a famous John Legend song. The night carried on beautifully as one performer after the other took to the centre of the room and either sang, rapped or made an offering of spoken-word poetry. They were mostly talented acts, with a few humorous ones who had no business on stage. Finally, it was Afolabi's turn. As he squeezed through the people sitting around us, he was cheered by the crowd, several drinks in and eating pepper soup or asun. When he got to the stage, he adjusted the microphone stand – I wondered if he'd sing and realised I didn't even know if he could. So when he cleared his throat, I crossed my fingers and waited. But to my surprise, he told the crowd he'd be reading a poem.

> I left the door to my heart unlocked
> Yet you walked in with one foot in
> And the other out
> Your love is dizzying and all-consuming
> How will I get to you?

As he began, his voice was soft, but it became stronger and more passionate as he continued. I felt as if everyone around me was watching to see my expression. I didn't know anyone in the room, so looked straight ahead at the man I was besotted with. I smiled at the brief humour in the second verse, and by the third, a couple of people in the audience were snapping their fingers and cheering him on. Finally, he ended, looking straight at me, throwing me a wink:

> Love is rich
> Love is warm
> Love will make you do incredibly stupid things.

I was flabbergasted, high on love. Before my brain could catch up, I was up on my feet, joining the others in a round of applause, laughing wildly and blowing him kisses.

CHAPTER 46

Osayuki

A few days later, I was fuming at work. I had just received the press release I had ordered to be drafted and run by me, and the copy had been sub-par. I rang Adaora and told her to come into my office to go through the edit with her. Since I had started at House of Martha, it had been clear that we'd never be friends. I accepted her stance and regarded her respectfully as a colleague, but I had borne the brunt of her malice for too long and a talk was in order. I had gotten used to things working slower than I was used to in London and had been advised to take it in my stride. This was simply the way things were done in Nigeria, I was told, but I refused to let any insubordination pass. Whether Adaora felt she had been the rightful heir to my role or not, I had a job to do and for the second time that afternoon she had pushed my buttons.

I was typing furiously at my keyboard, composing an email to call for a team meeting the next morning, when I heard the clickety-clack of stiletto heels. I heard a knock and slowly looked up from my computer to see Adaora walking in. I took a quick glance at her shoes and for the first time caught sight of her ankles. I was shocked. I guess I shouldn't have been – there were tell-tale signs of bleaching on all the parts of her body that were uncovered. But seeing her blackened ankles in a sea of yellow skin was startling.

I recalled how I'd been astonished the first time I visited a beauty store and saw the quantity of creams, moisturisers and soaps that proudly advertised their ability to whiten, tone or brighten the skin to shades lighter than it naturally was. I couldn't believe the audacity of parading such items in the clear view of impressionable young girls, who already had so many self-esteem and body image issues to deal with. I couldn't remember such products being so openly available when I was growing up in Lagos. Instead, it was a trade shrouded in secrecy, almost like drug dealing, peddled by door-to-door sellers who promised the latest items from Asia or beyond. Now these creams and lotions were on the shelves of high street shops, and skin bleaching was the 'in' thing. Wendy had told me it was a favourite pastime of girly meetups; one girl would trade the latest miracle product with another. It was no longer a taboo, but an essential part of the 'Lagos Big Girl' look. It was no wonder that people like Adaora believed it was the only way to secure themselves their dream job, man or whatever was their current goal; and to an extent, it was the truth. If so many girls had sworn that their upgraded look was to thank for whatever man or job they had bagged, who were those still aspiring to such achievements to disbelieve them?

I looked at Adaora with pity and motioned for her to take a seat. After going through the press release with her and highlighting what I needed corrected, I rounded off the conversation by informing her about the email I was about to send. She was to make sure that the whole team understood the importance of the meeting and arrived on time. I was tired of hearing stories about the morning traffic as an excuse for lateness. When I'd worked in London, there was also a manic rush hour – I'd be on my feet for over half an hour jumping from one train to another amid the crowds – and I'd still always get to work on time. They'd simply have to adjust their alarm clocks.

After I was done with my tirade, she hit me with some bad news. Just before I had summoned her to my office, she had received a call from the makeup artist who was due to work on the models for our lookbook photoshoot. The MUA had called to cancel due to an unforeseen emergency. Adaora was panicky about it and so was I, because we had less than twenty-four hours to get our hands on another, but then an idea suddenly sprang to mind. I knew exactly who to call.

CHAPTER 47

Cynthia

I was done with work for the day and was preparing to leave when Osayuki called. I was in the staff room with Harmony and had been laughing over the homework I had just marked. I knew it was cruel, but I couldn't help but laugh and wonder how the kids came up with their fantastic ideas. The week before, I had assigned my class an essay on what they were looking forward to the most about the summer holiday and some of the stories had me bawling. I had to share it with Harmony, who joined me in a fit of laughter.

Osayuki was calling to ask if I could fill in as a makeup artist for her shoot that was to take place the following day. I initially refused because although I was a self-proclaimed makeup addict, I had never thought of myself as a makeup *artist* – certainly not on a professional level. But Osayuki persisted, telling me she believed I'd be just as good as the MUA who had cancelled on her. Osayuki was one of the kindest people I had come across, and was one of the closest friends I could say I had in Lagos, so I finally gave in, knowing that it would make her happy. But when I hung up, I wished that I hadn't and hoped that she'd call back to say that she had found someone else.

Harmony had overheard the conversation and when I told her I was worried about it, she brushed aside my fears and said she knew I was capable of pulling it off. Why else did I spend all that time doing my makeup and posting it online, she asked incredulously, if I wasn't going to use it to make money? She looked at me like I was a brat who had been born with a silver spoon in my mouth.

I guessed she was right. But I had never thought about it in that way. I didn't remember when exactly my love for makeup had begun; all I knew was that the low self-esteem I felt as a teenager had begun to dissipate with the compliments I got from the makeup looks that I created. I hadn't suffered an extreme case of bullying at school, but I guessed that it was the effect of those little snide remarks during puberty that had simmered like bubbling soup in a pot, eventually boiling over. Very early on, I became used to comments about my body following me wherever I went. I was always secretly unsure if a guy liked me for me or if they were just seduced by my curves. In time, makeup became my veil and served as a shield. I felt in control with it on – it was a sort of armour. It didn't matter what other people thought as long as I looked good for myself.

Seeing me deep in thought, Harmony suddenly asked me if I'd come somewhere with her. Having nothing else planned for the rest of the day, I agreed. She insisted that we take public transport even though I offered to pay for a taxi. If we were venturing into the city we were going to do it her way, she joked. I surrendered and followed her into a crammed bus. The driver insisted on filling it to its utmost capacity, like a person trying to zip up a too-tight dress, in denial about an extra tummy roll. I leaned into Harmony when the passenger on my right moved even closer on the wooden chair. Its padding, once there to provide a level of comfort to Lagos' working class after a hard day at work, had worn off. As the bus sped towards Ikeja, I was grateful for the air that came in through the window. I breathed in deeply to offset the smell of sweat and grime that lingered in the dingy bus, though could do nothing about how squashed my left bum cheek was. By the time we got to our stop, called Under Bridge, because it was literally under a bridge, I couldn't wait to be released.

One minute I was following Harmony under the bridge to cross to an adjacent road, and the next, my path was being blocked by someone dressed in a masquerade outfit. Shocked and scared, I tried to turn away, wondering what was happening and why no one else around me seemed to be reacting. I walked to my right, and then to my left, but still the masquerade stood in my way, stretching out its hand and holding out a koboko – a long whip – to block my path. I panicked. *Was I about to get a lashing?* I turned around and frantically tried to look for Harmony, wondering if she too was about to be attacked. I saw colours of pink, cream and black, and beads, sequins and cowries in flashes as I turned around in confusion, screaming to be left alone. Suddenly though, it dawned on me – whoever was behind the mask wasn't trying to attack me, they were asking for money. Harmony hurried up to me and explained that this was how some of the street men lived. They stayed under the bridge doing random jobs and begging for money, sometimes donning a masquerade outfit to intimidate or pressure an unsuspecting person into giving them money. As we walked away, the adrenaline still flowing through my veins from the fright I'd had, I contemplated going back to ask for a picture. *How often did anyone from my side of the world come across a magnificently dressed masquerade?*

I walked back to the masked man, who was watching for his next victim, and offered him two hundred naira for a photo with him. Ten minutes later, I was uploading the picture to Instagram. The caption read:

My father once said I paint my face like a masquerade. Well, here's an actual masquerade. Who wore it better? xx

CHAPTER 48

Cynthia

We continued our journey on a Keke NAPEP – a doorless, yellow, three-wheel vehicle that was introduced into Lagos in the early 2000s. The Keke, as it is commonly called, already had two inhabitants on the passenger side, and once again, I squeezed my bottom to fit into the space that was left for a third passenger while Harmony joined the driver in his seat at the wheel. I watched as she slowly shimmied her bum into the seat and then slightly turned outwards to the right, her back towards the driver in order to maximise the space. As the Keke careened through bumpy and pothole-ridden streets, I held tightly to my leather Zara bag and prayed for it to be over. I had always wondered what it would be like to ride in a Keke, and now I knew – it certainly wasn't a fun experience.

Later, while seated at the beer parlour that Harmony had led me to, she asked if I had seen the ashawo girls on Allen Avenue, a street infamous for prostitution. Yes, I sighed – I'd been shocked to see them bravely parading themselves, scantily clad in broad daylight. What was it with humans, naked bodies and sex? We all have bodies and know what they can do, but still sex retains it mystery, driving the dark industries of prostitution and pornography. Prostitution had always been in existence and I had sympathy for women who were forced to do it, either by circumstances or victimisation.

Harmony was listening keenly and when I had finished speaking, she added that it was because of women like those we'd seen earlier that she was grateful for the home her parents had worked hard to provide for her. She hadn't been raised with much, just the bare essentials – a roof over her head, clothes on her back, and food to keep her alive even though, during some tough times, she had had to go to school without any. But even with all the strife her family had gone through to ensure that she went to university, she had never once thought of selling her body for money.

'Chai! Things are so bad now that they even work in broad daylight!' she spat in bewilderment.

I too was grateful for my relatively comfortable upbringing. I might not have appreciated it as often as I should have, but hearing Harmony's story, and getting first-hand experience of what other Nigerians had to go through, was a wake-up call. I realised I had perhaps been too whiny in the past, when I should have been more thankful to my parents. They had gone through a lot in order to seek greener pastures. Mum and Dad had often shared what it had been like growing up in Nigeria, but being there at that moment made everything sink in. I had been complaining about the uncomfortable bus ride but I'd only had to travel by bus once since I'd been in Nigeria; for millions of others, even in torrential rain or indescribable heat, it was a daily reality.

A waitress served the beef pepper soup and drinks we had ordered. I sighed as I drank the chilled Star Radler beer straight from the can. It had become my drink of choice since it wasn't as strong as normal beers. I found myself cooling down from the heat and watched as Harmony gulped her can. We were quiet for a moment, eating our food and lost in our own thoughts.

I found my mind drifting, as it often did, to a truth I carried buried within my heart. Looking across at Harmony, who had been so open and honest with me, and who had never judged me, I felt an urge to share my feelings with her – my shame, I thought, would be safe with her. The truth, I told Harmony, was that I was utterly clueless about what to do with my life. I had managed to scrape a 2:1 in Marketing and Management at uni, but besides that, I had nothing else to show for my twenty-one years on the planet. I had watched my older brother sail through university and secure a job in the City. Dad was so proud of him, but I worried he saw me as a failure. After my difficult teenage years, I had managed to temporarily restore my father's pride in me by working doubly hard to get the A levels I needed for university. But now that I'd finished my degree and already quit one job, my dad's disappointment had returned.

I always felt my appearance had been what had opened doors for me. I had learned to play the game early on, but I worried that there was no hiding behind it anymore. What else did I have to offer besides my looks? Facebook posts showing friends moving on with their lives were a constant reminder of how disappointingly my own life was panning out. It had always been about moving on to the next stage in education, but with that done, I was confused about which path to follow next. I was applying for all the jobs that I could, but it just wasn't working, and alongside it all, I had to try to put on a brave face and be the well-adjusted Cynthia that everyone wanted me to be. But the truth was, I was tired. Even being in Lagos, where I felt I would have the edge over the competition, was no use. I felt empty and directionless, with nowhere to run.

Harmony looked thoughtful. I couldn't imagine that she'd understand any of what I had just revealed. After all, what were my woes in comparison to hers? I still had the pocket money from my father coming in each month, while she struggled to survive on the paltry NYSC wage offered by the federal government. But her reaction surprised me. It didn't matter about our differences, she said – everyone went through phases of life where they questioned what their purpose was. Most working-class Nigerians had big dreams they were struggling to achieve, whether it was working themselves out of poverty by securing a good job, marrying a wealthy bachelor or winning the lottery. It was all relative. Harmony advised that I cease feeling sorry for myself and really think about what it was that I wanted out of life. I had to stop being scared, stop worrying about what others thought and stop comparing myself to my siblings. I needed to use the tools at my disposal. She teased that she saw how much work I put into my makeup every day, even though the children couldn't care less about my appearance and I wasn't interested in the attention of the male teachers. It was clearly something I was passionate about – so what was stopping me saying yes to Osayuki's photoshoot? Perhaps if I seized that opportunity, it might lead me to some of the answers I was searching for.

CHAPTER 49

Osayuki

We had just finished another photoshoot, this time for our press package for the small independent shows at London Fashion Week. I had been impressed again by Cynthia. Since that first photoshoot she had filled in for, she had gained in confidence and I was more certain than ever that she had a knack for professional makeup artistry. She'd surprised herself, I thought, at just how talented she was – and had no doubt been pleased to be paid for her efforts – so I'd been encouraging her to take it more seriously.

I left the team downstairs at our in-house studio, said goodbye to Cynthia and headed upstairs to complete some work before I left. When I got to my office, I walked to the far end where I could see the Lekki-Ikoyi link bridge. I looked at the lagoon and the landscape and was glad to be standing there. It's peculiar how life works. Only seven months before, I had arrived in the bustling city in search of an escape from my old life. Now here I was, still doing what I loved but surprisingly dating again. *Who would have thought?* I had certainly sworn to steer clear of men, but Afolabi had changed all of that. I smiled as I thought about one weekend when Wendy had stayed over at mine and had forced me to go for a jog with her on the bridge, a popular spot for island residents. Apparently the real reason most of the runners went there was to check out members of the opposite sex. She joked that since I had bagged Afolabi, it was her turn to find a man. I had laughed, but curiosity got the better of me so I put on my exercise gear and went with her. We didn't find her a boyfriend that day, but the experience of being chatted up by an old man slowly driving alongside us in a Lexus, eager to play the role of sugar daddy, had at least provided some amusement.

I sat down to begin my work. Suddenly, there was a rumble of thunder and the previously bright sky began to turn grey. It was evident that the two-week break we'd had from the rain had ended and the rainy season was returning in full force. I knew the roads were only going to get worse once the rain started, so I decided to leave immediately. I had arranged a time for Mr Nelson to pick me up but since I was leaving earlier than planned, I took a taxi instead. Everyone had left by the time I got downstairs. I ordered the security guard to lock up for the day as I made my way out of the compound. I joined other commuters making their way home and it seemed that the impending rain had added to the usual madness that characterised Lagos roads. Horns blared almost constantly and insults were traded from driver to driver. I asked my driver to be careful and was promptly met with: 'You no see the weather? Me self wan go house, because this kind rain . . . Ah! I no want make e catch me for road o!'

I understood his point as I was also in a hurry to get home before the rain got heavier. I turned my attention back to my iPad and was reading the latest post from one of my favourite Nigerian bloggers when the driver turned into a side street that I was unfamiliar with. I held my tongue – perhaps this was a shortcut. However, after another fifteen minutes, I began to feel worried as I was still not seeing familiar signs or landmarks. I voiced my concern and the driver told me not to worry as he knew exactly where he was going and we'd be at my house in no time. I suddenly remembered I could check Google Maps, and saw that, true to the old man's word, we were on course to my house. I relaxed in my seat again, but just as I pulled out my iPad I heard a loud bang on the other side of the window. The taxi came to a sudden halt, throwing me forward.

I was confused at what had happened. Then I heard the old man shouting: 'OK, OK, make I wind am down!' He pressed the window button and raised a hand to shield his head – there was a gun being pointed at him. I had heard of robberies happening at random in traffic and had hoped that I'd never experience it, but there I was in the thick of it; and I was scared for my life. There were three of them. One stood in front of the car with his arms outstretched, attempting to block it from moving forward. A second stood by the driver's side, alternating between pointing his gun at the taxi driver and at me. The third man stuck his head through the opposite passenger window and ordered that I hand over *his* bag.

CHAPTER 50

Osayuki

The rain marched in through the open window. The armed man spotted the iPad on the seat and barked that I hand it over. Then his accomplice demanded I give him my phone. But that wasn't enough. They shouted at me to hand over all the money I had, the gun-carrying thug still pointing the weapon squarely in my direction. But instead of giving them what money I had, for some reason – perhaps the state of shock I was in – I began to plead that they come to their senses. Maybe I could play on their consciences and they'd leave us alone. But the third man continued to make demands, asking me to hand over my bag. I hesitated, trying to reason with him, but was met with an angry shout from the taxi driver, who told me to stop messing around with our lives and give the man what he wanted. The reality of the situation hit me. The robbers laughed, joking that I'd better listen to the old man if I wanted to leave in one piece. I didn't hesitate any longer. I threw the bag at the man opposite me and cowered.

Seconds later, the engine revved and the driver sped away. I raised my head and didn't dare to look back. The car was silent as we continued the short journey home. I was brimming with fury. I couldn't believe that I had just been robbed by armed men – it felt surreal. I began to shake from fear, adrenaline and the cold – the windows, I realised, were still wound down. I shouted to the driver that they be closed. Staring at him in the rear view mirror, I suddenly felt like screaming at him for taking a route I was unfamiliar with, but I realised I couldn't blame him. *How could he have known what would happen?* He'd had his possessions stolen too. I could feel his eyes on me as they darted from road to mirror, but I didn't want to talk. I held back tears and forced myself to breathe slowly until we turned into my street and reached home.

As soon as we were let into the compound, I jumped out of the car and saw Mr Nelson walk out of the front door. I spat a greeting and told him to pay the taxi driver; he could find me later to be reimbursed. I didn't try to explain what had happened as I feared that any attempt to do so would lead to an onslaught of tears and emotion, and I didn't want to cry in front of him or the driver. Mr Nelson looked at me in surprise, no doubt thinking it was unlike me to be so abrupt, but I guess he knew that it was no time for questions, so he let me be. As I walked into the house, the taxi driver got out of his car and began describing our ordeal, but I didn't care to hear about what I had just experienced first hand. I quickly made my way to my room, where I crawled into bed and began to weep.

CHAPTER 51

Osayuki

I couldn't tell how long I was asleep for, but after what seemed like hours, I heard a series of knocks on the door and then Juliet gently asking if she could come in. I sat up and rubbed my hands across my face, wanting to remove any tell-tale signs of crying. She walked into the room and handed me a phone. I reached out and collected it, baffled at the gesture as she explained that Aunty Rosemary kept a spare phone in the house for emergencies and since she had learned what happened from Mr Nelson, she had come to give it to me. I wondered what Mr Nelson had told her and even what exactly the taxi driver had also relayed but thanked her anyway. However, she hovered, and I guessed that she had something else to say so I asked that she spill whatever was bothering her. Nervously, Juliet tried to reassure me that what had occurred was no fault of mine.

'Na so all these useless boys dey do. Tufiakwa!' she concluded and cursed.

I appreciated the gesture, but of course it hadn't been my fault. *Whatever could I have done to deserve such a fate?* She asked if I would call to tell her madam and I replied that there was no reason to worry Aunty Rosemary since she was so far away and couldn't do anything about it even if she was here. Then my tummy rumbled and I realised that I hadn't eaten since that morning. I asked Juliet what she had prepared for dinner. Thankfully, she had made beef pepper soup, which was just the thing I needed. As she walked out to serve the meal, she remarked: 'Aunty sorry o, take heart,' which made me smile. It was truly a Nigerian thing to apologise for what was outside one's control or for another's wrongdoing. It reminded me of how much I'd had to adjust when I first moved to England as a child. I had been in the dining hall one day when a friend I had been sitting with almost tripped on her way to the till. I had immediately said 'Sorry', but she had looked at me weirdly and replied: 'You don't have to apologise, it's not your fault.' Her response had seemed silly then because of course I had known that her almost tripping over hadn't been my fault. I had only been trying to empathise. But I came to realise that 'sorry' was seen differently over there and with time, I learned to stop offering my apologies for everything.

When I was alone again, I picked the phone up from my bedside and looked in my journal for Wendy's number. But after the third call with no answer, I stopped trying, remembering that she had a thing for not answering calls from numbers she didn't know. And although my first instinct had been to call Afolabi, I had refused to do so because I wanted any man I dated to know that I was strong. However, also knowing that to be soft and vulnerable sometimes was just as important, I relented and pushed aside the feeling that it was too soon in our relationship to play the damsel in distress role. He picked up and as soon as I spoke, he could tell that something was wrong. All I managed to say was that I had been robbed before breaking down in tears again. I knew I was an emotional wreck, but I didn't care, and nor did it matter. As horrible as the event had been, speaking to Afolabi made me feel safe.

CHAPTER 52

Osayuki

Forty-five minutes later, I was surprised to see Afolabi strolling in just as I had finished clearing away my dishes in the kitchen. The pepper soup had hit the right spot and I felt much better, despite the backdrop of the gloomy weather outside. I had told the gateman to let Afolabi in when he arrived but I hadn't anticipated him arriving that soon. He watched as I walked over and held on a little longer when I made to pull away from our embrace. He held my hand and led me to the three-seater couch in the living room, and asked to know exactly what had happened as he'd been worried on his drive over that I had been hurt. I narrated the whole event from when I left work to my arrival at home. Although I knew the driver couldn't be blamed, I still wished he hadn't taken the alternative route because the whole incident would have been avoided otherwise. I was surprised to see that Afolabi was also upset for me, but after wallowing in the 'what ifs' of the event, we decided to let it go and be thankful that I wasn't physically hurt. It pained me to lose my iPad, phone and all of the other contents of my handbag, but I was grateful to have come out of the ordeal alive.

When the phone Juliet had given me rang, I checked to see who could have been calling and was surprised to see Wendy's number on the screen. When I placed the phone to my ear, I heard a tentative voice asking who had called earlier. I laughed, knowing that Wendy was trying to tread carefully so as not to talk to any one of her many phone stalkers, who didn't understand 'the meaning of no', as she often said. When she realised that it was me, she asked why I had used a different number to call her and why I wasn't answering her calls to my usual number. For the second time that night, I recounted the whole story. But instead of the sympathy that I had hoped to receive, as I had from others, Wendy offered tough love. She was aghast to hear that I had tried to reason with the robbers. I tried to defend my rationale but she shut me down and said flatly: 'It's like you don't like your life abi? There's no reasoning with these people, just thank God they didn't try anything else!' Her remark gave me the chills and once again, I realised that it had been a precarious situation to have been in, and ironically, I was grateful to the taxi driver, who had brought me to my senses. When she was done with her scolding, Wendy asked if I was alright and if I wanted her to come over. I coyly said that she shouldn't bother, which piqued her interest, and so I had to blurt out that Afolabi was already with me.

'OK o, let me leave you with your boo!' she teased. After a good laugh, she said goodbye and put the phone down.

When I turned back to Afolabi, he was watching me. I suddenly felt shy and remembered that I hadn't offered him anything to drink since he had arrived. But he said that he had brought my favourite ice cream from Cold Stone, which was already melting.

'Your typical cheer up gift for a girl huh?' I teased.

'Good. I see that you've still got your bite!'

We both laughed and I stood up and took the tub of ice cream to the kitchen and placed it in the freezer. When I returned, the room felt charged, so I grabbed the remote and turned on the TV. We watched the screen in silence but I guessed that neither of us were really listening to what was on. I wondered if he too could feel the electricity in the air. I stole a side glance at him, and just as I was about to turn away, he turned to look at me too. I could tell he felt what I was feeling. Suddenly, everything happened so fast. One minute we were kissing on the couch like lovestruck teens and the next I was leading him upstairs. As we rushed into my room, I was glad that Aunty Rosemary was away.

I flopped on the bed and watched as he took his shirt off and then his singlet – I wondered how Nigerian men were able to cope with the heat while wearing such an unnecessary under-garment. In a flash, he was above me, pushing my robe aside to reveal the negligee I sometimes wore to bed when I wasn't naked. I sighed as his hands brushed my thighs and he slid my panties down. And when he took off the flimsy dress and placed his tongue on my left nipple, my sighing gave way to panting.

While his mouth sucked, his hands roved below my waistline and I was on fire. He was slowly stroking, teasing me, and I couldn't bear it. In a fit fuelled by passion, I pulled his head and embraced his lips with mine. I reached towards his lower torso and yanked his jeans button open, then grunted when I realised his fly wasn't made out of a zip but of more buttons. I frustrat-edly undid those too, giggling when I got stuck on the second and he had to help me to unbutton the rest. Seconds later, I held his engorged penis and rubbed at its tip slowly before stroking its length.

He flippantly brushed my hands away, unlocked his lips from mine and descended slowly while stopping to kiss every inch of skin on his trail, paying special attention to each breast in turn. When he reached the moon tattoo on my thigh, he sucked on the skin before looking up at me questioningly – 'Osayuki – "God created the moon",' I managed to gasp. He kissed it again and continued on his trajectory. By the time he reached my wet core, I was a writhing wreck – moaning and gyrating to the rhythm of my internal symphony.

By the time he put a condom on, and finally entered me, I had already orgasmed once from the foreplay, and I was ready to give him the ride of his life.

Hours later, we lay in each other's arms, spent and in a daze, smiling like fools. I had no nightmares that night.

CHAPTER 53

Osayuki

Since that first night together, Afolabi and I had grown closer than ever before. He seemed to understand me as much as I did myself. It was sometimes quite alarming how perceptive he was of my feelings – an outsider might have thought we had been together for years. Perhaps we had known each other in another life, Afolabi had suggested one night when he dropped me home after work. That had become a regular thing – ever since the dreadful incident, Afolabi had taken it upon himself to drive me home almost every day. I had worried that it was too stressful for him, but he brushed off my concern and said that he'd rather spend all the time that he could with me. I wondered if he was doing it as a way to ease my fear, or perhaps his, of something dangerous happening again. Whatever his reasoning, I wasn't going to bet on chance that I'd walk away unscathed from another robbery, emotionally or otherwise.

I felt myself falling for Afolabi. I couldn't explain why it was happening so quickly. I had advised myself against a relationship when we'd first met and had even avoided him, but it seemed that there was no stopping what was meant to be. He was everything and more, and when my demons returned to remind me of Nick and how our relationship had ended so abruptly, I told myself that Afolabi was nothing like my ex. He was neither as self-serving nor as lacking in ambition as Nick had gradually evolved to become. After three years, all the potential I had initially seen in him remained just that – unused potential. And no matter how much I had urged him to pursue his dreams, and how much he promised to take action, he had settled for his desk job at the bank. Tired of singing the same song over and over, I had let him be. I could only do so much to inspire someone else to change if they were unwilling to put in the effort themselves. We had been good together, but his mood swings during those last days should have been telling.

All this was running through my mind as I sat and ate breakfast on a Saturday morning. I looked at my phone and I'd received a text from Afolabi – he said he was coming to pick me up for an impromptu trip to the Lekki Conservation Centre. Before moving to Nigeria, I had read about the nature park when searching for things to do in Lagos, but I'd forgotten all about it until now. Excited, I finished my breakfast and got ready.

Afolabi picked me up and we headed to the conservation. When we arrived, I was amazed at the vastness of it all and couldn't wait to explore. If there was one thing I loved, it was an adventure, and I was glad that Afolabi was as willing and as spontaneous as I was. He was my kind of companion, always up for something fun and exciting.

First of all, we made our way through the nature trail, where we listened to the sounds of birds in the forest and saw peacocks, a tortoise and several capuchin monkeys. Next, I was eager to experience the canopy walk. Our tour guide had proudly informed us that at 401 metres, it was the longest suspended walkway in Africa. As we made our way across the precarious-looking bridge, I was in awe at the panoramic views it offered and understood why the tour guide had been so enthusiastic about it. Where others would have closed their eyes in fright, or refused to take another step, Afolabi and I marched on like seasoned veterans. I was an adrenaline junkie! After swimming in the Atlantic Ocean and bungee jumping in Switzerland, the canopy walk was simply another tick on my bucket list and I hungered for more.

At the end of the walk, the guide led us through another trail that led to a family park, with activities like giant chess and draughts games, a jungle gym and a koi and tilapia pond. Afolabi and I rested for a while then decided to play draughts, but I didn't know what I was doing and we ended up on the floor in a fit of laughter as he tried to prevent me from cheating.

Three hours had easily flown by, and after we had our picnic, we headed back to the car park and drove home. It had been a great day out – even if we hadn't managed to see any of the much-promised crocodiles.

CHAPTER 54

Cynthia

The fifteenth of September was always a big day. It was my birthday, and every year the days preceding it were filled with a flurry of activity in readiness for my party. This was the day amongst all others that I got to feel the most special, and I liked to make the most of it – so much so that my mother had teased me last year that I was no longer a little princess, as my dad still often called me, but an old drama queen. Even though last year had been particularly momentous – my twenty-first – my enthusiasm for the occasion was even more palpable this year as I wasn't only celebrating my birthday, but the halfway point of NYSC too. I had new hair extensions – a honey-brown body wave, twenty-two inches long – to debut at my party and was very excited for the night to unfold. But I felt a little weird for some reason. Perhaps it was because I didn't have my family or Veronica around.

Veronica and I were truly a pair. She was like the sister I never had. We had so many similar interests that when we had first become friends, it was like meeting a clone. Our love for makeup and fashion knew no bounds and soon enough we were inseparable. We'd go shopping together or share links to secret sales, or visit the cinema. Once, when we were teenagers, we sneaked off to an under-sixteen club when our parents wouldn't let us go, and as we grew older, our conversations turned to boys, and the wastemen who tried to get with us. By year thirteen, it was a no-brainer that we'd end up at the same uni. In fact, we sat down together and made a joint shortlist of universities to apply to. We both ended up studying Marketing and Management at the University of Manchester. Everywhere we went, it was

'Cynthia and Veronica'. You couldn't mention one without referring to the other. We planned each other's birthdays so meticulously that our parties became legendary. For my twenty-first, I had ensured Daddy provided everything I wanted. It was our biggest one yet, and a fitting way to round off our time at university. Our uni friends talked about it for months afterwards. But since then, we had all parted ways and were working to make a life for ourselves in the real world. I often wondered what some of them were up to and if they were finding it as difficult to adapt as I was.

I picked up my phone. Osayuki had sent pictures from her trip earlier in the day to the Lekki Conservation Centre. I wished I had been there, although I wasn't so sure about that canopy walkway. Aunty Ndidi had done her best to make sure I enjoyed my day though. She had gone to the market and cooked up a storm and even ordered one of the most expensive cakes in Lagos in preparation for my party that evening.

Harmony was the first to arrive, bearing the gift of cupcakes from the 'best confectioner' on the mainland, as she said with a flourish. It seemed every bakery or patisserie in Lagos hailed themselves as the best or most expensive. I thanked her for the makeup-themed cakes and placed them next to the other food. Then, within the hour, Osayuki and her bae arrived with Wendy in tow. I received a bottle of wine from Afolabi and a makeup brush set I had been banging on about from Osayuki.

When I tore the gift wrap off Wendy's present and saw the contents, I rolled my eyes. A vibrator – no surprise there. During our last meetup, I had hinted at my frustration with the men I had dated so far. Dating in Lagos was a conundrum. I had thought the Nigerian men in London were bad, but it seemed men everywhere were the same – suffering from a severe case of foolishness. I had met the first guy I went on a date with, Nnamdi, a week after I started teaching at the primary school. It had taken me three days to give him my number and in that time, he had shown me just how persistent Nigerian men could be. I had been walking towards the gates of the school when I

saw a Volkswagen pull up beside me. The man behind the wheel
was Nnamdi. He rolled the window down and called out to me:
'Angel!' I had been amused but tried not to laugh, carrying on
without even a glance back. To my surprise, when I finished work,
he was parked in the same spot, waiting. He tried again, this time
calling me 'baby' and saying that he just wanted to get to know
me. I ignored him again and jumped in the Uber that was waiting
for me. The next day it was the same thing, the day after that
too. But on that third afternoon, he had left the comfort of his
car and was standing next to it. I had looked at him in disbelief
and we had both laughed.

'Baby I just want to talk to you. Come on, just a minute of
your time,' he had cajoled. I cringed at the word 'baby', but not
wanting to draw any more attention to myself, I finally relented
and asked what he wanted. He was a peculiar man with big dry
hands that even the gold statement rings he wore couldn't embel-
lish. I had noticed his ashy knuckles when he stretched over the
car window to retrieve his phone from the dashboard. I reckoned
that I could block his number if I didn't want to speak to him
anymore, so I offered my digits, but turned down his offer to
drop me at my destination.

CHAPTER 55

Cynthia

Nnamdi had been quite sweet when I got to know him more over the course of two weeks, until the day we went out for our second date and I found out that he was married. I had been in shock when he had picked me up from the bus stop closest to the primary school with a gold band on his ring finger. The moron had forgotten to take it off. He had stammered, trying to explain it away. I had screamed at him and told him to shut up. He finally fell silent and looked out of the car, confessing to what I had never suspected.

'I hope this doesn't change anything?' he had asked slowly. I had jerked the door open, not bothering to answer, but he followed me so I ran all the way back to the school and waited until he walked back to his car and drove off. I had subsequently blocked his number and brushed him out of my mind. At thirty years old, he was too old for me anyway.

A month later I met Jason while getting Gala from a local vendor. Aunty Ndidi had been feeling peckish and had sent me to buy the pre-packaged sausage roll from the shop down the street. This time, I had made sure to ask if he was married and he had laughed. Jason was twenty-five years old and worked in the entertainment industry, and I came to learn that we had similar interests. Jason was stylish and charming, and I enjoyed his sense of humour. I began to talk to him most nights before bed, and it was always the best moment of my day. I had visited him once at the radio station where he worked and as he introduced his colleagues to me while flicking his short locks away from his face to the other side of his head, I realised he was full of himself. He had clearly invited me to the studio to show off to them that I was from England and he kept on asking me unnecessary questions so that I kept on talking. 'I tell you say she get accent,' I heard him say as I left the room to wait for him in the lobby. That hadn't turned me off though because I enjoyed the attention he gave me whenever we were alone. I also enjoyed listening to his tales about what went on in the industry and I'd laugh about the stories he had to tell about the celebrities he had interviewed and what they were really like in person. It was a frivolous affair that I was comfortable with, helping me to fill up my time when I wasn't working or meeting up with friends. But he had ended up spoiling it all with his tomfoolery. It came to an abrupt end when he decided he wanted to take me somewhere special after a month. He had chosen a relatively new pan-Asian restaurant in Victoria Island that overlooked the ocean. I had been excited for the date and had worn a black satin mini dress with lace embroidered on the cups. I had been astounded by the architecture and decor at the restaurant. The ambience was great and the waiting staff were polite and knowledgeable about the menu. Everything had been going smoothly until the food arrived. We had ordered sushi and spring rolls for starters and I was about to dip a piece into the sauce when Jason spat out the piece in his mouth. I asked if it had gone bad and he responded: 'God! It is raw fish?' in a bogus American accent and then proceeded to raise his hand, shouting, 'Get me the manager!' I was embarrassed and forced his hand down, telling him that sushi was mostly made using raw fish. 'Oh, I see,' he had guffawed in embarrassment and waved the waiter away. I was amused but said nothing, carrying on with eating the food as our other courses arrived and continuing our conversation. I really wish that had been the only thing, but when the bill came, Jason looked aghast and then started counting the money in his wallet underneath the table. He flatly asked me to 'borrow' him twenty thousand naira. I had first thought he was joking until he looked up and I saw the embarrassment in his eyes yet again. I brought out the requested wad of notes from my bag and placed it on the bill tray even though I could feel his hand tapping my knee telling me to pass it to him under the table. When the waiter took the bill away, I booked an Uber and waited for it to arrive before telling him I was ready to leave. 'Ahn ahn . . . I thought we were going to chill on the beach before going home together?' he pouted. 'No, I'm going home now,' I replied and got up, leaving him to follow on my heels. When we got outside, he held me on the waist and tried to lead me to his car, but I swatted his hand away and walked towards the waiting Uber, not bothering to look back.

All the way home, I was on the phone to Veronica recounting the whole experience. She couldn't believe he'd do that. I didn't get why he'd take me to such a lush place if he couldn't afford to pay the bill. 'Wasteman behaviour,' Veronica had concurred and I wished she was in Lagos with me. 'I mean . . . I had to pay twenty thousand naira! That's like forty-three pounds or so. What a fucking wasteman, and he had the cheek to ask me to pass the money under the table! Babe, I'm done with these Lagos men,' I screamed in irritation.

As the months passed with a few more encounters, I decided to take a break from woeful dates. So yes, I was frustrated with men in general.

CHAPTER 56

Cynthia

I had already begun to receive birthday wishes from my NYSC mates once the clock struck midnight, as was the custom amongst most Nigerians. I had learned that anyone who held you in great esteem was expected to usher in prayers and well wishes once it officially became your birthday at 12 a.m. There was no time difference at the time between Lagos and London but I didn't expect my family and friends back home to call or message that early. However, by the time morning came and I had finished breakfast at nine, I had begun to get irritated that no one from my family had bothered to contact me. So when my phone rang fifteen minutes later, I snatched it from the side table with enthusiasm. When I put the phone to my ear, I heard the booming baritone of my father's voice accompanied by my mother's pseudo soprano, which was unsuccessfully harmonising with him; and amidst their well-intended vocal chaos, I heard my younger brother Alex, also singing happy birthday along with them. I laughed at their resolve, but thanked them when they had finished singing.

I was finally in a good place with my parents since I was no longer bitter about my exile. In fact, I had begun to look forward to keeping them up to date with how I was faring and had relished the moment when I told them that I was working as a freelance makeup artist and making my own money. Since my sojourn, I had also learned that almost everyone in Lagos had a plethora of 'side hustles' and makeup artistry was mine. You'd be introduced to a lawyer one minute, only to find out in the next that she also sold Mary Kay products and sold jewellery online; or an engineer who also worked in showbiz and was trying to break into the music industry. In Lagos, no one did only one thing, it seemed almost a taboo to do so. Everyone was a hustler and it was truly a city that was ever evolving and never in slumber. There was always something to do and somewhere to be.

My mother had first scoffed when I told her about the jobs I got through Osayuki, but when Alex showed her the models I had posted on Instagram, she broke into one of her Igbo songs, thanking God that something good had come out of the trip after all, and I knew she was right. I completely felt the same. The day before my parents had broken the news that I'd be travelling to Nigeria had been the worst day of my entire life. I had lain in bed that day, unwilling and mentally unable to take any course of action in regards to my future. I had been at my wits' end and was totally disillusioned by the institution of education. I had thought: *What was the point of it all if I couldn't even secure a job after graduation?*

It had seemed all too easy. We were supposed to study hard at school for about sixteen years, get good grades and then land the job of our dreams, but I had learned that life wasn't as easy as that. Getting good grades even after studying hard was sometimes a struggle, and even after that, the employers that I had thought would be in line waiting were nowhere to be found. No one had taught us how to get that dream job. I had applied for more graduate schemes than I cared to remember, but after several tests, I never got to the final lap. Besides, Nathan had made it seem so easy. He had finished uni two years before I graduated and had a job waiting as soon as he was through. He had moved out six months later and was renting a flat with his friends who also worked in the City. It had seemed like the ideal life and I had naively thought the same path was in wait for me, but after a couple of months of applying for carefully selected jobs, I had quickly started applying for any graduate or entry-level job that I could find on job sites. I had applied so many times that I thought something was bound to give, and it eventually did but a few weeks later, I resigned from the lacklustre job and when Mum had perplexedly asked why I would do such a silly thing, I had spat that I hadn't gone through three years in university for a receptionist job. It might be true that a 'beggar has no choice', as she had spat back, but there were some things that were beneath me and that job had been one.

I had never felt as forlorn in my entire life as I did that day. I was truly heartbroken and had felt like my soul and worth as a human had been dragged through mud, stampeded and pissed upon. I hadn't been able to see an end to the gut-wrenching reality that had been my life and that night, I had cried myself to sleep amidst prayers to God that if he truly loved me, he'd do everything in his power to bring good news. The following day had arrived with worse news of what I had called a family-imposed exile to Nigeria and I remember thinking that I had been forsaken. Looking back now though, I wondered if perhaps that had been a glimpse of the light at the end of the tunnel.

CHAPTER 57

Cynthia

At 9.30 p.m., I finally left the apartment with my entourage. Aunty Ndidi had declined to go clubbing with us and Harmony had almost backed out too until I bribed her with a dozen Rose Apples. The girl could walk on broken glass for those things and I knew Osayuki had bucket loads of them at her workplace, although I believe it was the excitement of going clubbing for the first time on the island that finally swayed her. It was so with life in Lagos that the mere idea of the possibilities of what one could do and the sort of people that one could meet – the crème de la crème of Lagos – on that land surrounded by the lagoon, that even non-materialistic and usually unimpressed Harmony was sold.

By the time we got to our first stop, we were all pumped up with adrenaline from the shot of vodka we had drunk before leaving and the supercharged songs Afolabi had blasted from his playlist on the ride to the island. Our first stop was Pirate's Lounge. Osayuki and I had agreed that no rad night was complete without bar-hopping before the main shindig, so we took turns in suggesting a bar to take a couple of shots in before moving on to the next. I looked over at the Lekki-Ikoyi link bridge on the other side of the lagoon from where we were seated as we waited for the waiter to return with our shots and cocktails. It was the first time I had seen it lit up in all of its glory, fittingly so since it was blanketed by darkness due to the power outage in the homes and buildings surrounding it. I marvelled at how silly I had been to place so much judgement on a place and its people. I had had my many shares of frustration in the country since I arrived, but moments like these were magical. I was grateful for its beauty no matter how rare, and the optimism of the people. That night, I couldn't have imagined being anywhere else than in Lagos. It had quickly shifted from a place of derision to a place where the metamorphosis of my self-growth was spurred.

I almost choked on my mai tai when, during a round of truth or dare, Wendy cheekily suggested I walk up to the man on the opposite table who had been clearly staring at me since we arrived, and ask him to dance since it was my birthday.

'Wendy, no one is even dancing!' I shrieked and declined her preposterous idea.

We all laughed and then she suggested I say a truth instead. I told them I was having the best night of the year, and it was true, because the next morning I could hardly remember what had happened at our third stop before we headed to the club. By the time we got to the club, I was so tipsy that it was a bit taxing to walk straight inside. But before then, Afolabi had left us alone in the car to suss out the place. It was one of the most popular and prestigious clubs in Lagos and, as I had learned during my first visit with Aunty Ndidi's friends before I had left for Abuja, they had a strict policy where girls were never allowed into the club alone, and sometimes it was still difficult when a group of girls arrived with one man. This, however, was common knowledge with the locals. It was an attitude that bordered on the absurd, but one that made perfect sense to such establishments as they saw it as a way to crack down on the number of prostitutes who wandered in looking for their next client. That first time though, it had riled me up. I was irritated that if an independent woman was to visit such venues and public spaces, wanting to spend her own money on a well-deserved self-treat, she'd be turned away and wrongly mistaken for a harlot in search of a ride (pun intended). Such attitudes towards women were still one of the most upsetting things about the culture, but it was nothing that I could solve that night, so we left Afolabi to go uphold our honour.

Finally in the club, no one could have moved me from the

dancefloor. It had been like I was possessed by the god of dance. Every song was my favourite song and every beat deserved the *shoki*, a popular Nigerian dance style, or the dab, which had taken over dancefloors the world over. The DJ came ready, as did I, and it was an epic night even though some people smoking in the building had almost ruined it for me. We had walked in and were led to the seating area that Afolabi's friends, who had got there before us, had booked. The dancefloor was packed and the wannabes were trying to push their way through the cordoned area where we were seated. The music was on full blast, bodies were gyrating and big spenders called out to waiters who in turn hurriedly strode off to pop one or more bottles of Cîroc or Spades for their high-paying guests. An hour later, I was surprised to be the centre of attention as a semi-nude waitress, carrying a cake with sparklers, led her team, also carrying buckets of alcohol, to our table. The group started to sing and cheer and some of the people around joined in the gleeful charade. All of that was great until the pot-bellied man who had clearly missed his bedtime lit up a cigarette and blew out the smoke in our direction. It was disgusting that he couldn't care less about the health of those around him to smoke in such a confined space and even worse that establishments allowed it to continue to happen. *Just what was the Minister of Health doing to have not banned indoor smoking?* I wondered, but just as I realised the upset was rising in me, I quickly quelled it and declared that my night wasn't going to be ruined by the absurdity and idiosyncrasies of life in Nigeria.

I reminded myself that I wasn't only celebrating my birthday, but also being halfway through NYSC. I had my friends – Osayuki, Harmony, Wendy and even Afolabi and his friends – matching my every move with theirs. There was no stopping me, I was overcome with joy unlike I'd known in the recent past and I couldn't place my hands on what exactly was causing it, although I did know it was a culmination of things. It seemed that as I was celebrating being twenty-two, the scattered puzzle pieces of my life were slowly assembling into place and it was the most euphoric feeling I had known in a long time, even though I still didn't know what I'd like to do when I got back to London.

If there was one thing I loved most about Nigerian men, it was that they knew how to take care of their female companions. I had eaten more suya and goat meat than I should have, downed shots, drunk cocktails and been seated at the VIP area, all without a dent to my pocket. Afolabi and his friends had graciously covered all the costs for the wild night and I couldn't have thanked them enough. We had left the club belting the lyrics of Take That's song, 'Greatest Day', in our strained voices. And by the time I finally rolled into bed at 7 a.m. the next morning, it had truly been the greatest day of my life.

Minutes before, I had stood on my threshold and waved goodbye to Osayuki and Afolabi as they headed back to the island. Wendy had been dropped off at hers by one of Afolabi's friends, while Harmony had been with us and had been the first to be dropped off. I had for the first time seen where she lived and what she had described as the life she lived would have been clear to a blind man. Harmony's house was on a run-down street in a part of Lagos not many would have liked to be found in. I had seen a slight apprehension from Afolabi when he had asked for her address. As we drove slowly to the end of the street, Afolabi tried his best to miss the many wide potholes along the way. The gutters on both sides of the street were left uncovered and the grime and waste matter in its belly was open for all to see. There were overflowing bins and rubbish littering the streets and if our windows weren't wound up to keep in the AC, I bet there would have been a stink in the air. She pointed to a yellow building a few yards away and Afolabi pulled up at its front. What would have once been a vibrant yellow was faded and soiled with black markings that must have been the work of children playing with charcoal. The roof was covered with tin that was rusting and well due for renewal. I couldn't tell what might have been the colour of the wooden door although I could see patches of light blue. The side of the house was paved with brown sand and led to an overgrown back garden of some sort.

I could see the sides of a well and above, tall branches of a palm tree just above the house. I couldn't have imagined what it must have been like for her growing up or what it still was like, so I smiled and waved when she turned back at her door, betraying no signs of sympathy. I allowed her her dignity, she was more than worth it.

The night had definitely taken a crazy turn when a guy I had a couple of dance-offs with had assumed that he'd leave at the end of the night with me by his side. When he finally realised that I wasn't going anywhere with him, he had all but fallen on one knee to beg for my number until Osayuki teased that I live a little. I had shrugged at the lucky fella and scrawled my digits on his palm.

CHAPTER 58

Osayuki

As soon as we dropped Cynthia off, I stretched my tired arms and prepared for the ride back to the island. I was grateful for the quiet road that stretched before us as I was ready to jump straight into bed. Afolabi and I had a recap of the night's events and laughed a lot as we recounted all that had happened. It had been an amazing night and I was sure that Cynthia had a great time. Our strained voices and worn bodies were proof of that. As we inched closer to Afolabi's home, we grew quiet, both of us left in our own thoughts. I stole a look at Afolabi and thanked the gods for sending him my way even when I had been cautious about getting attached to anyone.

We both sat comfortably in the silence that surrounded us and had no urge to fill it. I was as comfortable with him as he was with me. He was so different to Nick, who had always felt a need to talk all the time and fill any gaps in our conversations. I felt that sometimes being in each other's company was enough without the need for verbal communication. Nick had always been the jester, which was what I had loved about him at the start. As I continued to ponder about the differences between the only two men I had ever loved, I also began to take stock of my life and how far I had come. It couldn't have been a coincidence that I met Cynthia when I did that afternoon at the market. I realised that we were both on a journey, one that each of us didn't have a detailed map of, but a journey nonetheless, and one that we might not have embarked on if not for our move to Lagos. Cynthia was clearly growing into herself and less resentful of her being in Nigeria, and I was slowly but wilfully mending my broken heart and finding happiness in romance. I had always challenged the idea that my life was incomplete without the attention of a lover or some sort of coupling, but Nick's transgression had been a heavy blow, one that had made me question a lot about myself and the three years I had shared with him.

I was grateful for House of Martha and all that I had accomplished since I began there. All the press coverage we had gained at the London fashion shows had been glowing and the success had gained me the seal of approval from the matriarch herself. I knew my stuff and was good at it, but working in Nigeria and with Nigerians had been a challenge. It had been stressful at times and the communication painfully slow, but it was proving worth it. I had come to grudgingly accept that there was such a thing as Nigerian time and I tried to roll with it as best I could. I was finding my way in the bustling city of Lagos and all fears about relocation that I had in the past were put to bed as I woke each morning, took the day in my stride and welcomed positive energies into my life.

I often wondered about my mum and how she was faring in London, even though I knew she had a great companion. Bob had come in and swooped Mum off her feet just when she needed it the most. If Dad's death had been what it was to me, I couldn't have imagined the pain Mum had gone through. In those years when I was just an adolescent and not as objective and open as I had grown to become, I had made it all about me. I had been in what seemed like an unending loss and Mum's pain had often been invisible. However, she was now happy and I sometimes did wonder if it compared to her first love with my father. How did she develop the will to move on and love again? I believed that I possessed such strength and instinctively reached out to caress Afolabi's hand, before wandering off into my thoughts again. I wondered what it had been like between his parents. The conversation I had had with his mother was telling – she had loved her husband tremendously and she had wished the same for Afolabi and his sister Lola. I wondered if they'd grow to love me like Nick's mum had, and would ever try to get us back together if we ever fell out as Nick's family had. I wondered just how far we'd go and how long the new relationship would last for. I was terrified that he might one day wake up and declare that he no longer loved me. *Would I know in time and shield myself from another shattering pain?* I clearly had been oblivious with Nick. I questioned how I had been so comfortable with a partner that I'd let my guard down and unknowingly given him a blade to slash at my heart. I questioned what it was to love another wholeheartedly and if indeed it was even possible. I continued analysing these thoughts and asking myself questions about the similarities and differences between Nick and Afolabi so deeply that I didn't notice we had pulled up in front of Afolabi's gate. Afolabi brushed his hand against my cheek, then gave me a peck to bring me out of my trance. I stared at him in surprise then giggled as I realised that I had been in my own world all the way home.

He asked what I had been thinking about. He felt that whatever it was seemed serious because he had seen several expressions across my face as we drove in silence. I didn't want to hide anything from him. Not that early, at the start of our relationship. So I laid my cards on the table and let out what I feared the most. Surprisingly, he dealt with all of my pent-up emotions well.

'I thought I was in love once,' I said.

'And now?'

'Well I was and now maybe I am, but they both feel so different and I guess I'm a bit worried because of my past,' I replied.

'Well, it should feel different. We don't have to talk about what your ex did or didn't do right now, but know that I'll always be here for you and with you.'

His words were reassuring. I felt content with the knowledge as he led me into his home and up to his bedroom. We were quiet for the rest of that night as we crawled into bed and stripped off each other's clothes. That night it was real, physical and heartfelt – we expressed ourselves in ways that could not be voiced. The only sounds that could be heard were the gasps of pure joy.

CHAPTER 59

Kian

After the incident with Eunice, Kian had no longer felt comfortable working with Beaterbox. But he could no more blame the producer for whatever had occurred than he could blame himself for the part he played in it, so he carried on. Each week, he clocked in and clocked out – enthusiastic about his music, yet impatient for his time at the studio to come to an end. He and Beaterbox continued like nothing had happened, but Adewale noticed that something was off when he visited. However, whenever he broached the subject, Kian denied any 'bad blood' between them, as Adewale put it. He offered that perhaps the producer was getting impatient with them for not paying his fees on time. Kian had become even more uninterested with the producer and his ways as he found himself more and more being used as an errand boy. Only the week before, he had been sent off to buy fuel for the generator and had queued for hours to fill the jerry can the producer's sidekick had thrust in his hand. Kian understood that he had to work hard in order to achieve his dreams, but felt that Beaterbox's upper hand in the situation was getting out of hand. He wanted to be rid of the producer and told Adewale it was time they worked with someone else after their songs with him were completed. Adewale agreed and revealed that he had got Kian a spot to feature on a song by some other young artists in the area. The collaboration would ensure that his name would reach a new local audience and cost them less in studio fees since they'd all be paying only a share of the price.

Kian was happy with the new developments no matter how slow they were. While he worked in the studio, Adewale had also managed to get him a couple of interviews on trendy blogs and his songs onto music-sharing websites. He was chuffed by every little win but knew he required much more exposure to draw the attention of high-calibre people in the industry. They were only grasping at straws as it was.

That evening, before he left for home, Beaterbox had said enthusiastically that Kian should bring the rest of his money when next he came to the studio. Their work was finally being concluded and Kian realised that Beaterbox was just as eager to let him go as Kian was to leave. Kian nodded and smiled ruefully as he made his way out of the door. He was haughty and in the mood for a fight. He couldn't wait to get to the flat and let out all of his frustration. Even the thought of sexy Caroline whom he had been seeing and loved to beckon whenever he was done at the studio didn't quell his thirst to vent. He felt that he was being cornered from every angle. Nothing seemed to have gone his way and what had his months of toil yielded? 'Nothing,' he mouthed as the taxi sped off to his residence. The driver glanced at him, wondering if he had picked up a drunk JJC.

Kian was glad to see Adewale when he got home. Immediately, he went for the jugular. He accused Adewale of feeding off him and doing nothing to better their predicament or boost the efforts he had put into making their dreams work. Adewale set down the Guinness in his hand on the side table and looked at Kian, baffled.

'Don't start again man. Na wetin sef?!' he screeched, catching Kian by surprise.

He took his legs off the coffee table, stood up and glared at Kian, waiting for his next move. They argued with raised voices until neither made sense to the other and Kian finally sat down – tired, hungry and no closer to a resolution. They had both said mean things to each other, and finally, in silence and both with their heads in their hands, broke down in fatigue and desperation. Each also felt the need, at the back of their minds, to impress their fathers, even if for different reasons. Adewale wanted to prove that he didn't need his father's help and would make it on his own. Kian wanted to prove that he would amount to something and that his father was wrong to have left him and his mother unloved and neglected. Their row had revealed a lot about their personal struggles and their drive to make it in life by all means.

'Bro, Beaterbox says we shouldn't bother stepping to the studio until we have all of his money. I'm draining man. This shit is scary you know?'

Kian's worst fear was coming to pass and he knew he was out of his depth in Nigeria. He no longer had the ability to live life on his own terms the way he had in London, nor the secure embrace of his mother, who was there to take his troubles away whenever he needed it. He realised that it was tough being independent and all his talk and bravado in the past had been possible because of the reliable comfort she offered. Finally on his own in a different world, he wished that the setbacks he had experienced hadn't proved how difficult it was. It was his secret and he promised to take that knowledge with him to the grave. For all anyone knew, he was Kian Bajo, the ever-so-confident young chap who would make it in the Nigerian music industry and emerge an international Afrobeat star like the others before him.

'You've got to chip in man. Maybe we can go see your dad tomorrow?' Kian said.

'OK,' Adewale reluctantly agreed. He stood up, heading straight to his bedroom, his beer left forgotten on the side table.

CHAPTER 60

Kian

The next day, both young men were playing video games and eating the yam and scrambled egg sauce the house boy had prepared while they waited for Adewale's father to return from work. Kian had more time to go around the house during the visit and had wondered why they couldn't stay there rather than living as shabbily as they had been. He tentatively mentioned this to Adewale because he knew his cousin wasn't fond of the idea and Adewale, true to form, shut him down. Adewale reiterated that he had to stand on his own feet as a man and pull through until he made it. He didn't want his father controlling him or the plans he had for his future just because he was dependent on him for a roof over his head. As far back as he could remember, his father had kept to the phrase 'As long as you live under my roof, you must abide by my rules.' It was a phrase that every young Nigerian knew all too well and it served as the push they needed to get their acts together and flee the family nest.

Hours later, Mr Babatunde walked in to find his son and nephew watching football in his living room. He was surprised to see both men as he hadn't been expecting them. He immediately knew what must have led them to his door and smiled as his son prostrated in greeting, something he had stopped doing a long time ago. Adewale was fooling no one; his boy, thought Mr Babatunde, already knew he had to join the family business if he wanted any aid from his father. His arms were always open to receiving his son back into the fold whenever he was ready to resume his position by his side.

Mr Babatunde set his briefcase down and joined the boys in front of the TV. Ten minutes later, the briefcase disappeared and another tray of yam and scrambled egg sauce appeared before him. He placed the tray of food on his lap and ate silently as he waited for his son and nephew to say what was on their mind. He secretly indulged in their nervousness. He listened as his son feigned a mild interest in how his work was going and how his staff were taking to orders and the store's activities. Then Mr Babatunde joked with Kian about personally showing him around his stores dotted throughout the mainland. When it was clear all the small talk was over and Mr Babatunde was ready to leave with his empty plate to the kitchen, Adewale made a stab at broaching the subject of what had really brought about their visit. But before Adewale could continue, his phone rang and he excused himself and left it to Kian, who rolled his eyes at the bad timing and Adewale's stupidity for not putting the phone on silent. Kian was still dancing around the subject, unable to ask his uncle outright for help, when Adewale returned with a grin on his face. The call had brought good news, he said in a voice too loud for the only two people in the room listening.

'We're performing at Industry Nite!' he said exuberantly.

'Congrats boys. Well you know where to find me abi? I'm going to bed, goodnight,' Mr Babatunde said dryly and walked out of the room.

'Goodnight sir,' the boys replied in unison. They began to fist bump each other, overcome by excitement and forgetting their impending insolvency.

The next day, they left at noon, eager for the following week to proceed, after stuffing their face with home-cooked food. They spent the remainder of that week prepping for the performance. Kian rehearsed incessantly while Adewale prepared for the potential contacts he would secure at the event. He tried his utmost to push out content on various blogs that owed him a favour and the ones who, in turn, he would owe a favour, to announce Kian's upcoming performance at the popular venue on the island. Industry Nite had become a popular affair for the knowns, and for the unknowns who wished to be known. The mini concert gave local rising stars a platform, and the prospect of performing at it gave Kian hope that a better tomorrow was just around the corner. There was always a surprise performance by an artist who had broken away from the fold and made it to mainstream. Adewale was on the hunt to find out who the scheduled star was. With all of his shortcomings as an inexperienced manager, he dared that even the devil himself wouldn't be able to take away his dream of a collaboration from him. 'Where there is life, there is hope,' was the saying that got Nigerians up every morning, even if life in the country was as tough as nails, or like rubbery meat that refused to break down in one's mouth.

CHAPTER 61

Kian

The night arrived and neither of them could have been more prepared than they already were. Kian had never been one to suffer stage fright, but as he stood backstage with the other acts, he made a silent prayer that this would be the day things began to turn around for them. The right person in the crowd could change their lives forever, Adewale had been saying again and again. So he prayed that his older cousin was right. They had visited Beaterbox the weekend before and collected the mastered song, which Kian had subsequently rehearsed. Everything was set and he was poised to show the crowd what he was made of. Unfortunately, the weather had a thing or two of its own to say. It had been bad. The downpour had caused the usual maddening traffic on the island to worsen and it took much longer for the attendees, who were already operating on 'African time', to arrive at the venue.

When Kian finally took to the stage at midnight, he looked across the hall and saw the charged crowd looking up expectantly at him. He looked at the sea of unfamiliar faces and wiped the sweat on his forehead with the back of his hand. He was nervous and became transfixed. He remembered the last time he had felt that way on stage. It was about two years ago, performing at his first full-room gig in Brixton. He had been lucky to have been put on by a friend from college whom he had fortunately bumped into the weekend before. He had been standing by the corner of an estate with Dan having just left the studio where they were recording some demos. He hadn't seen Jermaine since they had all finished their stint at Lewisham College, but there he was five years later. He didn't recognise him at first. Jermaine was no longer the scrawny Jamaican lad he had made fun of in class. He had grown muscles and somehow looked taller than he remembered. It was Dan who had first spotted him and called out. Seeing them both, Jermaine had bawled in surprise: 'I see yous lot are still like Bonnie and Clyde huh?'

'Get out of here man. Who you calling Bonnie?' Kian had replied jokingly as they shook hands. He could tell that Jermaine had been hitting the gym.

'You on the other hand though, my G, welcome to the club!' Kian had remarked, playfully smacking him on his left bicep and shaking his hand.

'You know how we do. You know how we do,' Jermaine had replied while massaging his beard.

As the boys reminisced about the old days, Kian and Dan were surprised to find out that Jermaine was an events organiser and had a rave they had heard about coming up the following week. Jermaine had been equally surprised to learn that they were still trying to forge a career in music. By the time they had finished catching up, they had left with Jermaine's number and a promise of a small slot to perform at his rave.

Kian had always believed in fate and as they jumped on the Victoria line at Brixton underground station, he had enthused that it could have only been fate that had brought them in contact with Jermaine. A week later, Kian had been on stage with Dan and was a nervous wreck when he realised the rave had pulled in a bigger crowd than he had been accustomed to. He was suddenly rooted to the spot, his hands sweaty on the mic. He had been lucky to have Dan on stage with him. His friend and hype man had pulled him out of his state and they had ended up performing brilliantly to a crazed crowd who couldn't get enough of him. Those were the days when he had wanted to be the next hip-hop star. For a number of weeks after that gig, Kian's song had played repeatedly on several pirate radio stations and if you had asked him then, he would have said the same thing he had always believed: his stardom was just around the corner.

Kian quickly glanced behind and Adewale encouraged him with a thumbs up. He cleared his throat and strode across the stage, launching into his set. He heard cheering, but it slowly died down as he continued. It was one of the toughest crowds he'd had to please and while they liked his style and swagger, his performance was not doing it for them. Nigerians weren't easily impressed. You either won them over or got a lukewarm reception that told of their defiance of anyone they felt was inauthentic. 'Fake it till you make it' was the saying, but Kian was quickly realising that faking it in Lagos was going to cost him more than he had imagined. They weren't buying his act of Africanism that easily.

Backstage, the runners and other artists sympathised with him. A performer wearing nothing but ankara trousers and fake gold chain necklaces walked over to him to offer some suggestions. He advised that it was a tough game, but with persistence and banging beats, Kian would eventually win them over. Kian nodded distractedly, wondering why his usual charm wasn't working on this Lagos crowd. The cousins waited until the gig was over and in the early hours of the morning, they left with a few contacts they hoped to pursue later.

CHAPTER 62

Kian

A month after the performance, Kian was no closer to his dreams and was finally at his wits' end. Facing the reality that he was broke had been a tough pill to swallow and he realised that it was no wonder Caroline, his Kalabari lover with the perky boobs, was no longer as quick to dash to his side. He had taken pride in taking her out to lavish bars and nightclubs, but as the weeks went by, he had realised that his sham lifestyle was no longer sustainable. If he were in London, he would have been in no way able to indulge in the way that he had and was only able to do so because of the crumbling value of the naira. The crash against the dollar seemed to have taken everyone by surprise. The country had been certain that their new president was the change they all sought. He was going to bring the dishonest to justice and improve the failing economy. *How could they have been so wrong?* Kian didn't bother himself with such thoughts though. The falling naira was to his advantage. As they say in Lagos, 'One man's meat is another man's poison.' The exchange rate, of one pound to about four hundred and sixty-five naira, had been his ticket to a flashy lifestyle, until even that could no longer sustain him. He had asked his mother to help transfer the rest of his savings to his Nigerian bank account, and its balance worried him. He felt that he couldn't go back home to London just yet. He had given up a lot to travel to a homeland that had welcomed him with open arms, but failed to warn him of its workings. If sociologists argued that meritocracy was a myth in the Western world, in Nigeria, surely, it was a mad man's conception.

Kian was quiet and unlike his boisterous self. He was sat in a bukka with Adewale and some other artists who frequented the place to fill their tummies and nurse each other's bruised egos. They all believed that their luck was just around the corner and that a change was about to come – a change they all awaited fervently. It was the same story every day. As they carried on, he wondered what his best friend Dan was up to and if he really enjoyed his supervisory role at the sports store where he worked in Lewisham. He assumed not, but Dan had chosen practicality and left him behind when after years of chasing the dream, he decided that perhaps music wasn't for him. Kian thought about their beginnings and the love they shared for music. Rap music of the nineties had changed their world and they had wanted to become like the stars they had idolised. At least Kian did – Dan had given up altogether. For a second, Kian imagined himself only working at a retail store, a bank or anywhere else that would require he start at 9 a.m. and clock out at 5 p.m. He couldn't imagine living that life and shuddered at the thought. He felt deeply that he was on the right path and believed that he was different from the men who sat around him. He didn't know their stories, nor did he care to; all he knew was that he was going somewhere and that place was unlikely to fit them all. He looked at the one opposite him who continued to laugh at the other's joke with his mouth opened wide to the heavens, displaying the half-chewed rice in its enclave. They repulsed him and he was certain that he was miles ahead of them. He just needed the right person to take notice and reprimand themselves for not finding him sooner. He, Kian Bajo, was the new 'star boy' waiting to take his rightful throne. He couldn't wait for the calls for collaborations that would pour in. His heart raced at the mere thought of it. He sighed. Dan had been wrong to throw in the towel.

As Kian came out of his daydream, he remembered that he hadn't returned his mother's call from the day before as he had promised to. He excused himself from the group and left his unfinished food, now cold, and walked off to find a quiet place to make his call. His mother didn't pick up. He tried again and was near to giving up when her voice came through. Matilda was always happy to hear from her only child. He was the fruit of her womb and the reason she had worked so hard to provide for him and fill the hole his rogue of a father had left. She asked how Kian was faring and said that she was proud of him. Tilda, as her friends fondly called her, was impressed that her son hadn't called to ask for her help since his departure. She was excited to learn that everything was going well for the son she had feared would return home worse off than he had left. She hadn't been back to Nigeria since her last visit as a teenager and had been shocked when Kian had first proposed the idea of going there alone. She had fought against it, but as was usually the case, had accepted that his mistakes and triumphs were his to experience. She just wished he wasn't so obsessed with what she saw as a foolhardy pursuit. She couldn't bear to witness any harm come to him and the thought that the effect of failing would crush the light that she knew was in him caused her many a sleepless night. It didn't matter that he was grown up. He'd always be her baby.

Kian had hoped to ask to borrow some money from her when he called, but on hearing the excitement in her voice and the hope it carried, he couldn't bring himself to do it. If his mother thought he was making something of himself in Lagos, and the mere thought of it helped ease her worries, in addition to increasing the faith in him that he had seen begin to fade away, he wasn't going to ruin it for them both. He indulged her curiosity, sent his regards to their extended family and hung up. He didn't like lying to her but he saw no other way out of the pit he had buried himself in. He walked back to the bukka and resumed his position next to Adewale, and to his surprise, found his food being devoured by one of the group. He looked at the scrounger in disgust and beckoned to Adewale that they leave.

'Ah, oyinbo! You still dey chop?' the man asked cheekily when he saw Kian's expression.

'You be ọdẹ o!' Adewale cursed, tipping his head forward. 'Fool!' chorused Kian, as the two of them left.

CHAPTER 63

Cynthia

I was seated beside Osayuki, watching as she glowed while speaking to her mother about Afolabi. Her whirlwind romance was going steady and she decided that it was finally OK to reveal the mystery behind her cheer to her family even though it was hardly a secret. It hadn't taken long for her mother to guess something was up a few months after she had first met Afolabi. Osayuki and her mother had a close relationship and I wished it was the same for my mother and me. I got along with my mum but our relationship had always been an uphill struggle. She had always seen my father as too liberal, so had taken the mantle of the disciplinarian even when it was uncalled for. I loved her, but I couldn't imagine gushing about a boyfriend to her as Osayuki did to her mother. I couldn't help smiling as she told her all about the date she and Afolabi had been on. She sounded so happy. I had always felt that Osayuki was open and a good influence, but with Afolabi around, she was an even better version of herself.

I heard her tone change – still warm but quite different – and I guessed her mum had passed the phone to her step-dad. Bob sounded like the best step-father or even *father* that anyone could have wished for. From what she had divulged about her relationship with him, he was exactly the male role model she had needed after her father's untimely death. Her initial reaction to her mother's partner had been the typical teenage angst, but Bob had quickly proved himself and she took refuge in him at the times when she and her mother had butted heads. Bob never saw any wrong in her. He had been as encouraging as her father had been, although it was also clear that no other father figure could take that place in her heart. I thought about my own father too. I couldn't wish for anyone other than him. And even though I had been terribly mad at him for sending me off to Nigeria, I knew that in his own way, it was his love for me that had pushed him to it. The sojourn was just as hard on him as it was for me, although ironically, it was Mum that hadn't wanted me to leave. 'Human beings are funny o,' Dad always said when someone acted in a peculiar way or did anything that beggared belief. I agreed with him. I thought that my mother's initial opposition to the idea of me doing the NYSC programme was unlike her. She was acting funny, but I had come to realise that although she'd rather not confess to it, just like a mother hen, she wanted me close.

In the middle of her conversation, Osayuki looked at me and I poked out my tongue at her. She couldn't help laughing as she finally ended the call with her parents.

'You're making fun of me right?' Osayuki asked, putting her phone away.

'What do you think? Afolabi this, Afolabi that . . . "Oh Mum, he's so wonderful!"' I said in an exaggerated impression and she threw a cushion at me.

'Am I that bad?' she asked with her hands over her face.

I responded with an eye roll. I was happy for her and told her not to worry about it. Afolabi seemed to be worth all the fuss considering what she had gone through.

I had some worries of my own and voiced my concerns to Osayuki. My service year was gradually coming to an end, and I was still clueless about what I wanted to do with my life on my return to London. I loved Lagos, I really did, but it wasn't the place for me. I couldn't envision a future in its borders and that was OK. I just didn't know what to do and I felt strongly that by the time I was set to return to London, I had to have a plan.

'Don't stress about it. It will come to you when you least expect it,' Osayuki advised.

Meanwhile, it felt surreal to think that in three months it would all be over. I recounted all that I had been through – my prior expectations and assumptions about what life was like in Nigeria, living with Uncle Peter and his wife Evelyn, my three weeks at the NYSC camp, living with Aunty Ndidi, teaching primary school children, and all that life in Nigeria had entailed. Looking back on everything, it was clear that I had grown a lot in that span of time. I was grateful for all the experiences that had led me to who I was becoming and Osayuki agreed that I had definitely grown and changed from the girl she had first met at the airport in Milan. I was happy about the development – in my mother's words, 'Thank God o!'

One thing still nagged at my conscience though, and I was bound to face it in the coming weeks. It was customary for my family in Nigeria to travel east to the village of their ancestors every December during the Christmas period. I was very excited to experience life in the village, but knowing that it meant coming face to face with Uncle Peter, and especially Aunty Evelyn, whom I had been rude to, was embarrassing. I had no leg to stand on when it came to my uncle and his wife; and I knew that I had taken their kindness and generosity for granted. I had hardly spoken to them since I left Abuja and knowing that I'd be living with them at the family compound in Anambra State made me nervous. I spontaneously invited Osayuki to join me, but as I already knew that she would, she declined my invitation because she had already made plans to spend the holidays with Afolabi. She was no longer returning to London to spend it with her family as she had initially intended before meeting him.

We spent the remainder of my visit poring over all the pictures that had come through from the Lagos Fashion and Design Week. The four-day event had been electrifying. It had drawn both fashion and art lovers alike to the city and the venue had been abuzz with activity. It had been incredible to have been a part of it and Osayuki, leading her PR team, had done wonders for House of Martha. The old fashion house was beginning to reclaim its prestige in the Lagos fashion scene and after wowing the audience at the fashion show that October, it was clear that House of Martha was there to stay. I had also shared in the success of the event as I was one of the makeup artists backstage working on the models for the runway. I would be forever grateful that Osayuki had taken a chance and given me the opportunity to work on an international platform, which hosted the likes of Julien Macdonald. Mrs Phillips had put her faith in Osayuki and she had delivered spectacularly. She had been able to get the top fashion bloggers in Lagos to cover House of Martha's new line, and had secured notable mentions in international publications. With things beginning to take shape, it seemed that House of Martha was on its way to getting back in there with the likes of Lisa Folawiyo and Deola Sagoe. All in all, it seemed that my friend was flourishing and my journey in our homeland was advancing, and that the year was going to round off fruitfully.

CHAPTER 64

Cynthia

The day I had been dreading finally arrived. Although the rest of the month had passed swiftly, the weeks remained the same. I went to work, taught my class, had my break with Harmony. Sometimes we went to a pepper soup canteen for dinner before heading home, or on other days, I had my dinner with Aunty Ndidi when she wasn't insistent on going to church for some praise night, singles fellowship or demon outcasting event. Aunty Ndidi was a self-assured woman who had lots of great qualities about her; however, she was one independent woman who was desperate for a partner. Although I had pointed out that she shouldn't stress herself so much about finding a suitor, she had shooed away my suggestions absentmindedly like one does a pestering fly. 'You won't understand,' she had said. However, I had come to understand full well what caused her incessant prayers to God for a husband. She lived in a society that was unkind to an unwed woman over twenty-five. It didn't matter that she was a graduate, had a job, was taking care of herself well enough, and was leading a good life in service of others. It still stood that 'God forbid' she remained single at thirty-five years old.

The world was rapidly changing although it was obvious that Nigerian cultural values were yet to catch up. Aunty Ndidi's strongest desire was to have children and that was exactly what she was unable to do without a partner. 'I don't even want a fine man sef. At least, let him just be hardworking and take care of his family!' I heard her once say when a friend chided that perhaps she was being too picky. After all she was a beautiful woman who knew how to cook and tend to a home – why was it that

she was still single? I had been livid that she had friends who
spoke such nonsense, but it seemed that such nonsense was what
the average woman had grown up learning and as such was their
norm. I felt for her. It couldn't have been easy as a single woman
in Lagos. My short time had already exposed me to the woes it
brought, so I could imagine what a lifetime of such inanity could
cause. I was thankful that my mother hadn't put such pressures
on me, and hoped that by thirty at least, I'd be married, although
my love life since arriving in Lagos had been up and down. I
had definitely enjoyed the dating scene Lagos had to offer. The
men were known to be big spenders (even though Jason had
turned out to be an exception), the 'Yoruba demons' included.
They had gotten their moniker for their philandering ways. Yet
cheating, as everyone knew, was not limited to a tribe.

I continued to date sporadically, even though every other guy
declared that I was the love of his life. I had come to understand
that Nigerian men loved the finer things in life, and it didn't
matter whether there was a connection or not; as long as they
deemed you beautiful in appearance, they instantly wanted a
relationship with you. It was quite different from what I was used
to in London where casual dating, 'seeing each other' or linking
up was the order of the day.

I waited by the living room door as Aunty Ndidi walked around
the apartment to check if every switch had been turned off and
nothing was amiss. We were finally travelling to the village for
the holidays. It was customary for most Igbo families. I had
wondered why it was a tradition especially reserved for the
Christmas holidays and Aunty Ndidi had shed some light as best
as she could. She narrated that it must have started around the
time after the civil war – the time of Biafra, as it was sometimes
called. The Igbos had wanted a secession from Nigeria. After
they lost the war, Igbos anywhere other than their hometown felt
the need to return every year to their villages. It was somewhere
they could reconnect with their roots and commune, no matter
what else happened in the world. It represented a sense of
belonging that the war had failed to erode. So, perhaps, that's

how it came about that every Christmas season, Igbos from far and wide returned to Nigeria and travelled back to their ancestral homelands. Of course, not every Igbo person stuck to the tradition. As far as I knew, I had never been to my village and it had been quite a while since either of my parents had visited Nigeria.

Although I had been dreading seeing Aunty Evelyn and Uncle Peter again, the more I thought about the trip, the more excited about it I was. I was looking forward to seeing what other places in the country looked like and to living in the same compound where my ancestors had been born. It was times like this that I treasured the sense of community and closeness that life in Nigeria offered. It was easy to see yourself as a single entity, an island of sorts, when you were away from your extended family. I wondered if my parents felt the same way and if they ever thought of returning to retire in the countryside, as I had heard other older Nigerians in London did.

Aunty Ndidi said she wasn't going to give away anything since she wanted me to see for myself and experience everything with fresh eyes. All she said was 'Wait and see,' so anxiously, I waited. We loaded our luggage into the taxi that would take us to the bus garage. From there we would board a bus to Anambra State. I looked back at the apartment and wondered what new insights I'd return with.

CHAPTER 65

Cynthia

The ride to the bus garage at Jibowu went without a hiccup. It hadn't taken long and for once I had hoped that it would. I had become anxious again about seeing Uncle Peter and his family.

The bus garage wasn't what I had expected. It looked more civilised – it was unusual to see Nigerians (who, I had come to believe, had a natural aversion to queues) standing in line, one after the other, waiting their turn at the counter. Luckily, Aunty Ndidi had already bought our tickets the week before in order to avoid missing the first bus out. She revealed that she usually flew part of the journey, taking a plane from Lagos to Enugu State, before continuing by car to Anambra State. However, because it was my first time, and perhaps my only time for a long while, she wanted me to experience the six-hour journey by road. When she said that, I had laughed. Six hours didn't seem like a big deal to me. I had taken a ten-hour bus ride from Edinburgh to London back in my uni days when I had a penchant for raves and was as broke as a child's piggy bank.

We had arrived early, so we waited for our bus to be ready. I left Aunty Ndidi and walked over to the tuck shop at the other end of the garage to get some snacks and drinks for the ride. As I carried my plantain chips, Oreo biscuits and La Casera to the till, I hoped that the sales assistant would have enough change because I had only one thousand naira, in notes, in my purse. The exchange of money between traders and me had been a stressful transaction throughout my time in Nigeria. It was still mind-boggling to me that on any given day, getting back my change from a simple transaction was such a mission. No one ever had change. They always expected the buyer to magically have the exact amount for the item they wanted to buy. I wasn't used to walking around looking for change in order to buy anything. The seller usually began asking fellow traders to split bills and if that failed, there was always a small child around to send off somewhere to procure the right amount. Never mind having a bank card – that was almost as good as useless in a country that proudly announced itself as a cashless society some years ago. It didn't matter that traders had POS machines and that I was actually willing to swipe my card on those sometimes dubious-looking devices – it never worked. Sometimes the internet wasn't providing a strong enough signal, but most of the time there didn't seem to be any justifiable reason why a store that had a signpost clearly stating the acceptance of bank cards would then go on to tell you – once you were inside and at the counter with their products – that they accepted only cash. Life in Lagos was full of unnecessarily stressful situations. A leisurely stroll to the local shop could easily become *Mission Impossible*.

When I moved over to the counter to pay, I smiled ruefully, showing my banknote. 'Aunty no worry,' came the man's response and I breathed out a sigh of relief. I collected my change and the bag with my snacks, and strode off. Aunty Ndidi hadn't wanted anything. For her, the best part of travelling by road was all the fresh fruit and snacks she would buy in traffic. As the bus sped from one state to the other, the snacks usually changed from the usual to the more unfamiliar provincial foods. I also couldn't wait to see and taste them all, but if I failed to enjoy them, my plantain chips and biscuits would come to the rescue.

At seven o'clock, we were beckoned to board the bus. We stowed our luggage, then found our seats and waited for the rest of the travellers to do the same. After another thirty minutes of trying to fit everyone's luggage into the compartment, and once those who had run off to quickly use the toilets had returned, the bus huffed into life and then drove off. I was by the window and continued to look back at the woman standing in front of the bus garage until I could no longer see her. She had begged to be allowed on board even though she had a ticket for a later time in the day. She had said it didn't matter that there were no vacant seats, she was willing to sit on the stairs of the bus. The driver had looked at her exasperatedly and after explaining to her again that it was no longer possible and that he had to follow the rules, he had left her still begging and jumped into the driver's seat. He had honked for her to get out of his way and as she grudgingly did, he turned out of the garage and began the six-hour drive.

The bus was alive with chatter. Some people were still talking about the woman in bewilderment, others in humour and I in empathy. The child tied to her back had begun crying as the driver jumped into the front seat of the coach, perhaps somehow sensing that his day was going to take a different turn from whatever his mother had envisioned for them.

CHAPTER 66

Cynthia

I enjoyed the sights as we sped out of Lagos towards Ogun State. It was interesting to see the different parts of the city. I was already accustomed to seeing the mansions of Victoria Island and Lekki, and had seen other parts of Lagos mainland when I had stayed, worked and hung out there. However, I had never really seen much of the so-called slums of Lagos. As we moved through the light traffic, children with different coloured uniforms made their way to school on foot. Lagos' labour force was already gathered at bus stops around the city. I looked at their faces as we sped past and wondered what memories their minds held and what stories their eyes would reveal if I was to stare longer at their depths. I had learned a lot since I had arrived in Lagos, but I still yearned to learn more of how it was that people who owned so little, and had seemingly even less to live for, woke up each day and took charge of their lives. They made it to wherever they needed to be with optimism for a better day even though the chaos all around them suggested otherwise.

How was it that a year twelve student, for example, continued to study hard to get grades that would get him or her into higher education while knowing full well that the journey to their chosen institution wasn't as simple as getting good grades? I had come to learn that the process of getting into university was another major hurdle most young people had to overcome, unless they had good connections, good money or both. I became grateful for what I had in London. I had been lazy at my sixth form college until my dad had whipped some sense into me and I had begun to take my A levels seriously. Through hard work of the like I had never known, I succeeded in securing a place at university. Dad had declared that it would be a shame if I got my place through clearing. But at least I had that option. I had first made five university choices, which I then narrowed down to two, depending on my final grades. I had been really lucky to get the grades needed for my second choice after I slipped up on my first choice. It had been as straightforward as working hard for the grades to secure my place at the institution. But as I had learned from Harmony, that wasn't always the case in Nigeria. It didn't matter if you were at the top of your class with excellent grades all year round, when it came to JAMB and then post-JAMB exams at the institution of choice, things other than grades mattered. Harmony had experienced it first hand. The taste of the disappointment still lingered whenever she spoke about it. She had sat the exams twice and failed to be accepted even though she had passed with good grades on both occasions. Learning from her previous experience, she had travelled to visit a distant relative whom she had begged for the money that helped secure the admission she finally got, after rubbing hands with one of the secretaries at her alma mater. Nothing was ever plain sailing, it seemed. Even when you knew you were on the right path, you still had to secure whatever it was you were trying to achieve by shaking hands with some kind of authority figure. This sort of life – different to what I knew in England – forced me to take stock of what I thought was the norm. It was becoming clear that life was tragically unfair because having the same sort of values or work ethic as someone on the other side of the world never really yielded the same results. It made the term 'hard work' quite subjective because clearly, what hard work yielded in London was different to what it did in Lagos. From London to Lagos, the story and struggle was different irrespective of what efforts each person put in. I let the thought sink in.

I was brought out of my trance by Aunty Ndidi, who was nudging my side and pointing. I didn't see whatever she was pointing at. When she asked, incredulously, 'Did you see that?' I absentmindedly mouthed 'Yeah,' and returned to my thoughts. As we inched closer to the border between Lagos and Ogun

State, the coach began to slow down. We were no longer speeding through quiet streets. Lagos had come fully awake and the streets had resumed their usual rowdiness. I prayed that the traffic wouldn't linger. I couldn't wait to hit the expressway and watch the clear road and vegetation speed by as we made our way to Igbo land. Thankfully, we were in a bus with AC, so rather than feeling the heat – the temperature was already high at that time of day – I had a scarf across my shoulders to keep me warm in the cold air.

As we drove on, I saw all kinds of phrases painted in big letters on the backs of the buses and lorries that were in front of us or went past:

> BIG MAN, BIG PROBLEM
>
> HERE TODAY, GONE TOMORROW
>
> NO MONEY, NO FRIEND
>
> NO CONDITION IS PERMANENT
>
> MIND YOUR BUSINESS
>
> NO FOOD FOR LAZY MAN
>
> HORN BEFORE OVERTAKING
>
> WITH GOD ALL THINGS ARE POSSIBLE

I shouldn't have been surprised – after all, the transport company that we were using for our commute was called 'God is Good Motors'. But after a lifetime of seeing fashion brands, movie blockbusters and 'beach body ready' models on the side of buses in London, seeing such phrases made me giggle. I guess there was my answer – everywhere people looked, there was an encouraging phrase or word of advice to help Nigerians keep the faith and get through the day. It was definitely different to the bombardment of messages about fashion and beauty must-haves that I was used to seeing. I had been so desensitised by all the glossy images Western media offered and I suddenly realised that I hadn't shopped as much as I usually did since I arrived in Lagos. Whatever L'Oréal had launched as their latest lip collection couldn't have been further from my mind.

CHAPTER 67

Cynthia

I didn't know when I fell asleep or for how long, but the next thing I heard was a thumping sound on the other side of the window, just where I was resting my head. I blinked and quickly remembered where I was and took my head off the glass. A young boy who was about fifteen continued tapping on the glass and then motioned at the rectangular package he carried in his other arm. I looked over at Aunty Ndidi and saw that she was also asleep. I looked back at the boy and the carton of Gala he was carrying across his arm. I disliked the packaged sausage roll, which I deemed too dry, so I shook my head. He walked alongside the bus in the slow-moving traffic and continued to gesture at me and then to the packaging box. I would have loved to buy something from him, but I really hated the things, and since he was selling nothing else, I shook my head again and turned away, hoping that he'd finally get the message and look for another willing customer. Moments later, the traffic seemed to clear as if ordered by a genie and the bus gained speed and took off, leaving the young boy in its wake.

We were finally out of the city and, with nothing else interesting to look at, I put on my earphones and selected my favourite playlist from my iTunes library. I was listening to 'One Dance' by Drake. The song featured Wizkid, one of Nigeria's finest. It had been the banger of the summer and I was yet to grow tired of it. I tapped my feet to the beat and let the rhythm of the song course through my body. The energy of the song was invigorating. I had often played it when I was doing my makeup and getting ready for a night out.

I closed my eyes and sank deeper into my thoughts. There was something that bothered me terribly. I had matured tremendously since the start of my stay in Nigeria, yet as the year was drawing to a close, my next move was still a mystery. I still didn't know what I'd do once I got back to London. I didn't want to feel like a failure. Dad had sent me off hoping I'd return wiser, perhaps a bit different, less nonchalant, than when I had departed. I knew I was no longer the girl who had stormed out of the living room when I had first heard about my 'exile', but I was still the girl unsure about where to turn next. Bar my little stint as a receptionist, and the jobs I had done in Lagos so far, I had no other professional experience under my belt. So without the proper experience of working in different fields, I was lost as to what sort of job I'd actually enjoy. All I had thought about was making money, but now I knew that whatever I did to make that money had to be something I was passionate about. And what that was remained elusive. I had watched Osayuki in her role at House of Martha and I couldn't imagine her doing anything else; even fun-loving Wendy enjoyed her job as an accountant. *So what was my deal?*

I drifted off to sleep again, but I was jerked awake by the bus when it came to what seemed like an abrupt stop. The other passengers also began to stir and get up, dragging stiff legs off the bus. The last time I had my eyes open was when we slowed down at the Lagos-Ibadan Expressway due to a broken-down vehicle, which some good-natured drivers had helped to push to the side of the road. Before that, we had sped through, the only signifier that we had crossed several borders being the change in language, from the usual pidgin on the streets of Lagos, to Yoruba in Ogun and Ondo State. Since she had been colonised by Britain, Nigeria's first language was English. However, in the other states, one was most likely to catch indigenes speaking their tribal languages.

I followed closely behind Aunty Ndidi as she got off the bus and made a beeline towards the restaurant by the roadside. It was already filling with travellers from other vehicles and we quickly joined the queue that had formed in front of the women's toilet. It was always the same anywhere in the world I travelled. The female toilet always had a queue while the men's always seemed free. What exactly made us take so long, I wondered as I powdered my face in front of the mirror when I was done using the toilet. I waited for Aunty Ndidi by the door and then led the way when I saw her approaching. Downstairs in the main dining area, the different traditional foods and local delicacies mixed together and wafted under my nose. There was no mistaking the sweet smell of fried plantains. Aunty Ndidi's eyes and mine followed the direction of the scent and found the dish in a sieve while ẹwa agọyin and its pepper sauce stood beside it. I was tempted to buy some but decided not to when I remembered that the mashed beans were most likely not the best option for my stomach on a long bus ride. Aunty Ndidi however was braver than me and went for it. I watched in envy as she quickly devoured the food and chased it down with a sachet of cold 'pure water'. We were at Ore and had been given a twenty-minute break before we had to resume our journey. I wasn't about to spend all that time sitting again, so we went off for a walk around the premises.

CHAPTER 68

Cynthia

As our driver started the bus and revved the engine, I waved at the small boy I had met outside the restaurant when Aunty Ndidi and I had taken a stroll. He had been selling fresh coconut water with his mother at a nearby stall made of wooden planks and a tin sheet roof. He had run out to us as we walked past. He had been so cute as he pleaded that we bought something from his mother's shop. Aunty Ndidi had shaken her head because she disliked coconut water, but the boy was so small and yet so persistent that I had turned back and not only bought the coconut water, but also replenished my stock of plantain chips. We learned that he had been sent home from school because he had been sick. I looked at him incredulously as he cheekily revealed how he had left school and walked all the way to his mother's shop by himself. He was clearly proud of the feat, but as he jumped around us and grabbed at the fur pom-pom that dangled from my bag, he reminded me so much of one of the mischievous kids I taught that I wondered if he had truly been ill or was looking for a bit of fun and an excuse to skip school to take in what little action travellers that came through the area could offer. His English hadn't been too good and when he spoke to his mother when she shouted that he leave my bag alone, I recognised that their Yoruba dialect was different to the one I had heard in Lagos.

As the bus sped off towards the Edo State border, I turned to Aunty Ndidi and asked that she tell me more of what I was to expect during our stay in Anambra State. I already knew that lots of our relatives and extended family would also be visiting, but what exactly did people do for weeks on end when they returned to the village? I couldn't help but think that it would bore the hell out of me.

'Look, this time of year is the best o,' Aunty Ndidi enthused and then lowered her voice as if she was about to trade an important secret.

It was always the time of the year she looked forward to as she got to see her cousins, uncles, niece and nephew, other relatives and childhood friends. There was always too much food, drink and gossip. And the parties that they had were unrivalled. There was always a celebration of some kind. Whether it was a traditional wedding, a big sixtieth birthday celebration, a baby dedication, thanksgiving, or a renewal of vows, the village was always bubbling with too much of everything that made for good living, compensating for the tough year they might have had. Although it was unspoken, or spoken only in hushed tones, mothers would draw aside their single daughters and inform them of one chief's son or the other who was visiting from abroad and looking for a homegrown wife. Last year everyone who had been single and of marriageable age had their eyes in wait for Chief Chijindum's son, although none of them would ever admit it. At this point in the tale, Aunty Ndidi laughed.

'Trust. Me self wait tire!' she exaggerated. She gave a belly-rumbling laugh and I couldn't help but join her.

But Chief Chijindum's son never came from America. And just as the single women had arrived at the village that year with great expectations, they had left dour at their fate. Aunty Ndidi sighed like it didn't matter, but I saw the glint in her eye and prodded. Feigning annoyance at my inquisition, she divulged that she had followed him on Facebook since then and had looked out to see if any of the posts on his timeline would indicate he'd be turning up this year. Her coy smile revealed the answer.

'Eeeh Aunty Ndidi!' I hailed and gave a thumbs up. 'I didn't know you were such a hustler,' I teased.

'Trust your aunty, I no fit carry last. Why do you think I've been praying and fasting?' she said and winked as I covered my mouth in shock, giggling at her honesty.

We continued to chat as the bus sped off and our conversation mixed with those of other passengers, chatting and laughing at unknown events in their own worlds. It seemed like we had all tired of sleeping and others played games of Whot cards and Ludo as we continued to head towards Edo State, also known as the 'Heartbeat of the Nation'. It had been interesting to learn that each state had a slogan. I was learning a lot about the country I had vehemently refused to call home, but finally at its bosom, I was realising that there was no other place I'd rather be.

By the time we got to Edo State, the language had changed again from Yoruba to the native tongue of the Benin people. This state also had several languages and I was just as amazed as I had been at the start of the trip at the vastness and depth that one country alone could embody; not surprising though, given that it had over two hundred and fifty ethnic groups and a population of about one hundred and ninety million, which was so much bigger than the UK's population of about sixty-six million people.

As we drove through the state, the bus began to quieten and I could hear the young man behind me snoring. I sank into the chair and looked at Aunty Ndidi. She was also sleeping. The scarf around her shoulder had slipped, so I tucked it back into place. I put on my earphones again and returned to the land of Wizkid and the like. African music was really taking a major turn internationally and I couldn't have been prouder than I was to be in the motherland. Before I had left London, Afrobeats was already being played at nightclubs and parties. I'd walk into Tesco and hear Afrobeats – it was mad. Even African print was doing the trendy rounds on various international catwalks and the dashiki was a fashion buzzword in itself. The days of being shy to place my roots as Nigerian were long gone. I let my mind drift and be carried away by the rhythmic trance of the African drums.

CHAPTER 69

Cynthia

I felt a tap on my shoulder and reluctantly opened my eyes again to the hum of life around me. I saw Aunty Ndidi – she was the bearer of good news. She let me know that we were finally crossing the Onitsha Bridge, which connects the southwest to the southeast of Nigeria over the Niger River.

My bum ached. I was tired of sitting down and was pleased we were getting closer to our destination. The drive had felt longer than I had expected and I begged that we return to Lagos by plane. I had done the arduous ride for the experience but I didn't need to torture myself with an encore. Aunty Ndidi said that I should speak to my uncle and he'd book us a flight if I really wanted it that badly. She had quickly learned how to sober me. Without saying a word to her, she had known that I was uneasy about seeing Uncle Peter again. I rolled my eyes, plugged the earphones back into my ears and stared out of the window. We were driving at a crawl and I couldn't wait for the last leg of the journey to be over. I looked at the cars and buses we drove past. It was clear that families making their way back to the east were ready for great feasts. I could see sacks of garri and rice bulging out of boots, and yams tied to car roofs. Having become accustomed to such things in Lagos, I found nothing unusual, until I saw a bleating goat in the back of a pickup truck. I sat up in my chair and tugged at Aunty Ndidi's arm until she saw what had drawn my attention. She looked at me and grinned. The goat was helping itself to the moi moi leaves that were tied next to a sack of flour, and I could imagine the assault the poor goat would receive when its owner found out what it had been up to.

An hour later we arrived at Awka, the capital of Anambra

State, 'Light of the Nation'. I asked Aunty Ndidi how the states had arrived at their slogans, but she didn't know so I wondered if it had anything to do with their natural resources.

Awka wasn't what I had imagined. When I said this, Aunty Ndidi clapped her hands in the mock way Nigerians tended to do when something was baffling.

'You're funny o, Cynthia. What were you expecting? Awka is the capital though, it won't be like the village.'

Whenever anyone mentioned the village, I always envisioned small mud huts with thatched roofs. I had watched too many 'village life' Nollywood movies with Mum to imagine it any other way. As I was discovering, 'the village' was just a way of describing the countryside, although true to the stereotype, some mud huts still existed.

Uncle Peter had sent his driver to pick us up at the bus park and I discovered that his Hausa driver, Danjuma, whom I had met in Abuja, had taken time off to be with his family, and had been replaced by a man I had never seen before. Aunty Ndidi recognised him immediately and divulged that he was their hired driver for whenever they were back in the village. He had brought both of us a plate of abacha from Aunty Evelyn. It was one of Aunty Ndidi's favourite foods and I had grown to love it. Also known as 'African salad', it never failed to disappoint. When I opened my tupperware, my tummy growled and I felt a pang of hunger that I hadn't known was lurking, while my mouth salivated. I happily ate my portion as Mr Chukwudi drove us out of the city and towards our ancestral home, humming to his Igbo songs, while Aunty Ndidi dug into her abacha too. The forty-minute drive to our village made the total journey time from Lagos just over seven hours, an hour more than I had been told.

As we got to our family's hometown, the differences between life in the city, whether in a big urban place like Lagos or a smaller town like Awka, and the village, were obvious. Once we left the main motorway, the tarred roads gave way to red earth and our path was surrounded by trees and vegetation. It was clear that not much thought had been given to the development

of the surrounding area. As we continued, we passed small bungalows and communal compounds, as I had expected – but they
then began to give way to what I would never have imagined
was possible given my idea of the village. Massive houses sat on
even bigger plots of land and if I had thought that the houses
on Lagos Island were impressive, those we had driven past were
even more astounding. Now I fully understood what people meant
when they said the Igbos were very wealthy. I could easily see
myself returning to retire at one of those estates and when Mr
Chukwudi stopped and beeped in front of one of the houses
with an impressive black gate, my mouth was agape – nothing
could have prepared me for it. For all the wealth that I could tell
that my uncle possessed, the house in 'the village' was a total
surprise. The black gate was fitted with golden spiked ends that
opened automatically. As we left the muddy road and turned into
my uncle's compound, I saw a security officer poke his head out
of the guard quarters to greet us. When he saw that Mr Chukwudi
was with guests, he raised his hand in salute.

'Wetin you dey salute me for? Abeg open the gate!' Mr
Chukwudi remarked, even though the gate was already opening.
'Na so him dey do any time e see say I bring person come from
big city,' he continued and grinned at me through the rear view
mirror. I smiled back at the idea of the security guard saluting
on my account.

Between the gate and the house was a perfectly manicured
garden, in the middle of which was an angel-statue water foun-
tain. Sprawled in front of us was a magnificent white two-storey
building with four guiding pillars at the entrance. The room
upstairs gave way to a balcony that overlooked the driveway and
I could see small LED lights fitted in the ceiling. The front porch
was flanked with potted buxus topiary plants similar to the ones
they had in Abuja.

After parking, Mr Chukwudi jumped out of the car to carry
our bags into the house while we followed the loud sounds we
heard towards the back of the house. Walking into the backyard,
I saw a gazebo at the left-hand side where some children were

playing ten-ten. I remembered that Mirabel had tried to show me how the game was played after I had asked her to tell me about her childhood games, when Munachi and I came back from our excursion. To play the game, two players had to stand opposite each other and clap their hands as they moved their legs to a rhythm. The goal of the opponent was to ensure that they didn't raise the same leg directly facing the other player. If they did, that first player would score a point and win the game. I had never tried it myself, but looking at the little children at play, it seemed like fun. Meanwhile, close to the back door that led into the house, some older women huddled together. They sat around giant plastic bowls filled with vegetables and rice, each with a task in hand – cutting, grating or chopping a food item. I wondered how many of my relatives were present and moment-arily got nervous to meet them all at once. But before I could protest, I was being dragged to where the women were working while sipping on cold bottles of Coke and Fanta.

'Good afternoon ma,' I greeted each and curtsied, paying my respects to people I didn't know.

'Una well done o! Ehihie ọma ndị nne,' Aunty Ndidi greeted.

'Nnọọ Ndidi, kedu ka odị?' the oldest woman replied.

'O dị mma! Le nwa Jonathan,' Aunty Ndidi replied and pointed at me. I couldn't speak much Igbo, but understood that she was greeting them and revealing that I was Jonathan's daughter.

'Eh, nwa anyị nwanyị a nata go ụlọ! Ehen, welcome my dear, welcome!' the woman exclaimed and got up to embrace me, squeezing tight. She smelled like curry powder and Knorr seasoning. Her skin was smooth and soft, folding in places that might have been once firm. I patted her back and smiled softly.

'Have a seat my dear, join us,' another invited, but Aunty Ndidi led me away promising that we'd return once we had greeted the men.

'Ah, you've not gone to greet Peter? Oya go now. Come back o!' she shouted after us.

The floor of the large kitchen was covered in grey granite. I smelled the aroma of cooking cow leg and looked towards the cooker to see a big pot bubbling over. Beside it was another pot of well-seasoned beef. I couldn't wait for lunch. Aunty Ndidi caught my eyes and wagged her finger, beckoning me to follow her promptly. I followed her through several rooms that finally led us into a hallway where we could hear the voices and guffaws of male relatives and guests. In their midst was Uncle Peter biting on a kola nut.

'Eh Ndidi you're here! I was beginning to wonder when you'd arrive. Cynthia . . .' Uncle Peter exclaimed.

I assumed my position again, and greeted them several times, turning around to catch each man's eye.

'Who is this beautiful young woman?' a voice boomed, and I turned to see the pot-bellied man sitting next to Uncle Peter staring at me.

'This is Cynthia o. Nwa Jonathan,' Aunty Ndidi answered for me.

'Ehen, our very own Ada! Come here, come and greet your uncle!' he barked and opened his arms for an embrace. I had no choice in the matter. I bent towards the rotund figure that was very much not an uncle and placed my arm around his expansive back in a side hug. His breath reeked of Guinness and I tried not to breathe in.

'Nwa dị ike na nke nwere obi ebere!' he concluded.

I had heard those words before and wondered why he was calling me a strong and wilful child. I looked up at him in surprise, wondering if Uncle Peter had said anything about how I had left Abuja.

'Ehhn, it's the Okoye blood in you!' he offered as a compliment and laughed, easing my worry.

The other men joined in too and I wondered where in the maze of a house my cousins and Aunty Evelyn were.

CHAPTER 70

Cynthia

We found Aunty Evelyn on the second floor. Her room was bigger than my room and Aunty Ndidi's room in Lagos combined, and as suspected, it was the room overlooking the driveway. I looked around as we walked in and I greeted her as soon as our eyes met. She responded and got up to hug Aunty Ndidi fondly while I stood in the centre of the room awkwardly. The room was lush and tastefully decorated. A wide antique mahogany table that displayed a box of jewellery, a wig stand and more designer perfumes than I cared to count were placed in front of a mirror on the wall that had gold accents. The four-poster bed had a canopy draped in a lavender and white gradient netting and the bed sheet was white silk. It looked very dreamy.

'So what have you ladies been up to in Lagos?' Aunty Evelyn asked as we all sat down on the bed.

I couldn't tell if there was a sting in her voice, but I decided to lay low and begin atoning for my sins. I had been unfriendly the last time that we had been together and I was determined not to leave her with the same impression before I left for good; she was family.

'My dear, the usual o. Work and church, you know me na,' Aunty Ndidi started, and before I could add anything, we were accosted by a group of children who swarmed in and joined us on the king-size bed.

'Adaobi, what did I tell you about keeping an eye on these children ehn?' Aunty Evelyn scolded.

'But Mummy . . .'

'Oya all of you, out now. Go and play outside!' she concluded, not wasting any time to mince words with her fifteen-year-old daughter.

Aunty Evelyn turned back to us, smiling, and Adaobi grudgingly led them out. It was clear that she wasn't happy about the responsibility that her mother had placed on her. I smiled ruefully at her turned back, remembering when I had been about her age and had also been responsible for watching over the younger kids at birthday parties. At first I had been happy to wield my authority over them, but it rapidly became taxing when I realised that the children didn't care that I was fifteen years old and not their mate. They'd keep running around, putting things into their mouths that they shouldn't and knocking each other down on the bouncy castle. Running after them had been no fun.

I felt like Aunty Evelyn was watching me closely as I told them how my NYSC was going. I hoped that she wasn't still mad at me for leaving, so I told her that I missed Abuja. Later, both women began speaking fully in Igbo and although I could barely keep up with what they were saying, I gathered that Aunty Evelyn was bringing Aunty Ndidi up to speed with some juicy gossip and I remembered Chief Chijindum's son. I couldn't wait to see the man who was driving the women of the village mad with lust. I bet he wasn't even good-looking but made up for it with his money and father's title. What I had come to learn about my Igbo kin was that just marrying wasn't good enough. One had to marry well and into a financially buoyant family.

Aunty Evelyn eventually led us to the first floor and showed us to our rooms. While the younger children shared the rooms next to their parents, Aunty Ndidi and I had been given separate rooms and mine was overlooking the garden below. My luggage had been brought up and was standing beside the bed. I thanked Aunty Evelyn and promised to join the other women once I had unpacked and freshened up. After my shower, I changed into my loungewear and walked to the window while brushing my long weave, which I had changed from the previous honey brown colour to jet black. I inhaled deeply. The air coming through the netted window seemed fresher than it was in Lagos. The aroma from the food being cooked downstairs in the open travelled up and I couldn't wait to indulge. I looked towards the gazebo and didn't see the children. I was wondering where they had bounded off to when I heard giggling and turned around to see that they had in fact made their way to my room. Adaobi slowly walked in behind them and closed the door.

'Aunty Cynthia I'm sorry. These children don't hear word!' she began.

I could tell that she wasn't sorry. The poor girl was tired of playing caretaker.

'When I grow up, I want my hair to be just like your own!' came a squeaky voice and before I could respond, the other little girls chimed in: 'Me too!' Adaobi rolled her eyes and told them to shut up before introducing them to me. I was taken by their childhood innocence and watched as the girls looked over the clothes I had laid on the bed and placed them against their bodies, while the only two boys amongst them sat close to the door and bickered over a toy car, showing no interest in our girly activities.

'Who wants plantain chips?' I asked, dangling the bag I had taken out from my luggage.

They all screamed with enthusiasm and waited for my gift. My clothes on the bed were forgotten as they joined the boys on the floor and munched on the crisps I had presented. I asked Adaobi how she'd been and learned that she had done well in her exams just before they broke for the Christmas holidays. She also revealed that she had grown tired of playing the flute and was considering learning the guitar although her mother preferred that she learn the violin because it was more feminine. The way her eyes shone when she said it revealed that she was up for taking her mother on about it, but I doubted that she had the will to; Aunty Evelyn was a strong character.

'Where's Onyedikachi?' I asked.

'Probably playing video games with the other boys,' Adaobi replied and rolled her eyes.

We laughed and then I called out for the kids to follow me and Adaobi to go check on the other boys. After saying hello to

Onyedikachi and being introduced to my second cousins, I left the children with the boys, then took my leave with Adaobi in tow, her left arm interlocked with mine as we went to join the older women. When we got outside, I saw that Aunty Ndidi and Aunty Evelyn were already there and were sat on wooden stools placed against the wall of the house. All the chopping and prepping was finished and the cooking was underway.

'Ndo ehn, I can see that Cynthia has saved you from those children,' Aunty Evelyn said, laughing.

We each grabbed a plastic white chair from where they had been stacked on top of each other and sat beside our kin. I learned that the older woman who had welcomed me earlier was my father's aunt. Her youngest son and Uncle Peter had been very good friends growing up and still were. I wondered if he had been the boomer from earlier on, but discovered that he was going to join us later that night for dinner as he had gone to tend to some errands of his own. His wife, however, was in our midst and broke into old Igbo songs one after the other with the other women joining in. Some were singing, others were humming to her falsetto. I smacked at my legs whenever a mosquito buzzed near and helped to stir the bubbling pot of meat and cow leg stew while Adaobi fanned the firewood stove, helping to keep it burning. The women had watched her in amusement, leaving her be even though they knew that the fire needed no help to keep burning. On the other stove was my favourite food, jollof rice, and as it cooked and its aroma bombarded my nostrils, I was glad to be home, where it had all begun.

CHAPTER 71

Cynthia

My stay in the village was going well and, surprisingly, I was enjoying myself. I had warmed up to my extended family and they had embraced me right back like they had known me all along. I had some relatives who visited and would swear that they had met me that one time I had visited Nigeria and spent a week in Lagos. They had helped to braid my hair or wipe my bum, they would claim, before pinching my cheeks and exclaiming at how much I had grown. I didn't remember any of those incidents, but smiled and nodded as if I did, wondering if they really believed their own tales.

We also went to visit other families around our compound and were given a little tour of the village. Uncle Peter took me and the other children to the local stream, because I had insisted that I wanted to see what one looked like, after seeing countless young maidens falling in love at a stream in Nollywood movies. On our way there, we had seen some small mud houses as I had imagined there being in the village. Our family didn't know anyone that lived there so we walked past and went on our way, but not before I took a quick picture to show my father later that night. The boys had brought along a football with them and started playing as soon as we got to the stream while the girls played ring-a-ring-a-roses. Adaobi and I sat beneath a moringa tree and Uncle Peter told us stories from his childhood and meeting his first crush while she fetched water from the very same stream. I wondered what it was like for him and my father as young boys being raised in the village. For the first time, I was really thinking about my father as just another male human being and not the man who had been my guide and provider all of my life. I wondered how he too had felt when he had first laid eyes on my mother. I sighed. I knew she would have given him a tough time because she wasn't a woman who was easily impressed. But Dad was a good talker and must have been good at winning her heart.

Christmas Day arrived. The cooking began at dawn and I heard a cock crow. I turned in bed and went back to sleep, later waking up with a start when my little second cousin Ifunanya crawled into my bed still rubbing at her sleepy eyes and crying for her mother. I drew her against my chest and rocked her to sleep again and then set her aside to find out what was going on. The inhabitants of the house had slowly begun to stir, although the older women were already out at the back prepping for the feast of the day. The older and stronger men had been with them earlier, killing the cow that was to be used in making beef pepper soup. There was also chicken fresh from the kill and frozen fish bought a couple of days earlier. I pulled up my joggers and set to work, joining the women in chopping the red and green bell peppers for the fried rice and beef stew.

By twelve noon, we were receiving a ton of guests, and they continued to flock in even till the late hours of the night. A canopy was erected at the front of the compound and it housed two large speakers and rows of white plastic chairs for guests to sit, eat and be merry when the living room got too full. The children were made to play and eat there also, avoiding them ruining the carpets with their food and fizzy drinks. We were expecting Chief Chijindum and his family, but they had sent word that they would regrettably be unable to visit. They had enough on their hands with their guests also arriving, in addition to preparing for their daughter's wedding. That was when I learned why Emeka had been able to make this year's visit. His younger sister was getting married and he had to be present. It was no wonder that two days before, Aunty Ndidi had informed me that she wanted me to go all out with her makeup for the wedding day.

On the day of the wedding, she had hurried to my room in her dressing gown and was already flustered before the day had even begun. She was going to tie a blue gele and wear a gold george fabric sewn into a blouse and wrapper. I decided to give her a mesmerising smoky eye and red lips. If she was to wow Emeka, she had to step out in style. Two hours later with a full face of makeup, she hurried back to her room to finish getting ready. Then, ten minutes later, I heard a rap on the door and saw one of my extended family members standing there. She begged that I also help with her makeup, and then another twenty minutes later, two more women trudged in. I was amused; and by the time a fourth visitor walked in, I had realised that the tale of my makeup mastery was floating around the house. I looked up to see Aunty Evelyn by the door. I gestured for her to sit in the queue and continued the work at hand, loving my unpaid job. The women were chattering while they waited, while by this time, Adaobi and one of the older girls had also joined us and stood next to me on either side, watching as I swept different brushes against palettes and then onto skin. Adaobi had asked what the different brushes were for and I was explaining their purposes to her when something clicked in my head and I had an epiphany. I finally knew exactly what I wanted to do when I got back to London. I was excited by my revelation and couldn't wait to share the blossoming idea with Osayuki. I loved teaching, but didn't like teaching children. I loved makeup and realised that I actually enjoyed teaching it to others, and loved the boost of confidence it gave my clients whenever I was done. I was going to start a makeup academy to help women improve their confidence and self-esteem; until they found themselves, just like I had. For once, I felt I had a purpose.

When we finally got to the wedding party, the hall was already filled with guests and the families of both the groom and bride. We sat at our camp, behind the bride's family, and joined in the wedding ceremony. The groom had already finished his customary duties and his bride was carrying out the palm wine that she would serve to her soon-to-be husband. Chief Chijindum had a large fan in his hand and nodded as his daughter kneeled before her fiancé and raised the calabash of wine to his lips. The Chief's wife was seated next to him beaming and Emeka was by her side, with a broad smile on his face. He actually wasn't bad to look at and I turned to catch Aunty Ndidi's eye and winked at her. When the rites were finished and the couple were announced husband and wife, the next part of the ceremony began and trays of food began to be served. There was an abundance of food and drink, so much so that I was stuffed before the dancing was fully underway.

Later that night when I went to look for Aunty Ndidi to tell her that it was time for us to leave, I didn't see her where I thought she'd be. Emeka was seated with another lady at the groom's tent and when I finally found Aunty Ndidi, she was seated with Festus, Emeka's friend from Lagos. They had unintendedly caught each other's eyes and before we left for the vehicle that would take us back to our compound, they exchanged numbers. It had been an eventful and thoroughly successful day, both for me and Aunty Ndidi, it seemed.

CHAPTER 72

Osayuki

I opened the curtain slightly, then looked back at Afolabi, who was sleeping peacefully in my bed. He didn't stir. It was foggy outside and I could barely see a thing. The harmattan season had finally come and I made a mental note to buy a better moisturising cream because my knuckles, elbows and knees were quick to turn ashy even when I creamed properly. I opened the windows to let the cool breeze in. We no longer needed the AC. Afolabi murmured in his sleep and I went back to join him in bed. The house was empty and I was all alone. Aunty Rosemary had stayed in America with her family and had promised to return early in the new year. Juliet had gone back to her village to spend the holidays with her family while Mr Nelson took his annual leave. So except for the gateman who lived behind the house in the boys' quarters, I was home alone. Afolabi had been spending most nights with me, not wanting to leave me alone in the big house, and I wasn't complaining. I had been looking forward to meeting the sister he had talked so fondly about, but when the tremors of an earthquake in a nearby state were felt in New York and flights were either delayed or cancelled, Lola had decided to skip her delayed flight altogether and return in the new year when things were calmer. Nigerians are superstitious people and she wasn't up for tempting fate.

I loved December because it always spelled a double celebration for me. I wondered what it was like for Mum giving birth to me on New Year's Eve. She'd have had to abandon her celebrations with friends or prayers at the church when her contractions had begun. I had spent Christmas Day with Afolabi's family, so I decided to throw a get-together at mine to celebrate my birthday and the new year with our friends. What I loved most growing up was that I got to get two sets of gifts: one for Christmas, and another just before the year came to a close. I had grown to enjoy celebrating with a glass of warm mulled wine in one hand, while trying to rip off ribbons on birthday presents with the other. When I was younger, I'd wait until the next morning, on New Year's Day itself, to find out what I had received from Mum and Bob, but as an adult, I had resorted to tearing off the paper as soon as I could. Nick had managed to surprise me every year we were together, but since there was no more Nick, I tried not to think about it. I had told Afolabi that I wanted nothing and he seemed to have heeded my wishes. Our relationship was blossoming and it was mental to imagine that it would soon be a year since we first met.

Later that afternoon at a local supermarket, I was astounded by the cost of most things. Juliet had warned me to shop at the local market instead of in the fancy supermarkets, which more often than not hiked their prices, but I had forgotten to buy the chicken until the last minute. With Afolabi around, I was in no mood to travel far to get one freshly gutted. I grudgingly paid for my goods and left. Even the frankfurter had been overpriced. After some months in Lagos, I had learned to stop converting the prices of goods from naira to pounds sterling. When it worked, it was good, but when it didn't, it wasn't worth the effort of getting annoyed over it. Affording the basic necessities of modern life while living in Lagos was costly and I wondered how the masses kept up. I guessed they didn't, they simply went without.

By 5 p.m., I had taken the stuffed chicken out of the oven and hoped that it would turn out right, just like the YouTube video that I had watched had instructed. Afolabi had helped with chopping the vegetables for the salad and fried rice that I had prepared and had been in charge of buying the wine. However, since I was a self-proclaimed master at making cocktails, that had been left to me. I was hosting my first dinner in Lagos, and an important one, so I had decided to go all-out. By 6.30 p.m., I was in a red strapless midi dress with a lace hem, while Afolabi was in deep red trousers and a white short-sleeve shirt. We sat hand in hand in the living room downstairs while waiting for our guests and I hoped that the infamous 'African time' didn't delay their arrival too much as they were already thirty minutes late. Eventually, the first guests arrived at 7 p.m. and we opened a bottle of champagne and toasted. Wendy had arrived with her new boyfriend and I was interested in getting to know more about the man who had captured her restless heart. We all laughed when I said this and Wendy pinched my bum as she followed me to the kitchen to serve the starters.

By 8 p.m., everyone was eating, sharing jokes and making merry. We learned about each person's triumph of the year as well as the trials. We ended dinner by sharing what we were most grateful for, and Afolabi and I said we were most grateful for each other. We ended up being teased, but I didn't care. It was good sitting next to the man who I now loved and celebrating my twenty-sixth birthday in the company of new friends who now felt like family.

After dinner, I opened my gifts and then set my iPhone to a playlist Afolabi and I had compiled the night before. We all danced and drank, waiting for the race to midnight. At 11.50 p.m., Afolabi asked that we go to the back garden and I realised that he so far hadn't given me a present, just like I had asked. He had made breakfast in bed that morning before another round of love-making, but I now suspected there was more. I smiled sheepishly and held onto his arm as we walked outside. We were all full of excitement and I wondered what he had in wait. I closed my eyes, not believing that it was actually happening. Afolabi gave a speech and for the last time wished me a happy birthday just as it struck midnight, and a bout of fireworks came to life in the sky. I had been surprised by the first blast, but was in awe of its magical twinkling colours. I saw that his best friend had snuck to the garden before us and was manning the fireworks display. It was a small gesture but one that meant a lot to me. We rang in the new year kissing, wishing that no one was there and we were, again, all alone.

CHAPTER 73

Kian

Kian was celebrating a small win. He had been accepted to perform at a neighbourhood's New Year's Eve party and had, for the first time in Lagos, received payment for his performance, even though it had been a pitiful amount, the kind that wouldn't keep him for a week. His thirst for a flamboyant lifestyle had returned in full force after he had begun a tryst with a married woman, his 'sugar mummy' as he liked to say to his friends back in London. Lagos was yet to beat his iniquitous ways and he was revelling in his little wins.

Although the Afrobeat industry was yet to pave a way of gold, he was determined to see things through. With more money in his pocket and a lover by his side, he was ready for another phase, one in which he believed that he would eventually come to call the shots and be crowned king. His performance that night had been met with some cheers, a far cry from his shoddy days. But before any of this had happened, he had been in deep waters and had been contemplating whether to buy a ticket back to London with the last of his savings, or whether to use them for another few months' upkeep. He had later bet half of the money away with little return and had eventually sold his beloved watch, using the money unwisely to foot the bill for his birthday bash. Adewale had preached that celebrating at Boogies was the thing to do if he wanted to land a page on the gossip blogs and luckily for him, that had marked his first encounter with Gladys, Mr Obijiofor's wife, his sugar mummy. By then, Caroline and her perky boobs had been long gone. He had been conceited and reckless the night of his birthday, yet he had somehow made an impression on the forty-two-year-old woman. Gladys was a

light-skinned housewife who had married early and was now
bored of her routine life. She had everything she could desire
at her disposal, but that which she sought most from her husband
was lacking. He no longer paid careful attention to her or her
thoughts on whatever was going on in her life whenever he
wasn't around. His trips abroad had become frequent and she
suspected that he was having an affair. At first she had cared,
but after waking up one morning to him pulling at her night
dress for sex with no romance or foreplay beforehand, she had
looked at his growing belly with distaste and given him what
he wanted with no passion. That day, she had decided that if he
was going to be inattentive and play games, she wasn't going to
waste her time seeking his attention. Kian was to be her first
conquest and he had to play by her rules if they didn't want to
get caught and risk her husband finding out.

Kian had grinned broadly when a waiter had passed a folded
paper to him and said that she wanted him to ring her the next
morning. Kian had high-fived Adewale after showing him the
note underneath the table. His cousin shook his head in amaze-
ment and thumped his back. Adewale knew they were back in
the race and said a prayer to the god that kept them going.
However, Gladys' company had come with a price, but Kian
didn't care. He was willing to play until he no longer had to. He
had come to realise that he had a comfort zone in Lagos after
all. There, he could be whomever he wanted to be and get away
with it.

CHAPTER 74

Cynthia

It had been a week since I left the village and I was missing the serenity that life there had offered. I missed the afternoons spent visiting relatives and friends of the family, listening to gossip and eating more than was needed; the food tasted much better and was healthier too. I even missed the older women singing while cooking outside in a large pot and telling tales of their youth. They had been funny and warm. I had been able to patch things up with Aunty Evelyn and had learned more about Uncle Peter. The trip had been a success and my brothers were jealous of the stories I had to share, especially when I had shown them pictures of the old house where our dad had grown up. Even Nathan had asked a lot of questions and we had spent longer on the phone than we had in months.

Aunty Ndidi was still on another planet ever since her first meeting with Festus. It had been love at first sight and Aunty Evelyn had teased that her name was truly fitting because it must have been patience indeed that had brought a man like Festus into her life. I shook my head as I could already imagine them planning the traditional marriage for next December. Things could happen that fast with the way they were going and Aunty Ndidi's incessant prayers. They had already been on a date in Lagos and ever since then, it had been Festus this, Festus that. She was so besotted and had revealed that Festus was going with us to church the next weekend. She couldn't wait to introduce him to her pastor. Festus seemed just as eager. Their nights were filled with calls and text messages and I was happy to see that side of my aunt. Gone were her nagging days. She simply shook her head at me and walked away. I was happy for her – a bit worried that she might rush into things, but happy nonetheless.

Everything was going to plan and I had resumed my teaching duties at the primary school. The days were no different than they had been, but I felt happier and took them in my stride. I felt that my kids were also doing better than when I started and I was proud to have helped them in their journey, although I still hated the commute and it never got easier. Everyone still seemed exhilarated from the adrenaline that usually accompanied the new year and I was revelling in it even though the end of my time in Lagos was soon to come. As a teacher, I knew that I wasn't supposed to have any favourites, but when little Mary came to my desk and asked if it was true that I'd be leaving them in a month, I had been touched. I had seen the once-shy girl gradually come out of her shell and knew that I'd miss her small round face. A couple of months prior, she would never have been confident enough to come up to me, but things had also changed in the lives of those around me and I knew that I would miss it all, even though I wasn't going to admit it to them.

I had met up with Osayuki the day before and we had caught up on each other's experiences during the holidays. I had filled her in on everything that had happened in the village, while she had told me about her party. I wished I had attended the dinner and seen the fireworks. The children in the village had secretly bought bangers, and Adaobi and I had run after them praying that none of them would get hurt, but we also ended up joining them in the fun, throwing the knockouts in the driveway and sometimes over the gate. When I had initially found them doing that, I had been aghast and hoped that the startling noise hadn't caught any passers-by by surprise or harmed them in the process. Village life had been fun; I couldn't help but smile every time I remembered it.

I had also shared my business idea with Osayuki and she hadn't been surprised, but glad that I had come to the decision in my own time. I was so excited that I was already looking up places that I could house my company – workshops in east London, so that I could be close to home. Where I'd get the money from, I didn't know, but she had advised not to let that deter my dream although I first had to come up with a business plan. I always loved having serious conversations with Osayuki because for as much as I loved my best friend Veronica, she wouldn't have got it as much as Yuki did.

Harmony had also been a breeze to talk to and I was finding that I also enjoyed the friendship that we had. Unlike me, her journey in teaching wasn't coming to an end. She had decided that when the NYSC programme was over, she would continue teaching for much longer. It was no news that jobs were hard to come by in Lagos, or anywhere for that matter, and since she enjoyed what she did, she didn't see a reason to quit just yet, but she had revealed that she was also on the lookout for another institution that would pay better. She did have a family to consider after everything her parents had done to put her through education. I wished she didn't have such a burden to carry so early on in life, but I already knew that fairness was a rarity in life. I hoped that she'd eventually make it and had come to believe in the famous saying: 'With God, all things are possible.'

CHAPTER 75

Osayuki

Everything in my life felt in place. My clothes fit well, my hair updos stayed in place, my food was delicious, my home kept me warm and my new family kept me safe. All was well in my world. I was in an indescribable state of elation and felt secure all at the same time, unlike with Nick where it sometimes felt like something was about to give. There was no worrying that Fola (as I'd started calling him) would find me too 'zesty' or 'spontaneous' as Nick had spat out when I had confronted him about his affair. The things I loved about my personality he had come to loathe and I knew that even if he hadn't cheated, there had been no relationship to save. I had long concluded that we had been too comfortable and that I hadn't stopped to think and analyse if, years down the line, we would still truly be good together. The cracks had begun to show, but I remained blinded by the love he once freely showered. *When did I turn numb to his indifference?* I didn't let the thought linger; I was in a better space. One that allowed me to bloom and be free.

I was in my office and happy despite the tedious day. I was speaking to my mother and was being teased again for not sticking to my initial plan of returning to London to spend the holidays with her. I laughed, then told her not to blame me but my heart, which couldn't seem to beat on its own. I could tell that Mum was happy for me and not really upset, although I did know that she had missed me because I had missed her also. I was catching her up on all my endeavours when a call came in. I looked at my phone and saw it was Fola calling. I explained sheepishly that I'd have to call her back, then cut the conversation before she gave me another probing. Fola sounded excited and I knew he was up to something. There had been something off I hadn't been able to figure out since the week before and I hoped that with time, he'd be willing to share, but he only called to say that he wanted me to meet him at his office. It was another spontaneous date I was excited for, but I had wished that he'd just spill whatever was on his mind. I agreed to meet him at six and hung up. At four o'clock when I realised that I'd be working longer than I had hoped, I sent a message to say I'd be a bit later. He replied that he'd be waiting for me till eternity coupled with a sad face emoji that made me giggle. But after thirty minutes, I wanted to see my man, so I decided that the work could wait till the next day. I abandoned my desk and left for his office.

By the roadside, opposite his bank premises, I saw a sugarcane seller and remembered that Fola had said he loved them as a kid. The sugarcane seller was a skinny Hausa man whose wheelbarrow contained about three dozen sticks. He was parked by the road-side while he mopped sweat off his face with a white-coloured handkerchief that was now cream. I told the taxi driver to pull over while I beckoned the seller to approach. When he was stood by my window, I pointed at a stick and he cut a small piece for me to taste. I ground the sugarcane in my mouth and sipped its liquid, immediately feeling refreshed from the heat by its sweet juice. I told him the amount I wanted and as I waited for him to cut the purplish bark off and then chop it into bite-sized pieces, I saw Fola coming out of his bank on the other side of the road. I was enjoying watching him from afar until I saw that the woman by his side had her hand in his. They walked up to a white Hyundai Sonata and she leaned by the driver's door. They continued to talk, his right hand still holding hers while the other drifted up to poke at her cheek. She giggled and I caught his twinkle smile I had thought was reserved for only me. She turned the key in the door and they hugged for longer than I cared to see. When they finally pulled apart, she moved in again for another hug. Then he opened the door for her and gave her a peck on both cheeks. I looked away, not wanting to see what else he would do, and then I heard the door slam shut. I closed my eyes as tears that I didn't know were mounting poured out of my eyes. Fola continued to wave until her car could no longer be seen in the distance. The Hausa man said something I didn't hear.

'How you want make he cut am?' the taxi driver repeated.

'Just give it to me!' I shouted and pushed the five-hundred-naira note into his palm, snatching the bag of sugarcane he had hurriedly packed.

'Oga dey go. Just dey go!' I screamed at the taxi driver with a trembling voice.

'No be this bank you wan stop?' he asked.

'I say dey go! Take me to VI!' I shouted, ignoring his valid but unknowingly absurd question, in light of what I had just witnessed.

I bit my lip as the taxi sped towards Victoria Island. It took everything in me not to write insults as I composed a text message to Fola: 'Never talk to me again. It's over!' it read. I wouldn't give him the chance to talk his way out of what I had seen. I couldn't believe I had so easily opened my heart to him after my initial reservations. I wondered if it was a curse for me to have suffered in love so. I folded my arms for the rest of the journey, not sure of what I would do. I wanted to scream so badly but held my tongue, not wanting to look like the mad woman I felt raging inside of me. The driver looked at me through the rear view mirror. His expression said 'Madam na wetin happen?' but he knew better than to utter a word. I looked out of the window until I saw the gates of my aunty's house.

The car drove in and I was surprised to see Aunty Rosemary's Jeep in the driveway. She had wanted to surprise me, she later revealed, because I had thought she was returning that weekend. I paid the taxi driver and ran out of the car, lunging to hug my aunt. Finally in her embrace, I was overwhelmed and didn't know when I began to sob. Aunty Rosemary looked at me, clearly the one surprised, and asked what was the matter. I was unable to form any coherent words, so she drew me towards the house while Juliet continued to unload her luggage from the boot.

CHAPTER 76

Osayuki

I was in the passenger seat of our BMW car staring out of the window as we drove into Victoria Island. The window was wound down and I welcomed the evening breeze as it hit my face, blowing at the tears rolling down my cheeks. Mr Nelson drove silently; he could have easily not been there. I didn't know how much he knew of what was going on; I did see the questions in his eyes, but was grateful for the silence. I had taken a couple of days off, my first since starting at House of Martha. I went to visit Cynthia, who was enjoying a day off thanks to her community development service meeting finishing early.

Cynthia was as gobsmacked as I had been when she heard the news. She hissed repeatedly, clearly disappointed. I needed to vent and she was a good ear to let out my frustration to. Fola had called incessantly during the weekend, leaving voicemails and text messages. I had read and listened to them all, angered at his audacity. I had finally decided to block his number that morning. I didn't want to be tempted into returning any of his numerous messages. I wasn't going to honour him with that privilege. He had ceased to exist and I was done with him and men, altogether. I was disgusted and deeply hurt that after all he knew I had been through with my ex, he had still toyed with me. 'Why are men so cruel?' I wrote in my journal after penning a poem I titled 'The Heart and Soul'.

> When I'm to explain which I feel,
> I'm torn between the heart and the soul.
> They are different, but yet the same.
> For when the heart bleeds, the soul hurts

and when the heart seeks, the soul yearns.
Different or the same,
they beat as one.

I had been talking to myself in my room and replaying what I
had seen so much that I had begun to lose my mind. I had
developed a migraine and taking time off work had been the best
decision. I didn't have to drive to work or deal with questioning
eyes. I wanted to be alone. I didn't want to face anyone and have
to pretend to be OK when my life had caved in on me yet again.
Wendy had heard the short version and had been livid; work was
still going to be a drain when next I went in and saw her.

Cynthia remained standing and paced while I narrated what
had occurred. She seemed poised to fight and her empathy was
comforting, and reassured me that I wasn't crazy. She was home
alone while Aunty Ndidi was still at work. The bottle of wine she
had brought out was left untouched. I didn't feel like drinking.
My head was still throbbing from the migraine, while my heart
felt trampled on. She listened to every detail and at first had
thought that it didn't make sense. She had been surprised even,
and didn't want to believe it was the same Fola that she had
grown to respect. But the fondness I had seen between him and
the woman had been real. *Why had they walked out hand in hand
like that?* He had never been able to hide his expressions and
what I had seen wasn't two friends getting along. I had never
seen that woman before – if indeed she was just a friend. His
feigning ignorance as to why I had cut him off was not shocking,
but it was annoying nonetheless. I sat and wept in my hands until
Cynthia calmed me down. *Why me? What had I done to have
been dealt the same awful hand twice?*

Cynthia agreed with me. It was best to cut off all communication with him. I couldn't tell what explanation he'd come up
with, and I wouldn't be giving him any second chances. Not
when it concerned my heart and wellbeing. *What was this thing
called love that had the power to ruin as much as it caused a sense
of passion and intimacy with another?*

I didn't know what I had expected going to Cynthia's. Perhaps I thought I'd feel better or drain myself out of tears, but it hadn't worked. I did not feel better after we had both cursed him. I still ached and I was even more tired. I drifted in and out of sleep as the car sped back home. I watched the skyline in a trance as the sun began to set. It was beautiful and in all of the years I lived in London, I had never imagined Lagos with a beautiful sunset. And amongst all the wonderful places I had dreamed of visiting, Lagos hadn't come to mind, but sitting in that car sad and alone, the pinkish golden haze of the sun setting on the horizon was a stark contrast to how I felt.

Aunty Rosemary had stunned me the day she had arrived and I had begun to sob uncontrollably. She had led me to our private dining area once we got in. I had been unable to contain myself and she had held me in her arms and listened as I described what had happened between tears and hiccups. She had lifted my head up to face hers and held both of my hands in hers. My hands had been sweaty and wet from wiping at my face but she hadn't seemed to mind. I could see the expression in her eyes soften as she composed what she was about to say. I had waited, sniffing. Her words had shocked me. They weren't what I had expected. Aunty Rosemary was a strong woman, I had always known her to be so, but I was also beginning to learn that some things came at a price.

'Osayuki, I know you're hurting, but I'll only say this once. There are some things that even as wives, we cannot change in our men. It's sad I know!'

I began to sob even harder. *What was my aunty trying to say?* I couldn't believe that Aunty Rosemary would subscribe to those beliefs and the shock in my eyes was telling.

'Don't look at me like that,' she continued. 'It's true. This is Nigeria not your London o. Here, it's different. We have to wait the nonsense out. So we just focus on our children, raise them up and shower them with all our love. In the end, the man will come back when he sees that his wife at home is better than the yeye girls outside. They'll respect you more for everything you would have done. Trust me, they always come back!'

'Aunty, but that's not the life that I'm ready to live!'

'It's not your fault, but that's their nature. Believe me, they always come back when they get tired of the nonsense. It's OK, don't cry ehn?' she said.

Aunty Rosemary's opinion had shaken me and I had begun to wonder what kind of relationship she had with her husband, Osi. *Had she also had to 'wait it out'? And for how long?* I didn't really know Uncle Osi. Over the years, I had met him in person only a handful of times and her little wives' tale was beginning to chip at the image of the marital bliss between them that I had previously envisioned.

CHAPTER 77

Cynthia

The end had finally come and I was teaching my last lesson. The day before, I had asked the principal if he'd prefer I meet at his office to collect my final clearance letter declaring that I had satisfactorily completed my NYSC duties for the month and he had told me that he'd deliver it himself. We all knew that Mr Fagbenle hated walking over to the staff room, so I had been amused, but when he came into the class at 3 p.m. that Friday with Harmony and a few staff members in tow, I knew why. Harmony carried a cake with pink and white lettering that said: 'We'll miss you Cynthia!'. Before I knew it, my kids got up and gave me a group hug. I could see Mary at the back, her big eyes clouding with tears. I looked over at Mr Fagbenle and the other staff members who I had got on with and thanked them. 'Cut the cake! Cut the cake!' the kids began to cheer so I took the knife from Harmony and obliged. They all clapped afterwards. I was holding back from crying when Mr Fagbenle thanked me for my service and said that the door was always open for me to stay, but I knew he was only teasing. He knew that retaining me as he did Harmony was out of the question. I had grown to like my role at the school, but there was no reason for me to stay longer than necessary. We cut a piece of cake for everyone and an hour later, I said my final goodbyes and left the premises.

The next week, Harmony and I met at our local government office to complete our final clearance in preparation for our passing out ceremony where we'd collect our National Service certificates. This day was commonly called POP (Passing Out Parade) and everyone had been given a mandatory two weeks' leave in order to take part in the various activities lined up for the end of our service year. These activities included getting our CDS card satisfactorily signed off by our Local Government Inspector (LGI), submitting our clearance letter, attending a job awareness seminar and undertaking the POP rehearsals. Harmony and I had already decided that we weren't going to be doing any of the latter, but knew that in order to collect our National Service certificate, we had to pass the other procedures. So that Monday morning, we headed out to get it sorted. We had been in different CDS groups, so we parted ways to find our LGIs to get our cards signed off and agreed to meet later to finalise our clearance. I had prepared myself for the worst knowing that organisation and efficient procedures weren't always the protocol with NYSC officials. When I got to the building, there were already a couple of people outside the LGI's office. I saw two of my CDS group members also waiting for their cards to be signed off and rushed towards them to find out what was going on.

'Aunty abeg don't use style to chance us o. We too have been waiting here,' someone in the queue barked.

I looked at the girl who had called out my ruse and sighed. My learned tactic wasn't going to work. I found out that the inspector was being unnecessarily strict to people who had missed their meeting more than once even though we had been given a grace of two misses, and then I walked back to the end of the queue. I had missed a meeting once when it had rained mercilessly and most roads had turned to summer pools. I hoped the inspector wouldn't have a go at me. I was already at the end of the service year and wanted the ordeal to be over already. I breathed in deeply, forcing myself to remain calm.

When it was my turn, he looked at me from head to toe like one sized up a shank of beef in the market and then he signed my card without a word. I didn't know what summation his size-up had come to and I didn't care, I was simply happy to have gone through without a glitch. When I got to the ebelebo tree that Harmony and I had agreed to meet at, I found her there waiting, so we walked towards the building where we'd complete our final check. It was the same place we went to every month to submit our clearance letter before our government allowance of 19,800 naira was transferred into our account, but that morning, the crowd had been more than we had expected. It seemed like everyone was keen to call it a wrap with the NYSC and were eager to do so sooner rather than later.

We had been standing in line under the hot sun for hours when an official came out and shouted that he wanted us to queue up by gender. Harmony and I looked at each other puzzled. The others around us also hissed and cursed under their breath. *What did queueing according to our gender have to do with anything?* We didn't have long to ponder because the pushing, fighting and skipping of lines began. Everyone was pissed off and the brash weather wasn't helping. No one cared about order, it was a tug of war to get to the front of the queue. Harmony and I held hands as we also pushed to get in front. Moments later it was all over and the queue was at a standstill again. I looked at my feet caked with dust and shoe prints from sole of the lady who had pushed in front of me. I hissed. It was going to be a long day.

An hour later, when we were told that the officials had gone on their lunch break and would resume forty-five minutes later, I almost cried. Tired of standing, some people had begun to kneel or sit on their handbags, newspapers or nylon bags. I looked at my already dusty ripped jeans – it didn't matter anymore. I placed my tote bag from the Lagos Fashion and Design Week on the floor and sat. Harmony did the same with a polythene bag she brought out of her leather bag from Yaba market. Forty-five minutes later we were still there and the queue hadn't moved an inch. I was frustrated but didn't dare to move. I had already suffered too much and wasted enough time to contemplate leaving my spot. *This would never happen in London*, I thought and stopped myself from crying. I was truly going to cherish going back home when it was all over. I finally appreciated what my parents' threats over all those years had meant. For all the happy moments I had experienced during my year in Lagos, I would never want to relive it.

An hour later, the queue had started to move, and it was my

turn to go in. By then, I was furious. When I handed over my clearance letter, CDS card and the other required documents to the inspector, she looked at me dully and, after a few keystrokes on her keyboard, announced that my file was missing. I looked at her in bewilderment.

'How can my file be missing?!' I asked, aghast.

'Young girl don't shout at me! You redeployed abi? I don't think your records were handled properly,' she spat at me.

'But I've been signing here every month!' I replied incredulously.

'Did you not hear me? Come back tomorrow abeg!' she said with finality and pushed my documents away.

I knew I wasn't going to get anything more out of the hateful woman. I was drained of energy to argue back. I snatched my documents from her table and left on the verge of tears.

CHAPTER 78

Osayuki

February was hard. I had been looking forward to spending Valentine's Day with Fola, but he had ruined any chance of that ever happening. It had been a weekday so I had buried my head in work. Wendy had left early to meet up with her boyfriend and had later messaged me to say that she had bumped into Fola on her way out and had seen to it that he wasn't let in. I had been nervous on my way out, hoping that I wouldn't be accosted by him. I still couldn't bring myself to face him, I didn't know what I'd do. Thankfully, he didn't lie in wait for me and I left for home unruffled. However, when I got home, a big bouquet of flowers and a gift box was waiting by my room. I had kicked it aside, knowing whom it had come from. I immediately called Juliet and told her to take them away. I didn't care to know what he had bought, I wanted nothing from him and told Juliet the same. I made her promise not to collect anything from him ever again and if he were to insist, she was to bin it, I didn't want to know. After our conversation, I pulled out the bin bag that contained everything he had ever given to me and told Juliet to keep whatever she liked and trash the rest. He was dead to me.

Cynthia had finally finished her service year and didn't let me hear the end of it. She had decided to celebrate with a party, which would also be her leaving party. I was going to miss her. I had also considered going back to London but had discarded the thought when I realised that it would mean running away for the second time because of a heartbreak. I was learning that love was warfare and I had decided to stand my ground. I couldn't let the men who had broken my heart dictate what I did with my life any longer. I enjoyed living in Lagos and was beginning to get used to the way of life, although I doubted I would ever fully come to terms with how things worked. I wanted much more for myself and had also realised that my life in London had become too comfortable. I wanted adventure and more challenges, and the newness of Lagos provided me with both. My contribution at House of Martha was invaluable and I loved what I did. I felt at home where I was and wasn't ready to leave yet, heartbreak or not.

Since the breakup, I had reduced my social activities, especially because I didn't want to bump into Fola at any of the events he was likely to attend. My itinerary had consisted of only work or meetups at friends' houses. I was torn about attending Cynthia's leaving do. On one hand, I knew that I had to be there for her, but I also had to do what was best for me, and partying was the last thing on my to-do list.

Cynthia was disappointed when I first told her that I'd be unable to attend. Wendy also hissed and asked what was wrong with me. She didn't expect me to stop living because 'Fola had fucked up'. Even Aunty Rosemary had encouraged me to go out on weekends, but all their pleas were unable to deter me from my mindset. I didn't care for much any longer and wanted to only focus on my work. This was until Bob called. He always knew how to get me out of a funk and encouraged me not to miss Cynthia's party. He knew I'd regret it and he also knew I had a thing about regrets. I really had no room for it, I lived on my terms, doing what was best for me and those around me, and I knew that he was right. I'd be upset with myself if I let a bad relationship ruin my friendship with Cynthia. She was leaving and I had to be there. Thinking about it got me excited and I messaged her to reveal that I'd be attending. I had a plan and it was time that the old Yuki resurfaced. I was single, free and ready for an unforgettable night.

On the day, Cynthia, Wendy and Harmony convened at my place for pre-drinks and Aunty Rosemary was in full support. She offered us a bottle of wine and had invited a private cocktail vendor to treat us for the night. By 9 p.m., we were all on our third glass and giggling like sixteen-year-olds drinking for the first time. We also had hors d'oeuvres delivered, what we fondly called 'small chops' in Nigeria. When Aunty Ndidi had learned of our plans, she had quickly decided to skip the pre-drinks, but promised to meet us at the club with Festus. Her courtship was going well and I was interested in meeting her man because I had already heard so much about him. Two hours went by swiftly and by 11 p.m., we were on our way to Boogies. We were all on a buzz, singing and screaming to every song, as poor Mr Nelson divulged the next afternoon when I was sober and nursing a hangover.

In the club, it was the usual Lagos scene. Both the VIPs and those pretending to be were at one end of the club. There were a few known faces that people pretended not to notice, such was life in the mega city. The paparazzi and celebrity culture of the West was almost non-existent in Nigeria. The music was loud as expected and the DJ was mixing the best tunes. We were taken to our reserved table and served more bottles of alcohol. Everyone was dancing and having a great time. Cynthia was enjoying herself and there wasn't a dull face in the crowd; we had all come to unwind from whatever was going on in our lives and to celebrate with Cynthia. We had suya, shisha and champagne on rotation. At that moment, nothing else in the world mattered. It was like an out-of-body experience and everything was heightened. I usually got this way when I had lots to drink and was feeling euphoric from the music and alcohol. I had danced for too long, holding in the urge to pee until I couldn't anymore and decided to go to the toilet. I grabbed Cynthia's hand and whispered in her ear to go with me. But on the way back to our table, making our way through the throng of people, I lost Cynthia. Looking around to find out where she had gone, I felt a tap on my shoulder.

CHAPTER 79

Osayuki

'Hey, hey, I know you!'

I looked sharply at the man who had touched me. I couldn't believe who I was staring at and laughed before I could stop myself.

'Hi Ms Badu, I haven't seen you around!'

I rolled my eyes at Kian. He hadn't changed. His demeanour still annoyed me.

'Well, we don't run in the same circles. What have you been up to anyway?' I shouted to be heard above the music and moved towards him.

'Lagos has been mad. I've been performing at sold-out gigs and shows!' he yelled over the music.

'OK, good luck with that,' I replied flatly and turned to leave, but he held onto my hand.

'Have a drink with me.'

'Why should I?' I replied caustically.

'Come on, let's catch up.' He nudged me.

I leaned my arm against the bar and sized him up. I looked around and still couldn't find Cynthia and hoped that she was back at our table. I decided that I had some time to entertain myself with the *great Kian Bajo*. I was beginning to come down from the buzz from earlier and could do with the distraction. I looked towards our table again. I could see some of our friends still dancing and saw that Cynthia was back with them. I turned back to Kian and stared.

'Go on then, I want to hear all about your accomplishments!' I teased, unsure if he knew I was being sarcastic.

I looked at the curve of his lips, the lines in his face and then the tightening of his jaw as he spoke. It had been a year since I first laid my eyes on Kian. He had tanned and looked older in a rugged way. He talked about the events he had attended and the shows he had performed at, but not once had I ever bumped into him. Not even at the places I frequented that he said he had been to. I could tell he was either lying or exaggerating his experiences. He looked good, but I had always been able to tell when someone was stressed and he looked spent. I nodded and provided considered interjections, but I didn't believe his ploy.

'So I guess you're a Lagos big boy now, where do you live?' I goaded.

I could see that I had caught him unaware. He stuttered, then regained his composure.

'I move around a lot, you know how it is. But I have an apartment in Ajah.'

I laughed. 'No, I don't know how it is. And your album, when is it being released?'

I couldn't stand pompous men like Kian. The brief time I had spoken to him had revealed more about his character than I cared to know. He was the type of guy that liked to show off, but had nothing really to show off about. He was arrogant and too proud. He probably had daddy or mummy issues, or perhaps even both. I didn't care to know. I was in the mood for pettiness and ready to call him out on his BS. It was sad actually when I thought about it and I looked at the emptiness of his eyes, not hearing what he was babbling on about, but then his eyes softened and I heard his last words.

'Things actually haven't been all that if I'm honest.'

'Oh . . . really?' I still teased.

I wasn't going to let him off so easily, but as he continued to talk and open up, I felt pity. It was a shame that he had given up everything to pursue his dreams in a new country and felt drowned by it. I wondered what sort of plans he had made before the move and what he had actually expected to achieve in the time since he arrived. I was no expert on the music industry, but I understood that it was one that was hard to crack.

Kian had talked up his cousin who was to manage him, but it had been a hoax. I pitied him mostly for that. Having been deceived myself, it was a situation that I'd have loved to avoid if I had been given the foresight. Our conversation was turning dour, so I changed the subject and asked that we go out for a walk. The air suddenly felt suffocating where we were, with smoke billowing from cigarettes.

Before we left, I went back to the table to get my purse and told my friends I was leaving. I told Cynthia to enjoy her night and not to worry about me. I got quizzical looks, but no one said anything and I joined Kian at the exit. It was calmer outside as we walked along the street; the only sounds were the zoom of cars and the chirp of insects. The air was cool and it seemed to make Kian more open and me more forgiving. We found a bar not far away and continued to talk. And as we drank, I forgot my disdain for him and let a camaraderie grow. I was listening to his childhood experiences and learning of his aspirations as well as sharing mine. His mother sounded wonderful, and I guessed that in his own twisted way, he believed that he was doing it all for her. He didn't mention his father, so I guessed I was right, he did have some daddy issues. I also shared my experiences in Lagos and revealed my recent breakup without divulging too much of what had happened.

'Why would any man cheat on you?!'

'Oh shut up, you do the same with other women don't you? So what makes me different?'

I was pissed off again and we became quiet, each of us lost in our thoughts. The one thing I hadn't wanted was happening. I was thinking of Fola. My mood had soured and I wanted to leave, but Kian convinced me to stay for another drink and promised not to ask any more questions. We talked more about ourselves and I sensed that he didn't have anyone he could be this open with, or to give him the audience he craved. Kian wasn't so confident about his abilities after all. He had moved from the genre of music he loved to something else that he hoped would bring him success. He was no longer sure of his decision and had considered going back to London to clear his head and recuperate. For the first time I was seeing him differently and realised he mostly put on a facade to hide his real emotions. I wasn't surprised. Men were very repressed in my opinion. That was why leaving Fola hurt so much. He was one of the few men I had dated who got it.

'Let's get out of here,' I said.

CHAPTER 80

Osayuki

Kian walked me to his car, a Honda Civic with scratches on its side. I could see the embarrassment on his face, which he tried to cloak before he got in. I said nothing and got in too, hoping that he could still drive sensibly. Driving after having drinks was a norm in Lagos and I had gotten used to it happening. Although I ensured Fola stopped drinking hours before we had to drive home.

'So where to?' he asked.

I didn't feel like going home just yet, so responded: 'How about you take me somewhere cool?'

'I know just the place,' he said and started the car.

We drove quietly, the songs on the radio the only backdrop to the thoughts roaring in my head. I leaned close to the door, looking out of the window, watching as we sped past houses and buildings. It was dark mostly, with some street lights marking the way. I didn't know where we were going and thirty minutes later, I looked up at him, wondering about our destination.

'Don't worry, I'll never take advantage of a drunk girl. Unless you want me to?'

I caught his wink and hissed. Ten minutes later, we rolled into a street and he parked in front of a locked gate. I looked around nervously as he brought out the key and opened the padlock used to secure chains across its bars. The electricity came on as we walked in and we both cheered, 'Up NEPA,' and laughed. It was a sad joke we had both learned. I followed as he led the way into the apartment on the ground floor of the duplex. It was sparsely furnished and I guessed it was the apartment in Ajah that he had so proudly talked about earlier.

'So this is the cool place?' I asked with arms akimbo.

'Wait here, I want to show you something,' he replied.

I walked around the living room, looking at the few pictures and pieces of artwork on the wall while he hurried into another room. My tummy growled and I remembered that I hadn't eaten much all day. When he came out, he handed me a bound book and put on his music player. I didn't know the music until I recognised his voice and realised that it was his song. I sat down and listened, while he went to the kitchen to make Indomie noodles. It was good, but I couldn't say that it was the best thing I had heard in years. I leafed through the book and read the poems he had written, but tucked in the middle were lyrics full of depth and emotion, totally different from what was booming out of the speakers. I was amazed by his expressions and the evocation of his experiences. I hadn't expected Kian to be so complex. I got up and headed to the kitchen. He was already on his way out, so we headed back to the parlour. I didn't say anything until we were done eating and had cleared our plates.

'Why are you so quiet?' he suddenly asked.

'Why are you hiding these?' I shot back, holding his gaze.

I threw the book at him and asked him to read. He refused, so I pleaded and sat next to him, leafing through the pages until I found the one I wanted him to sing. He was nervous, I could tell. I smiled reassuringly and told him that I loved it and wanted to hear what it sounded like coming from him. He started, and I realised that I must have been the first person he had sung it to. He started shaky, but by the third line I had my eyes closed and was rocking to his voice. I took off my heels and leaned back on the couch, folding my feet under my wrap dress. I hummed along and only stopped when I heard he was quiet, sensing a shadow above me. Kian's face was close to mine, he was too close and I couldn't tell what the expression on his face meant.

'What are you do—'

I hadn't finished asking before his lips brushed against mine. I hadn't exactly expected him to do that, yet I wasn't surprised. The air had changed between us and I had felt the heat between my legs. He kissed me again, and I sat there unmoving, telling myself to push him away, to ask him to stop, but when I grabbed at his shoulders, I wasn't pulling him away, I was pulling him even closer. I told myself that I was mad. *What was I doing?* But it felt good and I opened my mouth, my tongue searching for his. We continued to kiss and then his T-shirt came off, and then my dress was untied and pushed aside. I told myself to stop, but another voice said *Only a smooch, what harm could it cause?* I didn't listen to the silencing voice. I took my arms out of the dress and threw it on the floor. Left in my undies and still kissing, the voice again said *What of Afolabi?* and the other screeched *WHAT OF AFOLABI? HE'S DEAD TO ME.* I was having this internal monologue while Kian continued to undress, grope and rub every part of me. His hands found my breast and pushed away the cups of my bra revealing hardened nipples. I was panting as he sucked and played with them with the tip of his tongue. When he started to slide off my panties, I jerked. He looked up at me in question and I loosened my grip on his hand and smiled. I concluded in my head: *Afolabi is dead to me. All men are dead to me. I will do what I want, when I want, because it's my body and my choice.*

I was tired of being the heartbroken and virtuous woman who continually got let down. I had been unappreciated and used up like a sponge, then discarded when I was no longer needed. I was tired of the Folas and Kians of the world, both made no difference, good or bad, they all stood for ill. I wasn't trading one man for the other, I was simply taking what I wanted. Sleeping with Kian wasn't him playing me, but me using him. It was going to be my needs and wants moving forward.

The voices were finally silenced. I allowed Kian to take me right there on his couch and it felt good.

CHAPTER 81

Osayuki

The next morning I wasn't so sure that I had made the right decision. Not that I regretted my choice, but more that I shouldn't have given any man access to my body, they didn't deserve it. Kian offered to drop me at home, but I refused. I didn't want him knowing where I lived; we weren't going to be friends. What had happened was never going to happen again and I hoped that he got the message. He asked for my number and I gave it to him reluctantly, not wanting to be awkward, but I didn't plan on keeping his. I wished him the best in his endeavours as I hopped into the Uber I had ordered. I hoped that he found whatever he was looking for, but I really didn't care. He was still a dickhead as far as I was concerned. Men like him didn't change overnight. His arrogance was still unabated and stifling. He had come on to me that morning frisky again. When I refused he hadn't been able to stop from talking himself up and I remembered why he had originally annoyed me so much.

I had received lots of messages from the night before and I responded to everyone to say that I was fine and in bed at home. No one had to know what I had got up to after the club, not even my close friends. When I got home, Juliet had a letter for me and I had almost ripped it up when I saw that it was signed by Lola Morgan. *Why was Fola's sister writing to me?* She had no business meddling. I guessed Fola must have put her up to it and decided to read it anyway:

Dear Yuki,

I hope my letter finds you well. I'm sorry that our first correspondence has come about by an unfortunate circumstance. Fola has told me so much about you and I couldn't wait to meet you over the holidays. Even our mother had talked about you with so much regard and she has never been a person to give undeserved praise.

I returned home a few weeks ago and was so excited to finally meet you but Fola has been unable to explain why you no longer talk to him. I'm sorry if this sounds weird coming from someone that you hardly know but my big brother has been inconsolable throughout my visit. I've never seen Fola this drained, not even after our father's death and I'm truly worried about him.

An exaggeration, I thought, and continued reading:

Please what went wrong? Did he do something unforgivable? I've asked him to explain everything that happened the last time he spoke with you and he still hasn't been able to understand why you went from being excited to meet him, to sending harsh messages about ending the relationship.

I know there are two sides to every story and I would really appreciate it if we could meet and talk. I know that Fola is my brother, but I'm not here to take sides. I know that it might be unfair to ask this of you, but I would really like to give him some closure since you no longer want to speak to him.

I know that you love each other or at least you once did, so I'm begging you in the name of God, please let us meet and settle this matter once and for all. I'll be leaving Lagos pretty soon and I hope you'll consider my humble request before I do. My number is 08010614401.

From a loving sister,
Lola Morgan

I knew what she was going to ask for and I wanted to be done with the Morgans altogether, so agreed. I messaged the number she had provided in the letter and told her to come at 3 p.m.

Then I shoved the letter into my bottom drawer and rushed into the bathroom to scrub the previous night away.

At exactly three o'clock, my phone buzzed with a text message. Lola was waiting at the front door, so I asked Juliet to let her in. I had already informed Aunty Rosemary about what was going on and had begged her to stay out of it. She had agreed and asked that I call her if I needed anything. I wanted as few of my loved ones involved in the mess as possible and had told Lola to get straight to the point. However, when she walked in, I was stunned. Lola was the very same girl I had seen hand in hand with Fola. My stomach plummeted and I realised the mistake I had made. We shook hands awkwardly as she introduced herself. She tried to make small talk, but I cut her off and asked to know where Fola was. She was alarmed by my briskness and tried to plead on behalf of her brother. She stated that he was confused and depressed, unsure of what had happened to have caused my actions. I couldn't contain myself any longer and began to sob, which made her even more surprised. Unbeknownst to me, Aunty Rosemary had been lurking in the passageway and stormed into the room when she heard me crying. I assured her that everything was fine and revealed that I had made a terrible mistake. I looked at Aunty Rosemary and revealed that Lola was the woman I had seen with Fola. It finally dawned on everyone what was going on and I asked to speak with Fola immediately.

'You don't have to call. He's waiting outside in the car,' Lola informed me.

I didn't wait for her to say anything more; I put on my slippers and headed towards the door. When I got outside, I opened the gate and saw Fola pacing beside his car. He saw me and stopped. I hurried towards him then paused, unable to move closer, my legs trembling. He looked puzzled at the streak of tears on my face.

'Why are you crying? Yuki I—' he began before I cut him off.

'I've made a terrible mistake Fola. I'm so sorry—' I started, looking at my shaky hands.

I didn't get any more words out of my mouth before he crushed me in his arms in an embrace. I started sobbing again and turned to see Lola and Aunty Rosemary grinning behind me. I felt stupid and embarrassed. I told Fola that we had many things to talk about and I needed to apologise for what I had done.

Later that evening, when everything was said and forgiven, the air cleared and my heart restored, I felt really awful for shutting him out the way I had. I realised that my breakup with Nick had affected me more than I had even known. It had almost cost me my relationship with the man I loved. And then I later found out that another surprise had also been lurking. Aunty Rosemary had invited Fola and Lola to stay for dinner. I knew her real reason for the invitation. She wanted to know more about the man who was driving me mad, an inquisition also from my mother I imagined.

We were in the living room, talking and sharing family histories. Aunty Rosemary brought out a bottle of wine, while Juliet prepared the food in the kitchen. I was seated next to Fola, my hand in his, not wanting to leave him ever again.

At that moment, I found out what he had been hiding all along that had made me suspicious of his actions. He explained that he had been planning a special trip to the Obudu Mountain Resort in Cross River State. He stood up, then went down on one knee. He didn't have the ring on him, understandably since he didn't know if we'd be reconciling. Still, I was overwhelmed and looked on in shock, not believing what was about to happen. Aunty Rosemary was shouting for Juliet to bring out her camera, while I had begun to sob again.

'Osayuki, the apple of my eye, I love you more than you can ever imagine and I'll never do anything to hurt you. Will you marry me?' he asked tenderly.

'Yes! Yes!' I shrieked and grabbed his hand, pulling him up for a kiss. When we finally pulled apart, I turned around to look at our audience. Lola had her hands on her chest while gushing 'Aww' while Aunty Rosemary was clapping and beaming. She had left the picture-taking to Juliet, who was snapping away dutifully and happy for the responsibility.

We went out that night to celebrate, just the two of us. I sent pictures to Wendy and Cynthia and both were astounded and full of questions. It was crazy how things had changed over the course of the day and I was suddenly a fiancée. That night in our hotel room, Fola leaned over me and, staring back into his brown eyes, lost in the depths of them, I rediscovered why I had fallen in love with him in the first place. Above all else, he was kind, respectful and consistent in his love for me. I no longer doubted it. But when he asked how Cynthia's leaving party had been, I had almost cried again, remembering the tryst that had gone on between Kian and me. I said it had been fun, but I regretted how the rest of the night had panned out. He had looked at me closely, then grinned before rolling me over onto my tummy and kissing the nape of my neck. It was ticklish and I giggled.

'Osayuki Rachel Idahosa, the moon in my darkest nights, I beg that you never shut me out again,' he whispered before licking my ear.

I wanted to forget that the night before had ever happened. I turned around and held him by the waist with my thighs, pulling him down towards me. For that night, I did forget and would continue to will myself to forget about it every night thereafter.

PRESENT DAY

THE NAMING

Osayuki

Cynthia and I are sitting side by side in the house that Fola and I have nurtured and promised to keep each other safe in. I am dizzy from the whirring of my mind and unearthing of memories from the previous year. Cynthia is quiet beside me. I can see the shock on her face. She now understands what happened, but has still not said a word. I'm not surprised – even I am confused.

'So Nimi is Kian's?' she asks again.

'I don't know,' I reply again and begin to sob.

'Babe, what do you mean?' Cynthia asks incredulously.

I don't answer her. My eyes have caught sight of the scented candle in the bathroom. The pleasant memory of the sweet smell of Fairy Dust takes me back to a memory of the time when it was just Fola and me. My Fairy Dust candle had been burning in the same bathroom. It was the first time I had lit it after months of choosing just the perfect fixtures and accessories for the house, just like I had always dreamed of one day doing. It was the first night of being Fola's wife and I was tired from the long day of festivities celebrating our traditional marriage. 'What a beautiful couple' was on the lips of everyone in attendance and I brimmed with joy. How did I get so lucky?

That day, after thanking the elders and our friends for attending, we left the guests still partying at midnight to go home to our new house. Fola was so cheesy. He made me wait in front of the door and then carried me in his arms over the threshold for the first time like we'd seen in American movies growing up. After we both ate the piece of cake I had saved in a serviette and had our last dance of the night, I headed upstairs for a bath. I was bent over, kneading my sore feet when I felt Fola get in behind me. With our bodies meshed together, skins of a similar dark brown hue, we were like mother and father peas in a pod.

'It fits us both,' Fola had said, pulling me towards his chest, while his right hand caressed my tummy that had just began to show a small bump that could have been mistaken for a lunch baby.

'I know silly, that's why I chose it,' I said, smiling up at him. He pinched my nose playfully and stuck his tongue out at me. I turned and rested my head back on his shoulder and closed my eyes, the sweet smell of Fairy Dust soothing my senses. Only a minute later, I felt the shower cap I had tucked my hair into being flicked off and thrown to the floor. 'Fola! What are you doing? You should know about my hair shrinkage by now. Why?' I pouted and turned to straddle him. 'I don't care,' he replied with a mischievous grin and dug his hands into my hair. 'I can't believe we get to do this for the rest of our lives,' he whispered just before nibbling my lips. Breaking free, I replied, 'But not like this,' pointing at my crushed updo, which was now wet and missing several hair pins. 'But like this,' he said, sliding a finger inside me. My breath caught in surprise and I started to pant as he moved his hands slowly. Then he got out of the bath and carried me again in his arms, his eyes locked on mine, as we made our way back into our room. I could see his love through his eyes – raw, hopeful and absolute, and I knew that it would never be the same with anyone else and I promised to never betray him.

Now, I feel terrible that it was I who had been unable to keep that promise. I bury my head in my hands again, trying to smother my tears and stop crying. I can't let anyone find me like this. The truth that I have been trying to forget over the past nine months has finally rammed into my life, demanding transparency. I used protection with both men. I always did, it was one thing Mum and Bob had ensured I learned about before I went off to uni. *So how could it have happened? Why was it just my bad luck to have been among the small percentage of condom users who fell pregnant?*

Three weeks after I had made up with Fola, I knew I had

fallen pregnant. I felt like there was a stirring in my body and coupled with my missed period, it didn't take long for me to guess that it was a possibility. I rushed to a pharmacy to buy a pregnancy test and it revealed what I had been praying all the way back home wasn't the case. I wasn't settled properly in Lagos, nor was I ready for a baby. I also wasn't sure of how Fola would react and I started to cry. I wasn't ready for a baby at all. I cried every morning in the shower for three days until I finally decided it was time to share the news with Fola. I looked down at the carpet in his room waiting for his response but nothing came. When I looked up at him, I saw that he was speechless with happiness. It looked like a thousand thoughts were going through his mind until he began to laugh and scream 'Yes! Yes!' like he had won a grand prize. He pulled me up and spun me around. When he put me down, he spread his hand on my tummy and asked: 'So I'm going to be a father?' and all my worries dissipated just like that. I began to grin and jump, screaming 'Yes. Yes!' We finally collapsed on the bed staring at each other lovingly. Fola held my hand and placed it over his heart. I could feel it beating. He didn't have to say anything else, we simply stared at each other for a long time.

I truly don't know who Nimi's father is. Relatives have said he looks exactly like Fola; that he has his father's nose and ears. Mama Fola has even said that he looks exactly as Fola did when he was a baby, but seeing Kian there on the news has been a thundering wakeup call. The truth I tried to forget has come calling and I feel terribly guilty. I made Fola promise to always be honest with me, but I am failing at my own test. *Does anybody need to know now Kian is dead and the truth safe forever? If I was Fola, would I want to know? I feel that Nimi looks like Fola but is that enough proof or just wishful thinking?*

If it had been Fola's condom that split I know that he would have told me. He would have wanted me to take the necessary precautions not to get pregnant before we were ready, so I can't help but think that it was a nonchalant coward like Kian who would have kept such important information from me.

'Kian is gone and nobody will ever know, but I know you Yuki. Can you let this go? Bury it forever?' Cynthia asks.
I don't know my answer to Cynthia's question, but I know that a decision has to be made.

*****

Downstairs, Fola has finished seeing off the guests. Lastly, he waves at his mother and sister as they drive off in their chauffeured car. He tells the gateman to lock the gate and returns to the living room where Osayuki's mum cradles a sleeping Nimi while Bob continues to nurse the bottle of Guinness in his hand. The party is done and everyone is taking a breather. Fola is very grateful for the success of their child's naming ceremony and can't wait to have some time alone with Osayuki. He could tell that the stress of the day had gotten to her. He looks around, but doesn't see her or Cynthia, and he guesses that they are upstairs somewhere catching up or gossiping. He's excited for the years ahead with Osayuki and whistles as he climbs the stairs leading up to their bedroom. He feels blessed to have married the woman of his dreams, who has also given him a son, albeit that it had been in an unplanned circumstance. When they had found out that they were expecting, both of their parents had pushed for them to marry before its arrival, and Osayuki, being Osayuki, had rejected the idea. She didn't want to be one of those women people sniggered about for marrying only because she fell pregnant. She wanted everyone to know that she and Fola were going to make it down the aisle anyway. Yet culture makes demands and she had relented, accepting only a traditional marriage ceremony, leaving the white wedding until she was fully ready and without child. No matter what, she was going to see to it that she would eventually have the wedding of her dreams, society be damned.

Fola suddenly remembered that when they had made love that night after their relationship was mended, he had first been terrified when he saw that the condom had split. He had never been in such a situation and had almost woken her up to let her know, but when he had looked at her, so beautiful even in sleep, he had decided not to. He had left it up to fate and nature to take its course. He knew that they were soon to be husband and wife anyway and if a child was to come, then he was ready to be a proud father. He loved her so much and couldn't imagine her slipping away from him ever again and Nimi's coming had ensured it. He felt a little guilty but brushed it aside, although he knew that he'd have to tell her someday.

Author's Note

'It is an artist's duty to reflect the times.' Nina Simone

This quote by Nina Simone easily summarises my reasons for writing this novel. *The Returnees* was inspired by my experience as a woman born Nigerian but now living in the diaspora and my observations of others like me who were returning to our motherland for various business or personal pursuits. Due to social media, now more than ever, we're able to own our narrative and tell our complex and nuanced stories in a positive light – the positive stories that the western media has kept hidden while stereotypes and negative press abound.

I was inspired by the transformations I was seeing happening in Nigeria, especially in the creative and arts industries in Lagos; and like many others I'd assume, contemplated the idea of returning home to Lagos. Although *The Returnees* is a work of fiction, it was this idea of a diasporan returning home that I decided to use as a vehicle to archive these developments in our history, as a means to document some of our experiences in this decade. I wanted to capture a story that can easily be about any of the number of people who are currently navigating this path. This novel is very much about Lagos as it is the lives of the three characters.

For Cynthia, it is seeing Nigeria for the first time, with new eyes and not through the filter of the western media. For Osayuki, it is seeing Nigeria with curious but experienced eyes, having been born and partially raised in the country before migrating. And for Kian, there is no seeing or thought at all. He goes to take whatever he can, with no regard for the people, traditions or history.

Although the story could be one of an outsider looking in,

observing and experiencing things with a different lens (to the locals), the characters are also very much a part of the people. Migration is a complex journey that both Nigerians on the continent and in the diaspora experience. So it has its place in the history of the country and how its people living all over the world interact with each other.

The novel illustrates a nuanced experience of what it can be to live in contemporary Lagos in an era of digital media and rapid globalisation.

My dream is that if hundreds of years from now, someone asks 'How was life in the 2000s?', *The Returnees* can be given to them.

Nigerians, and indeed Africans, have lost a lot of our history because hundreds of years ago, we preserved it through oral storytelling which is dying out and of course, because of the ramifications of colonisation. I felt that it was important as an artist to contribute to preserving our history in this way, so that nothing more would be lost from us and our future generations.

Acknowledgements

First of all, I'm grateful to God for my gifts and for everything else; and to the wonderful people I was surrounded by at the time I found my voice and confidence to unabashedly pursue writing as a career:

Teejay, for sharing your journey and philosophies with me so honestly. The idea for *The Returnees* truly began when I replayed our interview recording and heard you talk about your work with passion. It inspired me to pursue a meaningful narrative about our culture and country, so that it can be passed down to future generations.

Aminata Koné, for always believing in me. For your excitement and encouragement when I shared the synopsis of the novel. Your friendship meant a lot.

Marcelle Bernstein, for your thorough and insightful Novel Writing short course at City University, my very first step to taking myself seriously in 'going for it'. The weekly assignments pushed me to develop the plot better and it was in one of those classes the plot for *The Returnees* was solidified. I still remember your enthusiasm when I shared my synopsis and how brilliant you thought it was. That gleam in your eye gave me the confidence to proceed.

There were also many other people who were crucial to the production of this book and for which I'm also grateful.

My wonderful editor, Francine Toon, for believing in me, championing the book during Hachette's Future Bookshelf open submissions and bringing it to fruition. Thank you for encouraging me to stretch myself even when I thought I was done. I'm deeply grateful. Also, to the Future Bookshelf team, I'm grateful to you for creating this scheme to amplify voices like mine. The world needs more diverse stories. And of course, to everyone at Hodder who made all this happen, thank you.

The Society of Authors, thank you for assigning me an amazing professional who helped me with the contract since I didn't have an agent.

My sister, Adole (the Tom to my Jerry), thank you for being selfless and answering all my questions. I know I ask too many! I'm grateful to you for going over every detail of your NYSC experience even after years away from service and you claimed not to remember. For cross-checking the facts and helping me find others who could give insight when you couldn't.

To my cousin TJ, thank you for taking me to the Lagos NYSC camp to see it first hand; and Vivien Omesiete my dearest child-hood friend, for sharing your experiences of studying in Abuja and for reading the NYSC chapters.

Tope Okonkwo, George Ikemefuna, Cindy Kelechi Ikpe, Dunsin Ruhle, Toyin Hamza, Kevwe Omoghuvwu, Kenechukwu Okpala, and the many others who filled out my questionnaires, thank you for sharing your NYSC experiences; and especially Uzoamaka Obijiofor for sharing your experience as an IJGB!

Chiamaka Obuekwe, Cassandra Ikegbune and again, Uzoamaka Obijiofor, thank you for sharing your Igbo traditions and trips to 'the village.' Chiamaka Obuekwe and Besidonne Moore, thank you for helping me with the Igbo translations. I couldn't have done it without you.

Daniel Obasi, Papa Omisore and Bright Uwaomah thank you for sharing your insights about the fashion and PR industry.

Soji Abifarin, thank you for connecting me with young artists in a moments notice; and Ono Mccaulay, for sharing your know-ledge on managing artists and giving me a wake up call to take my research more seriously when it seemed I was going to leave Lagos without accomplishing all of my goals.

Maryam Adeleke, thank you for asking me about the progress of the book after a long time had passed and I was struggling to continue. That seemingly inconsequential question, meant you had taken me seriously when others didn't. Your show of care gave me the boost to continue writing during my darkest days. Writing this book was truly a lonely journey and for this, thank you.

Yemi Adisa and Leah Adenaike, what wonderful friends and cheerleaders you've both been! Thank you for everything and your endless support and care.

To the team at Project Noir, thank you for creating a safe space where for the very first time I was able to share some chapters with an audience. The round of applause after reading the first chapter, the questions and the feedback I got at that reading (a few weeks after I finished writing) gave me a great boost of confidence that I hadn't wasted my time and energy in vain.

Finally, I'd like to thank my mother for simply letting me be. For not giving me any 'Nigerian-like' ultimatum or pressure to abandon my foolhardy dream. Even though as a Nigerian mother, she couldn't help herself as the years went by to cautiously ask if it wasn't time I look for a good paying job and get going on the housing ladder. Now you can proudly tell all of your friends and our relatives that your daughter is an Author. God is good.

This book is brought to you in partnership with

At The Future Bookshelf we believe that publishing should be open and accessible to all people, from all backgrounds, from all communities. As part of Hachette – one of the UK's largest publishers – we are always on the lookout for books that surprise us, inspire us, make us laugh, make us cry or tell us something that we didn't know about the world.

If you are an aspiring writer who would like to understand more about the process of writing, editing, submitting and publishing your work, then we'd love to hear from you. Whatever your story, we can help you tell it.

**Visit us at thefuturebookshelf.co.uk
or on Twitter @FutureBookshelf**

BookDrop

Ready for your next read?

Join BookDrop and get the best
e-book offers, available for a limited
time only, on authors you'll love direct
to your inbox. Discover new favourites
and great hand-picked offers across
a host of genres, tailored to you by our
team of expert publishers.

Whatever you're in the mood for,
we've got you covered.

Join today at
bookdropdeals.com

Or follow us on social:
f Bookdropdeals
🐦 @Bookdropdeals